JUSTINA

DAUGHTER OF SPARTACUS

RYAN LEW

PROOF OF
CONCEPT
PRESS

JUSTINA: DAUGHTER OF SPARTACUS©
Published by Proof of Concept Press
Henderson, NV 89009

Published in the United States by Proof of Concept Press.

Hardbound ISBN 978-0-9996148-2-2

Paperback ISBN 978-0-9996148-1-5

Ebook ISBN 978-0-9996148-0-8

Cover design by Elizabeth Mackey

Visit us on the web at www.iamjustina.com

5 6 7 10 8 6 9 1 3 2

❀ Created with Vellum

ACKNOWLEDGMENTS

I would like to thank the following people who have helped make this book possible.

Paul Papa who has been with me on this ride from the beginning. You kept me calm and focused throughout the past two years.

Tonya Dennis, Mike Molony, Adriana Lopez, Nancy Meija, Juliana Marchand, Whitney D., and Danny Manus who all shared some knowledge and insight in making this possible, and Elizabeth Mackey (Cover Art) and Jennifer Severino (Editing, Formatting) for putting the final touches on.

CONTENTS

CAST OF CHARACTERS
(In Order of Appearance)

GLACIOUS, 36, Slave
MARONA, 29, Slave
DOMITIUS, 52, Slave
CAMILLA, 48, Slave
BRACCIUS, 32, Legatus
FABRICIUS, 23, Centurion; Oldest Brother
ANTONIA, 17, Slave
HERMINIUS, 21, Middle Brother
JUSTINA, 17, Sister
ATILIUS, 17, Youngest Brother
ALBA, 44, Mother
JULIUS CAESAR, 45, Senator
CATO, 51, Slave
LUCILIUS, 18, Soldier
LIVIUS, 45, Father
BRUTUS, 30, Senator's Aide
SERVILIA, 50, Mistress
CRASSUS, 60, Senator
POMPEY, 51, Senator
MEDICUS, 58, Doctor

CHAPTER 1

MARCH 4, 55 BC

Slaves were not permitted to walk the halls of their master's house by night. They were to be locked in chains in the basement, not allowed to roam as they please. But this night was different. This night, her husband Glacious, the *primo servus*, the head of household, the most-trusted slave, the one responsible for ensuring the locks on all the other slaves were secure, had not performed this required task. This night, Glacious, Marona, and two older slaves were making their way upstairs, in a forbidden area.

"Deep breath, my love," Glacious said to his wife in little more than a whisper. "Freedom is near."

The quartet had made its way up the stone stairs to the mezzanine floor and were just down the hallway from their master's sleeping quarters. It was dark. Candles that had once lit the way had long ago burned their last, leaving only trails of melted wax, frozen in time as they dripped down the walls and formed pools on the floor. That the flames had been extinguished was no concern of hers. Marona preferred the dark. It was a comfort, for it was in the dark that the slaves of this house found relief. It was the shade of night, not the light, that gave the slaves repose, welcoming them every eve, when long after their masters retired to their luxurious bedchambers, they fell, exhausted, into their cots of hay. Darkness was their friend. The light meant only that their day was to begin again, the cycle starting anew.

Marona and her husband had a plan, a well-thought out plan, and tonight was its execution. Their masters had a son in the Roman army, but tonight, he was on patrol, making this the night to strike. In anticipation, Glacious had concealed a hammer, a hatchet, and a dagger. Now only steps from their tormentor's bedchambers, Glacious stopped, pulled the hatchet from his tunic, and handed it to his wife.

"Now, as the cobra strikes, quickly and quietly, just as we planned."

The curved handle was made of fine polished wood, and though her hands were small, she was able to grip it tightly, firmly. Glacious was tasked with caring for all his master's tools. He had learned how to treat them and, more importantly how to maintain them. This included taking edge to stone to keep it sharp. It was something he had perfected, and the hatchet reflected the precision of his work. She held the weapon tightly against her bosom.

"Is there no other way?" Domitius, the older male slave, whispered from the darkness behind them. He and his wife Camilla had been cautiously following behind.

Glacious turned. "If you will not hurry your steps, I will have you hide in your cages until our freedom is secure. Then you can take your chances when the sun rises and our intent is revealed."

"I only meant that we have always been treated fairly by this house," Domitius said. "Were we to leave now, there would still be time to reach the aqueducts by daybreak and escape to…"

Before Domitius could finish, Marona spun around and took

hold of his steel collar, catching him off guard and off balance. The shorter Marona yanked hard, pulling him down toward her until they were face-to-face, eye to wide eye.

"Treated fairly?" she said. "What do you know about being treated fairly? You and your wife hide in the kitchen while the rest of us are fair game. You know nothing about what happens in this household!"

Marona's fingers tightened around the steel, her knuckles pressing against the older slave's throat. She was glaring at him. The hall seemed somehow smaller, darker, as if the whole world had stopped spinning for the briefest of moments. Suddenly, Marona was back in her master's bedchambers, bent over his bed as the grotesque man, many years her senior, violated her again and again. It was something he did routinely, grunting and groaning, more with exhaustion than pleasure.

Marona shuddered, and as quickly as it had appeared, the memory left.

"Do you have any idea what it's like being touched by that gangrenous swollen eel?" Marona asked, her words biting. "To have him bend you over as he pleases and thrust himself inside you. Saturating your body with his wretched odor?" She paused, and then looked down. Her voice grew quieter. "Never being able to cleanse yourself of that vile smell," she continued, "no matter how hard you scrub? His fetid breath still stings my nostrils." Marona had drifted away to another place, reliving what she had been forced to endure.

"Apologies," Camilla said, placing her hand gently on Marona's arm. "Neither of us had any idea."

The words brought Marona back. She was met with fear. Not her own, but in the eyes of the man whose collar she had in her grip. A grip she suddenly realized had tightened increasingly as she spoke. She looked down, almost embarrassed, and released the collar, then wiped the tears that had formed in both eyes.

As always, Glacious came to her rescue. "Standing outside our masters' bedchambers, weapons in hand," he whispered forcefully, "is hardly the time for second-guessing. This is what we all agreed upon. Now, do your part. Both of you." He pressed a hammer into Domitius' hand. "Take this and be ready to use it."

Glacious cradled Marona's face. He leaned in and gave his wife a kiss. His lips were warm, and they helped remind her why they were there, what their goal had been and still was. She grabbed the back of his head and returned his kiss, more forcefully. After a moment, Glacious pulled back and gave his wife a knowing nod, which she returned. He then flashed Camilla and Domitius a stern look before turning to the door of the bedchamber and pushing against it slowly.

Their masters were in bed, sound asleep, lying on their backs. The man of the house, dressed in nothing but his lower undergarments, was snoring loudly, his huge belly rising and lowering with each breath. His wife was clad in a sheer white gown, a strange smile pasted on her face. Glacious pulled a dagger from underneath his tunic. Marona looked at her husband, and the two shared a quick smile. "Freedom is but a thrust away my love," Glacious whispered.

They turned to face their masters and rushed into the room.

Marona leapt from the end of the bed with an energy she had never before experienced and landed squarely on her master's bosom. The instant weight and motion startled the woman, and Marona took full advantage of her confusion. She raised the hatchet high above her head and thrust it downward with both hands, plunging it deep into the woman's skull. She heard a dull crack, and a streak of bright red blood shot from her master's head, striking Marona directly between the eyes. She reeled back slightly, then brought her hand to her face and slowly wiped the blood from around one eye.

She was instantly flooded by a wave of emotions. Anger and guilt, power and vulnerability, the sweetness of revenge and the coldness of murder. She hadn't expected to feel all these emotions, and as the tears began welling up, she forced herself to push them deep inside. She looked down at her handy work. Her master's eyes reflected a mixed state of surprise and horror—the gruesome realization of what was happening forever frozen on her face. As the blood began to leak from the wound, Marona allowed herself a wry smile.

Glacious' advance hadn't been quite as smooth as that of his wife. Perhaps it was the swiftness of her movements, or the eagerness of her endeavors that caused Glacious to hesitate, but that hesitation came at a cost. Before he could thrust his dagger into their master's chest, the man woke from his slumber and managed to sit up straight. Wide-eyed, the master of the house looked over at his wife, then at his attacker, before crying out.

"Assassin! Help!"

Glacious jumped atop the man, trying his best to get the large, unruly mass under control. His master wasn't strong, but fear and panic had energized him. Facing a life or death struggle, he had found the strength of Hercules and was quickly getting the better of Glacious.

"Help me with this pig, you cowards!" Glacious yelled to Domitius and Camilla. But they seemed unable to move. Camilla hid her head in her husband's chest, and Domitius wasn't much better. He had wrapped his arms around his sobbing wife and was pressing her tightly against himself, shielding her face. His mouth had dropped, his eyes were wide, and his knees were beginning to buckle. The hammer lay on the ground before him.

Disgusted, Glacious turned his attention to the mass of fat before him. He raised the dagger high, but before he could slam it full-hilt into his master's chest, the man got ahold of his arm, clutching it with the might of a gladiator. His opponent managed to turn onto his side, rolling Glacious and almost causing him to fall to the floor. As their master cried out a second time, Glacious screamed an almost primeval cry, kneed him just below the ribs while twisting his own body, and somehow managed to maneuver him once again onto his back.

Marona pulled on the hatchet with both hands, but the blade was deep and she struggled to dislodge it. The blood on her hands made it hard to gain a hold on the handle. If that wasn't bad enough, she was being tossed like a ship on an angry sea, the conflict next to her making it difficult to keep her balance. Just as she was about to fall off the side of the bed, she got a firm grip on the hatchet and pulled herself back up. The action loosened the blade, and she was finally able to dislodge the weapon from the dead woman's skull.

As Glacious pressed his knees onto the large man's shoulders, pinning him down, Marona called upon every ounce of her strength to slam the hatchet into the man's throat—cutting his voice in mid scream. Blood spewed in all directions, splashing their faces, and staining the already bloody sheets. Marona was covered. She took a deep breath and fell back on her knees. Their captor was dying a slow, terrible death, his once commanding voice having been reduced to a life-ebbing gurgle. Glacious suddenly let out a scream and thrust his dagger into the man's chest—ending his master's life once and for all. He sat up, breathing heavily, and looked over to his wife.

"Our first step toward freedom," Marona said, pulling the hatchet from the dead man's neck. "Now, let us move quickly, lest we risk discovery."

Glacious removed the dagger and stood to face Domitius and Camilla. They remained pressed against the back wall but had now slid all the way to the floor. Glacious wiped the dagger on his tunic and moved toward them.

"Where were you when needed?" he demanded, hovering over the couple. "Neither of you did anything to help." He held the newly cleaned dagger, pointing the blade directly at them as he continued, "We give you the freedom you desire, yet you take no part in deserving it." Camilla's head was still buried in her husband's chest. She was sobbing, shaking her head from side to side. Domitius went to speak but was quickly quieted by Glacious. "If either of you slow down our travels, you may see the same fate," he said and left the room.

Marona followed her husband, pausing only momentarily, her disdain clear. "Get up," she ordered. "We need to move."

CHAPTER 2

MARCH 5, 55 BC

$\mathcal{M}$orning came early.

When Glacious rose, the others were still deep in slumber. He didn't mind. They would have to be woken soon enough, but for now, he wanted a few moments alone to ponder the night's events. Murder was a grievous act, and the thought of it weighed heavily upon him. It was not an easy thing to take another man's life, but it was necessary, if not deserved, for what his wife had been forced to endure. It was the justice their masters had deserved. A justice Rome would never have dispensed.

He pulled an apple from the satchel they had taken with them and bit into it. The juice spilled out the sides of his mouth. They had never been allowed such an extravagance. Everything in the pantry had to be accounted for at the end of each day. If even a nut was missing, it garnered a severe beating. The apple was just as sweet as he expected. Sweeter still because it was the first food he tasted as a free man. He walked over to the edge of the aqueduct and peered out at the world that lay before him, truly experiencing it for the first time. It looked like freedom. It smelled like freedom. It was freedom.

At first, he didn't feel it. He was too busy stretching his arms to the sky, soaking it all in. Too busy envisioning his future to feel the blade cut into him. But it did. It pierced him with the precision of a soldier. By the time he felt it, by the time he looked down to see the glistening steel protruding from his chest, by the time he realized what had happened, he wasn't even able to cry out. He coughed, spit out blood, and turned to face a squadron of Roman soldiers. He wanted to speak, wanted to know how they found him, but the words would not come. He looked over at Marona, saddened, and dropped to his knees. Then everything went black, and as he fell forward, he finally found that freedom he sought for so long.

❦

*T*hey were all there, the four slaves of the house— Glacious, Marona, Domitius, and Camilla—when the squadron found them. It hadn't been hard; slaves always followed the same route out of Rome. When the young legionnaire who had found his parents murdered in their own beds came to him, Braccius knew just where to look—the aqueducts. Slaves always ran to the aqueducts. It was the fastest way to escape the city. If they could make it there before they were discovered, freedom was almost a certainty. His young soldier had wanted to come, but more than twenty years' experience in the Roman army had taught Braccius not to let an emboldened pubescent boy, whose mind was filled with revenge, accompany them on this hunt. Actions taken out of anger instead of thoughtful purpose were seldom productive, and a member of the Roman Legion unwilling, or unable, to follow orders could find himself on the wrong end of the executioner's sword.

Braccius was a brut of a man, one well-suited to commanding

respect. He towered over most other men, but he wasn't just tall, he was big. His back was strong, his shoulders wide. Braccius was a hard man. Hardened on the field of battle. Hardened by twenty years' service to Rome. Killing came easy to Braccius, and he was particularly good at it—some might even say he enjoyed it. Those people would find little argument on his part.

His silver helmet and crest of a Legatus shone brightly in the morning sun, as did the metal strips that, when laced with leather, formed the armor protecting his torso. He pressed his over-sized boot into the back of the slave, took hold of his bone-handled gladius, and pulled it from the dead man's flesh. Before he could return the weapon to its scabbard, he heard a woman's scream. Turning, he saw a female slave lunge toward him. A smile formed as he raised his bloodstained sword. He was preparing to strike when a tall legionnaire grabbed her and yanked her backward.

"Well positioned, Fabricius," Braccius said to his centurion, but he received no answer. Fabricius' attention was focused on the tormented woman, screaming as she tried, in desperation, to reach her fallen husband.

"It would seem you have a wildcat on your hands, Fabricius," Braccius observed. He laughed heartily as he watched the legionnaire struggle to gain control.

"Calm down, woman," Fabricius called out, tilting his head to avoid being scratched. Fabricius had been under Braccius' command since he entered the service at age sixteen. Fabricius now celebrated twenty-three years of life. He came from a good family, house Livius, the son of a soldier turned butcher. Fabricius was a soldier's soldier. He took command and followed orders without incident. But more importantly, he was respected. Braccius saw a little of himself in Fabricius, who although only an inch shorter, had the same muscular build and the loyalty of those under him.

Marona was still screaming when Fabricius finally gained control and shoved her to the ground. He hovered over her, looking every bit the warrior. The slave tried to meet his gaze, but the silver on his helmet under the Mohawk-style crest caught the sun, forcing her to lower her eyes. She took hold of the young soldier's tunic as she yelled Gracious' name, but he pushed her away. She cried out her husband's name several times more, before those cries turned to sobs.

Domitius had taken a protective hold of his wife as two legionnaires approached. One of them reached down, grabbed Camilla by her hair, and ripped her from her husband's grip. She called out, but when he stood to protect her, he was hit sharply and knocked to the ground by the second soldier.

"Careful," Braccius yelled out, a chuckle in his tone. "Caesar wants these dogs alive. Their punishment, this day, is his pleasure."

With Marona under control, Fabricius returned to his commander's side. "Perhaps I was a bit hasty in killing this one," Braccius said, returning his weapon to its scabbard. He leaned closer to his centurion. "It may be best if we tell Caesar the dog fell by your sword."

"As you command, Legatus," Fabricius replied.

Braccius called out to one of his legionnaires. "You there, see that this collar is freed from his head." He pointed to the dead slave that lay before him. He turned to Fabricius. "I want to present it to Caesar."

The legionnaire approached the body, then bent down to examine the collar. He fiddled with it for a moment but was unable to free the collar from the dead man's neck. Braccius expelled a heavy breath. "Fool," he said. "Have you not a brain inside that thick skull? Must I do all the thinking for you?" He unsheathed his gladius and lifted it high in the air. The legionnaire's eyes grew big, and he started to cower when Braccius stepped past him. "Shall I wipe your ass as well?" he asked and heaved his sword into the dead slave's neck, hacking until the head came free.

He tossed the severed head a short distance away. "There, you see? Much easier with the head out of the way."

The legionnaire removed the blood-soaked collar and placed it in the leather pouch he had around his waist.

Braccius wiped his weapon clean, then sheathed it, and turned to his centurion. "Fabricius, why don't you take leave?"

Fabricius looked puzzled. "I am well able to stay as long as needed," he said, the worry evident in his eyes.

"I know you are," Braccius explained, placing a hand on the man's shoulder. "But, you have been on patrol long enough for one day. Rank has its privileges. Go home and rest. These men can handle two women and an oaf."

"As you command," Fabricius agreed. He hesitated for a moment, and then took his leave.

Braccius watched the young man as he walked away. It's not that he wanted him to go; he could not care less how much rest his soldiers had. Duty was above all, and if one of his men couldn't handle the burden required of a legionnaire, then he had no business being in the service. But he knew Fabricius was not one of those men. He would fight until his last breath, would do as commanded, but he had a fatal flaw—he was honest. Braccius understood the morning's event would likely require a bit of creative license when being reported to Caesar. He wasn't positive Fabricius would understand. He was even less positive his young centurion would be able to resist the truth when questioned by Caesar. It was better he wasn't there when the remaining slaves were presented. He returned his gaze to his men and began barking orders.

CHAPTER 3

"*B*egin!" she said and stepped out of the way.

Antonia cherished times like these when she didn't feel quite so much a slave. It's not that she really enjoyed watching swordplay, but here, in this room, with skills at the test, she could escape her fate—if only for a moment.

The match was painfully unbalanced, even she could tell that. Antonia had been in this room many times, and she recognized the look of one who was ready, if not eager, for battle. One of the two circling in front of her had such a look. The other did not. Herminius, the middle son of house Livius, clutched the wooden practice sword in his shaky hand so tightly, his fingers were already losing blood. If his shield were larger, Antonia was sure he would have hidden behind it completely. His steps were tentative, sluggish even. He moved as one resigned to his fate yet wary of its arrival. Every thrust of the sword met with an expert parry. Every step countered with sure placement of foot. Had she a denarius, she'd have bet on Herminius' defeat, but slaves didn't have coin.

What he lacked in swordplay, Herminius more than made up for with the spoken word. Even Livius, his father, didn't speak as well as his son. Rome had come to love two skills, those who could fight with weapons and those who could fight with words. Herminius' skill with words far exceeded his skill with any weapon.

When his opponent took a small step to the right, Herminius jumped into action. He raised his sword, lunged forward, and swung a downward diagonal blow. But his adversary was primed. Herminius' sword slammed into the opposing sword with a loud smack. Antonia caught his grimace from under his face shield. She had seen many such battles in this room, and though she had never taken sword in hand, she had listened. She knew Herminius' advance had been slow and was easily blocked. But it wasn't his only mistake. In his lunge, he reached too far and neglected to cover his body with his shield. His challenger took advantage of the opening. The wooden shield slammed hard into his chest, forcing him backward. His opponent smiled.

Being the middle brother of three and the only one not choosing combat for his path couldn't have made life easy in a household that saw their father serve in the Roman Army two decades prior. But Antonia wasn't surprised at the path Herminius followed. He never seemed suited for battle. He didn't have the stature of a fighter, not like his older brother Fabricius. There was a soldier. Rippling arms, powerful chest, Fabricius was a man made to wear a uniform. To look at Herminius' stomach, you would not see a muscle exposed. Although not overweight, he had a politician's mold more so than one of a gladiator. Antonia had observed many occasions when Fabricius had tried to teach his younger brother the ways of battle, but it all too often ended with frustration by Herminius, and thus, the ending of the session.

Today's battle wasn't going any better. Herminius barely got his shield up in time to deflect the blow that echoed off the stone walls. He tried to counter, but his efforts were blocked. Every thrust, every blow, blocked again and again. Antonia winced each time his opponent's blow found its mark.

Then, as if out of nowhere, a thrust forced improper footing, placing his opponent slightly off-balance. Herminius took advantage, lunging forward with a battle cry. His opponent barely managed to defend the lunge, offering a weak blow Herminius easily blocked. With his adversary still trying to recover, Herminius seemed emboldened. He lunged a second time, swinging his shield high toward the head. Maybe this time, the outcome would be different. It was a good swing, but his opponent's actions had been a ruse, one meant to goad Herminius into making a foolish maneuver, and that is exactly what he had just done. His opponent ducked smoothly, but Herminius was already committed to the move and was unable to change his motion in time. The blow to his back knocked him to the ground and stole his breath. Antonia gasped. His sword and shield flew across the room. Herminius turned himself over, but before he could rise, his opponent was on top of him, pointing the tip of a sword at his groin.

"I yield! I yield!" Herminius said, raising his hand in submission. "You've left me nothing to fight with but harsh words." He took hold of the tip of his opponent's wooden practice sword with his thumb and forefinger. "And I desire to keep what little manhood you have left me," he said and repositioned the sword slightly to the side.

His opponent laughed heartily. With the practice sword removed from his groin, Herminius took a deep breath, pulled off his helmet, and tossed it to the side. "It would seem clear I should discount combat from my list of potential vocations," he observed. "What is not clear is why you insist on continually challenging me."

"You rush your attack, brother," his opponent said and removed her helmet. Her long black hair swung freely as it fell past her shoulders. "And you lack planning."

If it was hard to lose to a girl, it must have been harder still to lose to one's own sister, but Antonia had been rooting for Justina anyway. The two had grown up together in house Livius, Justina being only six moons older than she. At the time, Antonia had been the only child in the slave's quarters. She was always getting into trouble. Playing where she wasn't supposed to, touching things she was not allowed. She had been caught more than once under the dining room table moderating a discussion between the apples and oranges. It was probably why she had eventually been allowed to play with Justina.

While house Livius was well-appointed, it wasn't so large that people did not come in contact with each other during everyday activities. When she was young, the word "slave" meant nothing to Antonia. It was only after her parents passed that it gained meaning. Before that, all she understood was she lived in one part of the house with her mother, father, and several other adults, while the people called Livius lived in another. She also understood the people who lived with her had different rules from those who lived in the other part of the house, but she didn't know why.

Antonia had seen her in the house many times, but the two were never allowed to play. It didn't make any sense to Antonia. She would sneak over to the room where the little girl named Justina sat, playing with her dolls or a horse on wheels. Antonia played the same games, only she had to use fruit—until it got taken away from her. Then she'd use nutshells. If they were playing the same games, why couldn't they play together? Why did they have to stay in different parts of the house? Still, every time she was caught there, she would be shooed away by one of the adults from her side of the house. It didn't matter, Antonia's fruit had better conversations than Justina's dolls anyway.

One day, she was allowed into the room. She couldn't believe it. She was finally going to get to play with Justina. She held her hands up under her chin as she entered. She wanted to run but was warned against it.

"Why didn't you come sooner?" Justina asked her.

"I don't know," Antonia said, twisting her foot back and forth. "I was told I couldn't."

"I saw you watching me, you know. You should have come in." Justina handed Antonia one of her dolls. "Her name is Cassia. She can be yours."

The doll didn't look like much. It didn't even have hair. But it smelled of cinnamon. Antonia hid it under her cot, only taking it out when it was time to play or when she was alone. From that day forward, the two were inseparable. They played together, shared each other's secrets, and dreamed of the future. Justina was the only one in house Livius who treated Antonia like an equal, even after they both learned what the word slave meant.

Now Justina was standing above her downed brother. She held her sword and helmet in one hand and offered Herminius the other. At first, he simply laid there, looking at the ceiling, most likely pondering the collapse of his manhood. But eventually, he took the offered hand and allowed Justina to pull him to his feet.

"Whether it proves to be your chosen vocation or not, improving your abilities with a gladius is a skill that will always serve you well, brother."

Herminius seemed unconvinced.

"Well then, if you do not care to practice for battle, then spar with me to aid my own self esteem," she said, and with a sly smile, added, "Besides, I'm taken to understand women are fond of a man who has a certain skill with his sword."

Herminius returned his sister's smile. "Such a beautiful woman. Long flowing dark hair, tall, with a smile that could melt any man's heart. And yet, you would prefer to stab his heart instead." The two laughed at this observation.

Just then, a slow, deliberate clap came from the opening of the room. Justina glanced over and frowned at the source. Antonia looked too and immediately shifted her gaze to the floor. The sight of the youngest male in house Livius was not one that was welcome.

17

"Well played, Justina," Atilius said as he entered the room. "Your skill is more than adequate for a competitor who hardly knows which end of the gladius to point at his opponent."

Antonia kept her head down, raising her eyes only slightly. She saw the look Atilius flashed at his older brother. It was not well received. Herminius walked heavily as he retrieved his sword and shield.

Justina's eyes narrowed, and her mood darkened. "It is your utter lack of charm that amazes, Atilius," Justina said. She crossed the room, seeming to walk deliberately in front of Atilius, though she did not look at him as she passed. It was only when Justina stepped in front of her that Antonia dared raise her head. When their eyes met, Justina smiled.

Atilius continued, "Though, I fear the outcome may be vastly different should you fight someone with actual skills."

Justina didn't comment. Instead, she began to remove her armor. Antonia allowed herself a quick glance at Atilius. He was looking directly at Justina, and the expression on his face wasn't pleasant. She turned her attention back to Justina, taking the armor as it was removed.

"You would serve this house best by spending your free time finding a husband and leaving the fighting to the men," he said. "Those who can defend themselves anyway."

Antonia didn't have to look at Atilius to see where his gaze was directed.

Justina turned to Herminius. "Bare him no mind as little minds are consumed with meager thoughts."

Even from across the room, Antonia could feel the heat emanating from Atilius' brow.

"I will take my leave, dear sister," Herminius said.

"As will we," said Justina, still wearing most of her armor. "Come, Antonia. Leave the equipment. I'll return later and put it all away."

Atilius was standing at the doorway, arms folded. Herminius

stepped to the side and slipped by him. Justina, however, didn't adjust her path or move to go around. She simply walked right up to Atilius. Antonia stayed a couple of steps behind. The two siblings locked eyes. Justina's mouth went thin. Before she could react, Atilius suddenly made a grand display of stepping aside to allow Justina passage. But as Antonia moved to follow, Atilius stepped back in front of her.

"And you had best remember your station in this house, slave," he barked and placed his hand on Antonia's chest to stop her. She shrunk and immediately lowered her head, daring not to respond. "You are neither friend nor confidant," he continued and slid his hand down her chest until his fingers had moved just below the edge of her tunic. She gasped. "You live solely for the graciousness of our father," he paused, "and the glory of Rome." Antonia froze as Atilius' fingers swept downward, outlining her breast.

ustina was done with this, done with Atilius, done with the way he treated Antonia, and she was not about to let it go on any further. It was one thing to say ignorant things to make yourself feel powerful, quite another to fondle an innocent woman. She forced herself between them, knocking Atilius' hand away with her body. She faced Antonia, positioning her back against Atilius to create a barrier. The two women were almost the exact same height, so when Antonia would look towards the ground, it would almost appear as she was looking down at Atilius. Justina tried to catch Antonia's eye, but she would not look up. "It's okay, Antonia," Justina said quietly. "Just leave and tend to your remaining chores."

"Of course," she whispered and moved to leave, but Atilius stepped right back in front of her, blocking her path.

"Be sure to pay particular attention to the latrine, slave," Atilius said. "I plan on filling it again for you."

Antonia was still looking down when Justina turned and touched her arm. "Go now."

"Stay where you are," Atilius barked. "I have not yet given you permission to leave."

In one swift move, Justina turned to face Atilius. She was taller than him—taller by a good two inches—and she used those inches when she stepped in closer with a glare. Atilius met her look with one of his own. In many families, when siblings are the same age, they form a bond so strong it endures long past their own lives. That was not the case in house Livius. Instead of being born into the house, like Atilius and Herminius, Justina had been brought in as a baby by their father. An act done without discussion or consent. Not that Atilius would have had a vote, being Justina's age, he too was but a baby. But he seemed to take it personally. For almost his entire life, he had done everything he could to show Justina that in his eyes, she wasn't his sister at all. She was simply an interloper existing under his own roof.

"At least when I spar with Herminius, he has gladius in hand," Justina said. "Is it your habit to attack a person unarmed? Or am I mistaken? Perhaps promoting your prowess with bowel movements is how a boy flirts these days."

Atilius grinned. "A person unarmed, you say? A person *unarmed?*" he repeated, emphasizing the second word. Then with a slight chuckle he continued, "Justina, you have mistaken a slave for a person."

"Oh, trust me, dear brother, I am well aware who does and who does not deserve the honor."

"Then you should know how to treat a slave."

"How? By fondling her breasts? Is that how you treat your slaves?"

"I treat them as I see fit."

Justina was trying her hardest not to curl up her fist and slam it into her brother's face. She knew how to do it. Fabricius had taught her how to throw a punch. How to curl her fingers tightly into the palm of the hand, tuck her thumb back so it didn't get caught, and make the surface of her fist flat to do the most damage and protect the hand. Her resistance was waning. "Is that the first breast you've touched, brother?" she asked. "Did you get a good feel? Did your meager penis rise at the touch? Does your puny brain even grasp the sensation?"

Atilius did not back down. "You worry too much about the size of my cock, Justina, when what you should be concerned with is the magnitude of my arm and its ability to wield a sword. As I recall, it is one you have yet to better."

Justina stepped even closer to her brother. She wanted nothing more than to wipe that smug grin from his face. But Atilius was right. Try as she might, she had not been able to beat him. While her skill matched, if not succeeded, his own, he was just too strong and too fast. Still, she was not afraid of him. Nor did she have any desire to listen to his mouth run.

"It may bring you some small comfort knowing you have bested me in the past, but that was by but a breath. If you desire, I am more than willing to put it to the test right now," she said and slammed her practice sword into Atilius' chest. The blow sent him backward a step. Antonia let out an involuntary laugh, and though she immediately brought up her hand to muffle the sound, it was too late, Atilius had heard her. He grabbed Justina's sword and pulled it from her hands.

"Challenge accept..."

"Children of house Livius!" The sound of their mother's voice was all that was needed to command presence in the room. Justina took a step back from Atilius, and Antonia seized the opportunity to slip past and leave.

"Have I interrupted?" Alba asked.

"Justina was just expounding on her prowess with a sword," Atilius said.

Justina wasn't about to simply stand there and be mocked by her brother, even with her mother in the room. "One day I will master the sword," she said, "and then I will show all who care to see, the role a woman can play in the Roman Army."

"Oh, Jupiter's Ass!" Atilius cried out. He tucked the sword under his arm, looked to the ceiling, and clasped his hands in prayer. "Please carry me to the underworld and spare me such an unlikely aversion."

Justina's face tightened.

Atilius pulled the wooden sword from under his arm. He tested its balance and smiled, then looked at his sister. "Date soldiers, Justina," he said. "Stop trying to be one."

Before she could react, Alba spoke, "Son, friend Lucilius awaits you upstairs. Terrible news accompanies him. His parents were killed last night by their own slaves."

Justina gasped.

Atilius' face hardened, and his grip on the sword tightened. "How is he holding up mother?"

"Poor child, he is distraught," Alba said, "I'm afraid that Lucilius feels responsible for being on patrol last night instead of being home where he could have prevented such a tragedy. You are his closest friend. Go, bring solace to his heart, Atilius. He is in deep mourning." Atilius dropped the wooden sword and rushed from the room.

Justina was about to leave as well when her mother stopped her. Alba was a proper Roman woman whose presence filled the room with the fresh scent of flowers. Her multi-colored silk robes cut low enough to expose a good portion of her ample breasts, which were decorated by a modest necklace adorned with garnets. Matching earrings dangled from her lobes. Her brown hair was mostly wound up behind her head, but strands of curls hung down from both sides, accentuating her face. Alba was striking, yet had a tired look about her.

Disapproval painted Alba's face. "Look at you, dressed like a man. You've been sweating," she said, curling her nose, "and you smell."

This was not the first time Justina had heard these words, but hearing them once again did not lessen the severity of their cut. She looked down at the floor as her mother stepped closer. "Believe it or not, Justina, you are a woman. You are not a legionnaire and you never will be. It is time you cast away this misguided pursuit. You may not have been born into this house, but we have taken you under our crest. You represent us just as if you had come from my womb, and while you are not one of us, you bear our name." Alba lifted one leather strap on Justina's shoulder and let it drop back in place. "Now remove this clothing meant for men and wash yourself. Put on something more befitting a woman of stature. Then treat your body to the essence of flowers before presenting yourself again. Lucilius has suffered enough and needs not his eyes, or nose, assaulted by this absurd charade of yours."

Alba stepped aside as Justina left the room, still looking at the floor. She would have looked up at her mother, but she didn't want her to see the tears welling in her eyes.

CHAPTER 4

*H*e had invited them to a lunch, and they had come. Most of Rome's most noble, of her most rich. There to be seen, to show their respect, to be included. Caesar had no delusions. He understood why his dining hall was full. Why they were there eating his food, drinking his wine. It wasn't out of respect. No, it was fear he saw in their eyes when he spoke to them. Not the fear a soldier feels before a battle. That fear must be pushed deep down inside or a man would never make it out alive. No, it wasn't that fear. It was the fear only the rich knew, the fear of losing one's rank, one's position in society. But he had earned their fear on the battlefield, and he would take it. Respect was for fools.

He took another bite of lamb. There were times when Caesar was amazed at how his life had progressed. Though he was born with his father's given name of Gaius, he chose long ago to discard that name and, instead, go by his middle name Julius, though now he was mostly referred to simply as Caesar. The decision on his name was purposeful, one designed to separate him from his current place. While his parents were aristocrats in Rome, they were nowhere near as wealthy as most, if not all, of the people in this room. Few would have expected him to rise to such stature. But even as a young boy, Caesar had higher aspirations than his birthright may have granted. And now, here he was in his own estate, a room filled with nobles, all there to kiss his ass. The thought pleased him.

The festivities were in full swing when Braccius, accompanied by several members of his legion and three shackled slaves, made a grand entrance into the dining area. His sudden appearance drew the attention of both the nobles and their would-be leader.

"Hail, Caesar!" Braccius called out, slamming his fist into his chest, before extending it outward. The metal clank echoed through the room.

Caesar, a mouth full of food, sat at the head table when the interruption came. He looked intently at his general and waived him to speak.

"We have captured the slaves from last night's massacre, Caesar, and have brought them here as commanded."

Caesar stood, as the nobles looked on. The eyes of the entire room were now on him and he basked in the attention. He was in his element, relishing it. Breathing it in like one would a fine wine. As the nobles watched, he slowly finished chewing, deliberately wiped his mouth on a red cloth, then dropped it and approached the group.

Though he was younger than many of his guests, just in his forties, Caesar moved easily with the assurance of a man who had headed great armies. A man unaccustomed to defeat. He was clothed in the finest fabrics Rome had to offer a purple-striped tunic loosely fastened by a belt, muscular arms exposed on each side. A gladius hanging from his waist. Atop his head was a flamboyant laurel wreath, which he had taken to wearing when in public. It hid, or more appropriately distracted from, his baldness, a burden of weakness he was forced to bear. He looked first at Braccius, then to the three slaves, before returning his attention to his guests.

"The work of an emperor is never complete," he said. Though he had not yet gained it, he used the title intentionally. He paused ever so slightly, scanning the room to gauge the reaction of his guests. If the nobles objected, they dare not show it openly. He continued, "It appears Caesar cannot even finish a meal without Rome demanding his attention."

The comment brought resigned laughter. Caesar smiled, then turned back to the slaves.

"Excellent work, Legatus," he said without looking at Braccius, "but I see only three slaves." He paused purposefully, "The report was that four had escaped."

"Yes, Caesar," Braccius said keeping his eyes forward. "During the capture, my centurion was a bit, overzealous."

Caesar raised an eyebrow, but before he could speak, Braccius quickly snapped his fingers and extended his hand. One of the legionnaire stepped forward, pulled the blood-soaked collar from a pouch, and went to hand it to his commander.

Braccius made a motion to wipe off the collar. The legionnaire searched for something with which to wipe and finding nothing returned Braccius a blank look. The Legatus motioned to the soldier's cloak. With all watching intently, the legionnaire did his best to wipe the mostly dried blood from the collar, then handed it to Braccius, who immediately presented it to Caesar.

Caesar nodded, leaving Braccius to hold the collar. He returned his attention to the captives. "I asked for four," he bellowed, "I get three and…" he eyed the item in Braccius' hand, "a collar where a slave is supposed to be." He glanced at Braccius as he said the words, then turned to his guests. "I suppose a loss of one slave shouldn't be a concern. I suppose I should be happy with the three that are left."

Braccius shifted his weight, sweat beginning to show on his brow.

"Gaze upon these ingrates. They have turned against their masters. Masters who fed them and clothed them, kept them out of harm's way. Let it be known that Rome wastes no time in capturing insolent, disobedient slaves. And you can rest assured, we will move just as quickly in dispensing punishment."

The crowd cheered. Caesar smiled.

He turned to the slaves. "Your fellow conspirator was given a merciful death," he said, more for the benefit of the crowd than the slaves kneeling before him. "Much better than he deserved. Let that bring you solace as you dangle from the cross." The words brought approving cheers.

Caesar paused and turned to his guests. He soaked in the attention, then continued, "Your broken, bloodied carcasses will best be served as an example to others of your kind who may plot similar treachery."

As the crowd cheered yet again, a lone voice yelled out, "I welcome death for I shall at last be free in the afterlife."

The room went suddenly silent, Caesar's guests collectively intent on the female slave Marona, who now stood in defiance. Her tunic was covered in dark maroon splashes of dried blood, as was her face, hands, and legs.

Caesar turned slightly. Braccius leered at the legionnaire behind the slave. Seeing his commander's look, the legionnaire grabbed hold of Marona and tried to force her to the ground. But it was no use, Marona was resilient, intent on standing. Caesar eyed his guests. Their attention was quickly shifting from the slave to him. Action was needed, and it was needed quickly. Just as Braccius moved to unsheathe his sword, Caesar waved off the soldiers and walked purposely to the slave.

Marona was bold. Her head was high and her chest puffed out, challenging her captors. He almost admired her. He would take a challenger over a coward any day. He moved until he was directly in front of her, his gaze fixed. His eyes didn't convey anger. Instead, they sent the message that this slave carried no weight in his sight—no purpose, no worth. As if he didn't see her at all. As if he were looking past her, through her. He didn't stop his approach until he was sure she could smell the meal that had just crossed his lips.

With the room quiet as a tomb, Caesar and Marona stood facing each other. She tried to return his unblinking gaze. Caesar stood motionless. It didn't take long for her resolve to fail. He saw it in her eyes. Her courage receded, and she looked to the ground. Caesar leaned in so close his lips almost touched her ear.

"You are a slave," he said softly. He could almost feel the nobles leaning in to hear him. "Lower than a dog. Since the very day you vomited forth from your demon mother's womb you were a slave. That is your fate." He continued, saying the words slowly, forcefully, emphasizing each one, "You will always be a slave." Marona shook.

Caesar took a step back. He turned to his guests but resumed speaking to the slave, "Do you not think there are Romans in the afterlife? We rule this world, and we damn sure rule the next one. If all were equal, there would be no reason to die."

The crowd was on their feet, cheering their leader. Caesar basked in the moment. He scanned the crowd, watching them clap, taking in their cheers. Then, when he was sure he had the attention of each and every noble, he drew his sword and drove it deep into Marona's gut.

The crowd went silent. Women gasped.

Marona's eyes widened in surprise. Her mouth opened involuntarily, but there were no words. Blood soaked her tunic and began collecting on the floor below her legs. Caesar took a step closer and looked directly into her eyes. "I condemn you to Tartarus," he said and moved the sword from one side to the other, disemboweling her. With the crowd looking on, he stepped back and pulled the weapon from her midsection. Marona stood motionless, staring forward, blood pooled in her mouth. She was more dead than alive. Caesar smiled. He used the slave's tunic to wipe the blood from his sword, then he turned to face his guests.

Just as her husband had done, Marona dropped first to her knees with a heavy thud and then fell slowly forward.

The nobles were stunned. Caesar sheathed his sword. "Once a slave, always a slave."

"And what of these other two?" Braccius asked. But Caesar didn't really need to answer. When one slave disobeyed, the entire household of slaves was destined to suffer the same fate. It was Roman law.

"Crucify them," Caesar ordered, "and let the crows feast upon their eyes."

In the back of the room, one of the nobles slowly began to clap. The others quickly followed suit, clapping and cheering for their leader, and as the cheers grew louder, Caesar smiled and took a bow. It mattered little if they respected him, but they did fear him and that was all he needed.

CHAPTER 5

"*P*ardon for the intrusion," Lucilius said to Livius. "I knew not where to go. But I couldn't go back to..." His words trailed off.

Only moments earlier, the young Roman legionnaire, who just that morning had suffered the loss of both his father and mother in a brutal slave uprising, knocked at the door to house Livius. Cato, the primo servus, had a decision to make. His first instinct was to turn the boy away. The murder was so fresh, Lucilius had not changed from his uniform, and the stain of his parent's dried blood yet covered his chest plate. Cato didn't much care for the young soldier. He was impetuous and had disturbing opinions on the treatment of slaves, ones he had little qualms voicing.

Had he been able, Cato, whose height and weight towered over all who entered, would have sent Lucilius home to change and gather his thoughts, but Cato understood well that the decision was not his to make. The death of Lucilius' parents put every house in Rome on edge. Tensions were high. On this day, even the most well treated slave was viewed through suspicious eyes, and every slave felt it. This was a day not to provoke the masters. This was a day to know your place in the house, so he let the boy enter, hoping the soldier's stay would be brief.

"There is no need to apologize, Lucilius," Livius said quickly. "You are always welcome in this house." He placed a hand on the boy's shoulder. "Especially on a day like today. We cannot have a legionnaire wandering the streets of Rome."

Lucilius nodded.

Livius had asked Cato to show Lucilius to the peristylum, an interior courtyard lined with columns. "The fresh air will do him good," he said. Though not as grand as some, the peristylum of house Livius was well equipped with all manner of plants, flowers, shrubs, and trees. It was Livius' wife Alba whose hand was evident here. Flowers hung from pots swinging from a veranda between each column, their colorful buds overflowing. Trees, many of which were fruit bearing, sprouted from large clay pots at the front of every column. Chairs and tables were scattered about to encourage relaxing in a leisurely setting. This was where guests were received.

Herminius entered the courtyard. Cato had a high regard for the middle son of house Livius. He carried himself well and was kind to slaves. He was a thinking man with an eye on the senate, and he certainly dressed the part, wearing a bright orange tunic, covered by a patterned robe, a color Cato was sure was intentional. Herminius was the middle son in more than just name. He was shorter than his older brother and taller than his youngest. He had his mother's soft features and his father's dark eyes. It was a pleasing combination. If Herminius had a fault, it was his youth. Barely into his twenties, he had much to learn about the ways of men.

Herminius' eyes fell immediately on Lucilius. "Profound condolences for your loss, Lucilius," he said, taking hold of his forearm. "Rome will forever celebrate the lives of your parents with tribute and defend their honor. No Roman should ever be forced to suffer such a tragedy, and no son should have to endure the loss of a parent, let alone both parents."

Lucilius smiled. "Gratitude, Herminius. Your words bring me comfort."

Atilius was the next to enter. While he resembled his father in appearance, Atilius favored his mother in character. He was not kind to slaves. In fact, he was not kind at all. At seventeen, Livius' youngest son was eager to take the leap into manhood, to follow his friends into the army. He had been held back a year by his parents. It was a prudent decision on their part. Atilius was not ready to take sword in hand, not ready to listen to orders, or contain himself when the need arose.

As Atilius strode into the courtyard, Cato was reminded of something his father had once told him. *Those who run off to sea change their climate but not their mind.* Atilius had something to prove, but what that was, Cato did not know. He wasn't sure Atilius knew either. But he was sure the young man's troubles would follow him wherever he went.

Atilius rushed over to his friend. "We had heard tale of an uprising, but had no idea the tragedy had fallen upon you and your house," he said, taking Lucilius' arm. "Were I in the legion with you, we would hunt down these murderers and ensure their place on the cross." Lucilius gave Atilius a slow nod.

"It is my understanding their capture has already been secured," Livius said, looking to Cato for confirmation. Cato nodded.

"Fabricius has already proven his worth," Lucilius confirmed and was about to continue when Fabricius himself entered the courtyard, still in uniform. At twenty-five, Livius' oldest son was as tall as he, with a similar build. His face was angular, his eyes deep and sharp. Though they were the color of his mother's, they had his father's intensity. Of all his children, Fabricius mostly resembled Livius. So much so, that Cato imagined Fabricius to be Livius' younger twin.

"Fabricius!" Lucilius called out. He released Atilius' arm and almost ran across the peristylum. "The centurion who avenged my parents' murder with a baptism of blood!" Instead of taking Fabricius' arm, Lucilius took him in a full hug. Caught off guard, Fabricius first raised his hands in the air, then eventually patted Lucilius on the back.

"My thoughts are with you," Fabricius said, pulling back a bit awkwardly. He was visibly uncomfortable with both the attention and the revelation. By the look on Livius' face, the announcement was news to him. It certainly was to Cato. Had Fabricius intended to speak to his father about the incident before word could get out, that opportunity had clearly passed.

Lucilius seemed intent on keeping a grip on the centurion. He took hold of his forearm and continued, "Word spread quickly of their capture and your swift disposal of one of the scoundrels. My debt to you, Fabricius, knows no bounds." He placed his other hand on Fabricius' shoulder. "Come, disclose to us the speed and circumstances with which you dispatched my parents' murderers." He motioned to Cato. "These slaves are shown our hospitality and they return favor with barbarous butchery. For too long, they have enjoyed sustenance and shelter without."

"We can only imagine the loss you've suffered, Lucilius," Livius said, interrupting. "But we must temper our actions with wisdom and measure our response with intent." He moved toward the pair. "Fabricius, I'm well assured, acted as commanded, nobly, and with honor." He extended his hand to his son. Cato knew what he was doing. By offering Fabricius his hand, he gave his son the opportunity to be freed from Lucilius' grasp. Fabricius seized upon the opportunity and moved away, glancing at Cato over his shoulder, as he walked. Though noticed, Cato did not let the recognition show. He simply stood there, stoically, eyes forward.

It had been nearly seventeen years since Cato offered his services to house Livius. Seventeen years that he could have lived as a free man or died alongside one of the most honorable men he had ever known. But he had an obligation, and he had done well in its realization. He had found another such man, Regulus Duilius Livius. A butcher by trade, Livius had once swung a gladius in the Roman army. Since the time he left the service, Livius had managed both his finances and his position in society with prudence. In the time he had served him, Cato had grown to respect Livius.

Slaves in house Livius were treated well, respected even, as much as slaves can be respected in Rome. At least by Livius. Reprimands were, for the most part, genial and a hand was seldom, if ever, taken. Their quarters were well appointed—better than most Cato had seen, or experienced—and food was never withheld.

Livius turned and put his arm around Lucilius' shoulder. He walked the young soldier across the courtyard. "You, Lucilius, have been brothers-in-heart with Atilius since you were both young boys. Your presence is always welcome in this house."

Lucilius had been in house Livius many times. Their domus' were in the same borgo, and the two boys had become the best of friends. Though Lucilius was a year older, they had spent many hours together sparring, talking, and doing the things young boys do. Now, Atilius was eager to follow him into the Roman army.

"My father speaks all of our thoughts, Lucilius," Atilius said. "You are a brother to us all."

"It is settled then," Alba said, suddenly entering the courtyard. "Until you find your house in order, you will share our roof as your own. It will do us great honor if you would accept."

Cato raised an eyebrow.

"It is you who honor me and my family," said Lucilius. "I humbly accept and offer all my services to you and your household."

"Your presence is service enough, dear Lucilius," Alba replied, placing a gentle hand on his shoulder. "You will stay with Atilius.

His room is the most accommodating. Atilius, have you any objection?"

"No objection here," Atilius said with a wide grin.

Alba's eyes went to the blood and Lucilius' followed. "Perhaps you could start with a washing and change of clothes." He was noticeably embarrassed. "I'm sure the night's events have left you drained and disheveled. I will have a bath drawn and fresh clothes brought."

"Gratitude," said Lucilius, bowing his head.

"Let's get you settled in, my brother." Atilius slapped Lucilius on the back. As the pair left the courtyard, each sent Cato a glare.

Fabricius stepped closer to his father. "Is this the wisest move?" he asked softly, leaning in. "Lucilius has demonstrated an impetuous nature in the past. I can only imagine his state of mind at this moment. I fear Atilius idolizes him more than is healthy. His influence may not prove a positive one."

Though he had intended to be discreet, Alba had heard every word. Cato knew he wasn't the only one in the house who caught more than he let on. "This was not your father's decision," she said interrupting. "It was mine. But I'm sure your father and I share the same thoughts on the matter."

The change in Livius' face was almost undetectable—a slight tightening of the lips, a drop at the corners of the mouth. But a good slave knew his masters. Knew when something was amiss, knew when a change in mood had taken place. The only other person who would have noticed it was possibly Alba, but it did not register with her. That, or she did not care. In fact, it seemed more and more lately that Alba did not concern herself with the cares, or needs, of her husband. There were many things of late the two hadn't agreed upon.

"I meant no disrespect, mother."

"Rest your mind, son," Livius said. "I am well aware of the effect Lucilius has on your brother. Your mother's decision is wise. She understands it is much safer to keep him here, under watchful eye, than to have him running about inciting others with his prejudices. Give him time to settle. It is the right move." Livius glanced at Cato, who returned the look before facing again forward. It was an exchange noticed by Alba, and it garnered both men a disapproving glare.

The tension was broken when another slave entered the room announcing a guest.

❀

"*W*ell, Livius, it would appear you have lifted young Lucilius' spirits," Brutus said as he entered the courtyard. The comment was met with puzzlement. "I passed the two young men in the hallway," Brutus added to clarify. Livius smiled.

Alba did not.

Marcus Junius Brutus, the Younger, considered himself a family friend of house Livius, especially to Livius himself. Just into his thirties, Brutus worked sparingly under Caesar, more appropriately, he was Caesar's lackey. It was a position he put up with, for now, hoping it would lead to an appointment in the senate. Still, the position allowed him some refinements, such as the robes he was wearing, ones that easily denoted his station in society, not quite a noble, but possessing a fair amount of wealth —something also supported by his girth.

"Given the gravity of events, it will do him good to stay a few days in this house," Brutus told Livius. "May the gods guide him on his journey to, shall we say, acceptance." As Brutus made his way toward Livius, he stopped in front of Herminius and flashed him a quick, almost unnoticeable smile, then continued to Fabricius. "And gallant centurion who nobly expedited the criminals to the cross. Their suffering in this world will ill prepare them for what awaits in the underworld." Fabricius nodded. Brutus turned again to Livius. "I was informed Lucilius was here and came to pay my respects."

"Would you please excuse Brutus and I to some conversation?" Livius said to the house. Alba made no attempt to hide her displeasure, but she conceded, leaving with her two sons. After everyone was gone, Livius directed Brutus to a nearby table and offered him a seat. Cato approached with an ewer of wine and two glasses.

"So, you are quite abreast of the past day's events," Livius said smiling. "Wanted to pay your respects? I was not aware you knew Lucilius or his family."

"I am privy to many things here in Rome. You should not be surprised by that." Brutus grinned. "Besides, it gave me reason to see an old friend. It has been too long."

"Have your travels served you well?" Livius asked as Cato poured.

"Enlightening, alarming, refreshing!" Brutus said in a loud voice and raised high his glass of wine in feigned celebration. "The songs of Caesar and the Triumvirate echo in the valleys and resonate in the heart of Rome. Caesar is revered as the only son of Rome, conqueror and statesmen." He took a drink, then continued more caustically, "How safe the people feel with him at the helm of the senate. And with him in partnership with Pompey, the man who made my mother a widow so many moons ago."

"And how is your mother?" Livius inquired.

Brutus peered from the glass against his lips and smiled, "When our business here is completed, I am to meet her at Caesar's domus."

"Servilia is with Caesar now?" Livius asked. There was perplexity in his voice. It was clear he did not know Servilia had taken up with Rome's soon-to-be emperor.

"Unfortunately, yes," Brutus said and took another drink. "This day, and every day that suits him." The words fell from his tongue like bitter fruit.

"You seem troubled, dear friend. Is there something wrong with your mother?"

"With my mother? No. But I must admit, their relationship brings me no comfort." He leaned in toward Livius. "Caesar seems intent on rubbing my nose in their affair as one would a dog in his own feces. Despite my continued requests, he refuses to allow me the dignity of collecting my mother outside his place. Instead, he demands I pick her up," he stopped and scrunched his face as if he had just eaten a piece of distasteful fruit or spoiled meat, "in his bedchamber. He has me collect her in his very bedchamber." Brutus again paused. He searched the inside of his glass for comfort. "He gives me assignments to aid his future but will not grant me a higher position. He treats us just above dogs, but we have no other choice. If I want one day to be a senator of Rome, he is my best path."

"It grieves me to hear this, Brutus," said Livius.

Brutus looked up and smiled a thank you. He paused briefly then said, "My dear friend, how I wish you had found love with my mother and saved her from this abomination. Tell me Livius, why was it not so?" It was a question he shouldn't have asked. It was unfair, and he knew it, but he loathed the situation his mother was in and couldn't help but wonder what life might have been like had he been the son of Livius instead of a man he never got to know.

Livius took a deep breath and paused a moment, letting the weight of the past settle, before he answered. "Your dear mother and I have a complicated past." Like Brutus had done, he searched his own glass for the right words. "But we are two different people," he said looking up. "I long for the simple things in life, while your mother reaches for the heavens."

"Is that a bad thing, Livius?"

"Of course not, Brutus. But it does complicate a relationship, and it brings difficulties." Livius looked off in the distance clearly reliving a memory. But whether that memory was pleasant or hurtful, it was not possible to tell. After a moment, he continued, "You are fortunate to have a mother of such fortitude and spirit, Brutus. She beds the most powerful man in Rome. She certainly could have done worse. I am but a humble butcher, far from the enticement of power and exuberance to which your mother is drawn."

"You sell yourself far from station, my friend. My mother serves Caesar only in the bedroom and not the heart. He keeps her solvent with scraps and charity. I would have much rather had a simple butcher as a father."

"You are kind, Brutus," Livius said with a gentle smile. "I cherish the moments your mother and I shared and recall most with warm memories. I've been fortunate to watch you grow from a young child to the man you are today. Rome will be better served when you are in the senate." Livius paused and looked again to his glass. After a moment, he continued, "Plus, Servilia had much larger aspirations than I could ever, or would ever, achieve. Both of our lives have taken different paths. I am more than content with mine."

"To contentment, then," Brutus said and lifted his glass. Livius raised his own, and the two men shared a drink.

Brutus took a quick glance around the room, and seeing Cato standing in the corner, realized the slave had stayed the entire time. Cato was an imposing sight, tall and dark of skin, with a body forged in battle. Cato didn't dress like a slave, something Brutus was sure Livius arranged to blur the lines. While most slaves were clothed in a nondescript tunic, Cato was allowed a more conspicuous wardrobe. In fact, he could have easily been confused with a soldier, instead of a slave. He wore a seasoned-leather vest that left his well-scarred arms and shoulders exposed. Leather pants covered his legs.

"Tell me Livius, do you not fear a similar fate as our dear friends last eve with an unshackled brute but a dagger thrust away?"

Livius looked over at Cato, then back at Brutus. "Cato keeps the house in order, and that includes the slaves. For the better part of two decades, he has shared a roof with my family and me. Perhaps knowing of my skill with a knife and cleaver," he said with a grin, "or having a centurion under our roof alters any thoughts of treachery."

Livius stood, holding the wine under his nose and taking in the aroma. "But I'd like to think it is how I treat my slaves that makes the difference. I am stern but fair, and that currency fares well in keeping a certain understanding. Lucilius' house was not of this manner. His parents were more heavy-handed, more cruel. Abuse has a way of festering until one day, it bursts. If you give slaves no other choice but to attack, they will do so. Men have nothing to lose when dying is a better option than living. Tragedies such as the one last night will continue as long as Caesar focuses less on Rome and more on his desire to rule the world." Livius took a drink and then continued, "Maybe, one day, Caesar will become the great leader he thinks himself to be."

Brutus stood and extended his arm. Livius put down his glass and took the offered arm with a smile. "I have always considered you a sage disciple of truth. Your graciousness is, as always, coveted and honored. I am glad to know that Caesar has not fooled every Roman. Now I must take leave before darkness covers my path. Give my best to all in your household."

❀

*A*s Brutus left, Livius' thoughts returned to Servilia and the time the two shared. It was a lifetime ago, but the memories played like pictures in his mind. After a few moments, he finished his glass and looked over at Cato, who remained standing, arms crossed. The two men shared a knowing smile.

CHAPTER 6

L oud, provocative moans filled the bedchamber
Caesar had her bent over the bed and was taking her
from behind, his thrusts hard and purposeful. She reveled
in the power, the force, and the confidence with which the thrusts
were delivered. But it was all about Caesar. All about how he felt.
It's not that Servilia didn't enjoy sex with Caesar. She did. It's just
that every act was designed to ensure his pleasure. When he
mounted her, he did so for one reason only—to drive himself into
her as hard and deep as possible. If she reached orgasm, it was
simply an accidental byproduct of his enjoyment. And she knew,
no matter what, it was her responsibility to made sure he always
believed she had one. Caesar needed that; he needed to know he
always, without fail, satisfied his woman.

But today, she would have no problem reaching orgasm.
Today, her Caesar was satisfying her. She moaned with every
thrust, clenching her fists as she tightly clutched the bed sheets.
Caesar groaned loudly, and she felt him climaxing inside her.

"Yes, yes, yes…" Servilia yelled out over and over again as the
throws of pain and delight racked her body.

When he was finished, Caesar withdrew himself, grabbed his

tunic, and began dressing, leaving her spent, still bent over the bed. It took her several minutes to catch her breath and regain her composure. She finally climbed onto the bed and lay in the sheets, her body still tingling. Caesar had made her feel sexy this evening, and she wanted that feeling to engulf her.

Servilia watched her man attend to items on his desk. Caesar was a tall man with a body forged in battle, one he took great care to keep that way. He had powerful arms, a strong, firm chest, and sturdy legs. But it wasn't just Caesar's body that Servilia found attractive. Caesar was a handsome man with a full face, fair complexion, and intense, dark eyes. Though he spent most of his time with a furrowed brow, when he did smile, it lightened her heart.

Servilia had been married once to Marcus Junius Brutus the Elder, a tribune in the Roman Republic. Like Caesar, Brutus the Elder was a powerful man, one who went to war for his beliefs after the death of Sulla the Dictator. But then, Brutus was opposed by Pompey and assassinated by one of his men. When he died, Servilia's dreams of status and position died with him. It had taken her years to recover. Now she was here, in Caesar's bedchamber, playing the role of his mistress.

Servilia had been blessed with a body built for pleasing a man. Though she just turned fifty, she hadn't lost her touch, and her appearance looked much more of someone fifteen years younger. She moaned as required, even screamed out his name at the appropriate time, much to his assured satisfaction. Servilia knew exactly how to satisfy a man, how to make him feel he could stay harder, last longer, and fulfill her more than any other could possibly even try.

"I hope I helped bring you to a satisfying finish, my love," she said.

Caesar stood with his back toward the bed. "You meet a need," he said, "and Caesar will do just fine when you address me."

The comment brought an abrupt end to Servilia's tingle, and

she sat up straight. Servilia understood her position. She knew she was not Caesar's wife, but she also knew Caesar's union to Calpurnia, his third wife, was a marriage of convenience, one meant to cement his position in society. She was much younger than him, and he did not love her. He most likely did not love anyone. Still, Servilia did not enjoy being reminded of her position.

"Well, I'm glad I could be of help to the mighty Caesar," Servilia said and began gathering her clothing from around the bed. "Your wife should join us one eve."

Caesar moved closer to Servilia, putting his face next to hers. "My wife cannot please me the way you do."

Servilia smiled, despite herself.

"You also keep me from having to bed a slave," he added. "I suppose I should be grateful. The thought of sticking my cock inside a dog sounds more pleasing. At least you keep me from making that regretful decision. If ever you find me bedding a slave, please have me crucified for that transgression." Caesar kissed her, smiled, and returned to his desk.

Servilia was no longer smiling. "We have shared a bed for years. Can you not look beyond the flesh and see the woman? Will you not look upon me as a proper Roman woman?"

"Sex is sex, Servilia," Caesar said. "Do not confuse it with anything else. I show you favor by not keeping you close. You would only bring me distraction and tempt my enemies with dreams of large ransoms. If you want me to show you favor, simply keep your legs spread and your mouth closed. You are not part of Rome's elite. You are not my wife. Be patient and enjoy what we have."

Servilia stood at the side of the bed and finished dressing. Her mood had soured. "I'll take my leave when my son arrives. Pray your 'whore' finds safe passage home or you may be forced to take that slave girl after all." She paused. "Or would it be a slave boy? Sometimes I cannot be certain with you." Servilia couldn't help but test Caesar's patience. He had hurt her, and she wanted to hurt him back.

Caesar showed no reaction to the comment. "Where is that son of yours? Off to the market for his fifth meal of the day?"

"He is paying homage to the boy whose parents were murdered last night."

"Ahh, yes!" Caesar said with a smirk. "I quickly dispatched one of those slaves myself just this morning. Her hands were still stained with Roman blood. It is a simple pleasure. The importance of which, the senate is far too ignorant to comprehend. Instead of the sword, they deal death with words that put to slumber anyone foolish enough to listen. There is no fear generated by killing with words. Thrusting a sword through a man, or woman, now that commands attention. Attention that demands respect."

And just like that, Servilia's mood changed back. The man in front of her was powerful, intoxicating. She felt the passion spreading through her again. It was the same power she felt only moments earlier as he thrusted himself inside her. She involuntarily placed her hand under her robes, between her thighs, and would have moaned had not a knock come on the door to Caesar's bedchamber.

Caesar granted permission to enter, and a young legionnaire came into the room. Servilia quickly pulled her hand from beneath her robes. Caesar did not look up from his desk. The soldier hit his chest plate with his fist, then extended his arm. "Caesar, Brutus comes for Servilia."

Not waiting for permission, Brutus entered the room. Caesar looked up, dismissed the legionnaire, and then walked over to Brutus.

"Tell me, Brutus, did you pass any whores on your way in? Boys or girls, either will do." Caesar flashed Servilia a quick glance, then returned his attention to her son. He placed his arm around Brutus and drew him close.

Brutus stiffened. "I know of no whores, Caesar, but I have met with the centurion who killed the murderous slave this morning. A great man to have in your command."

"Your centurion takes credit undue. It was Legatus Braccius who butchered that pig," Caesar told him. "You should guard that naiveté, Brutus. It could become your undoing." He patted Brutus on the chest.

"They seemed so sure, I…"

"I know men, Brutus," Caesar said as he withdrew his arm. "I know men who choose to do as they wish and men who follow orders." He walked backed to his desk. "Braccius and I are of similar mind, and while I do grant him some liberties, it is fortunate for him that he left me some fun of my own." He picked up a set of documents and continued without looking at Brutus. "No Brutus, your centurion did not kill this day, but he will have ample opportunity in the future. Now take leave with your mother. I need to wash off her stench. My guards will see you home safely."

Still intoxicated, Servilia walked up to Caesar and kissed him deeply, intently, pressing herself against him. As she pulled away, she let her hand fall slowly down Caesar's chest, turned and walked away. "Come Brutus," she said. "It's time we go home."

❀

*B*rutus stood for a moment looking at Caesar who had returned his attention to his documents. If he had just been kissed that way, his knees probably would have buckled, but not Caesar. It didn't even seem to affect him at all. Brutus was about to speak, but thought better of it, turned, and followed his mother out the door.

45

CHAPTER 7

*J*ustina was on Fabricius' mind as he made his way down the hallway. When he heard voices coming from her room, he stopped. It was imprudent to peek inside, but he found himself unable to resist.

"Who does Atilius think he is?" Justina asked. "What makes him think he's better than you? Just because he was born a free man?"

There sat his sister on the bed, uncharacteristically clothed in a maroon dress with a fine lace bodice, looking more like she'd rather be wearing the coarse woolen tunic and metal strips of a legionnaire. Justina was speaking to Antonia, one of the house slaves, who was combing her hair. Although she seemed to enjoy it, Fabricius knew Justina would be just as happy tucking it up inside a helmet. The thought brought a smile.

Fabricius understood his sister. He knew she never felt comfortable in what their mother would call "the robes appropriate for a woman of her stature." She never understood the need to bathe oneself in the aroma of flowers or to garnish oneself with sparkling jewels. Still, he was surprised at how the dress and accompanying jewels suited her. His sister had long ago discarded the strappings of a young girl and had grown into a comely young woman.

Something must have happened between her and Atilius. Fabricius wasn't surprised. Justina and Atilius never seemed to bond. Even as children, Atilius never held back. When they all would play, sword in hand, Atilius would strike Justina just as hard as he would strike his brothers. At times, Fabricius even had to step in. Justina would run crying to their father. Atilius would find himself in trouble, but it would have no effect on him. The two tangled constantly as children. Lately, those tangles were growing in intensity.

"You didn't ask to be a slave," Justina continued, "You haven't committed some crime that would cause your station. You were simply born into slavery. How is that just? How does that make Atilius, or anyone else, better than you?"

"He scares me," Antonia admitted. Justina turned. There were tears in Antonia's eyes. "This is the only room in which I do not feel like a slave."

Justina cupped Antonia's face in her hands. "Oh Antonia, in this room, you are not a slave," she said. "In this room, you are not even my friend. Here, you are my sister." Antonia smiled and the two hugged.

Antonia was the youngest slave in the house, just slightly younger than Justina. She had no siblings, no one with which to play, argue, or confide. Her parents had died when she was young. Being both an orphan and a slave, growing up had to have been difficult. Being so close in age, and with neither having an actual sister, it was only natural that Antonia and Justina formed a bond —a sisterhood. Something that was a most certainly a comfort to them, but an annoyance to others on both sides of the wall.

"The thought of his hands on you," Justina said, as they embraced. "I will never let anyone hurt you."

"I long for the day that we are truly sisters," Antonia said.

Fabricius took the opportunity to knock. "May I enter," he

asked and pushed the door open just enough to stick his head inside. The aroma of flowers drifted from the room.

"Of course, brother," Justina said and sat a little straighter. "You are always welcome," she added, then rose to greet him with a hug.

Fabricius embraced his sister. He glanced over at Antonia who quickly looked down when his eyes caught hers. If he wasn't mistaken, she was blushing.

"Come, sit." Justina took her brother by the hand and lead him to the bed. Antonia moved as the two sat. "Is it true that Lucilius favors us with his presence for, perhaps, more than a day?"

"Are you sure politics isn't where your heart truly lies, dear sister?" Fabricius asked. "You ask questions to which you clearly know the answer."

Justina flashed a coy smile. "Answers, brother, which I'd prefer not be true. I am concerned with the bitter concoction Atilius and our new guest brew by their association."

Despite what his father had said, Fabricius was worried as well. He patted his sister's hand. "It is only temporary, Justina. Father says he is better here where his anger can, shall we say, be curtailed." He hoped his words would reduce her apprehension, even if he didn't believe them himself.

"I suppose," Justina said.

"You know, Justina, you are the only one who has not asked to hear what happened last evening. Are you not curious to learn the gory details of Lucilius' parents' murder or wonder who might next befall a similar tragedy?"

Justina slid closer to her brother still holding his hand. "I do not need to hear gory details to understand the tragedy that has befallen Lucilius." She squeezed his hand. "I fear Rome has not seen the last of these attacks, and you standing between them brings me nothing but worry. What would I do without my big, strong brother to guide me through this life?" Justina smiled and gave him a kiss on the cheek.

He returned his sister's smile, then addressed Antonia. "Would you give us pardon?"

Antonia looked to Justina for guidance. When Justina nodded, Antonia stood and headed for the door.

"Please close it behind you," Fabricius said and watched her leave, waiting before he continued. When the door closed, he returned his attention to Justina.

"Your concern for me is appreciated, but unfounded. You must put your faith in the gods Justina, for what happens to your big brother. It is in their hands."

Justina gave him another hug.

He returned her embrace. She was warm against him and smelled of fine flowers. There was little in the day's events that had made him happy, or brought him comfort. This was one. After a moment he pulled back, then stood. "We have other matters to discuss."

Justina looked concerned. "What is it, brother?"

"Your words, Justina, so outspoken." He paced. "It is not womanly, and it is not wise. These words, these ideas, the ones you so freely say within these walls must now remain purely your thoughts, not to be uttered."

Justina sat upright and crossed her arms. "I do not favor being censured or quieted in my own house, Fabricius."

He stopped and faced his sister. "You create danger, Justina. Lucilius could take your opinions as not favoring the empire. He is a member of the Roman army and anyone who does not believe as we do, or as we are told to believe, causes friction. Dangerous friction."

"So you would have me remain a dumb mute?"

Fabricius sat back down and took his sister's hands. "Of course not, Justina. I am perfectly happy with you just the way you are, and in this house, your thoughts are always welcome."

"For the most part."

"Indeed, for the most part," he conceded. "But with an outsider staying among us," he paused. "Certainly, you can see the danger in speaking one's mind, acting as one is not expected to act."

"As a woman, you mean."

"Yes, and as an owner of slaves. Just now, your encounter with Antonia was more of equals. I know that is your nature, and it is one of the many things I love about you, sister, but you must keep vigilant and act the part until our guest is gone. I cannot stress this enough. It is of the utmost importance."

Justina's face turned a ruby red as the heat rushed to her cheeks.

"Really Justina, it is but for a little while. I am not asking you to change. I am simply asking you to use caution. There are wolves among us."

Justina suddenly stood, arms still crossed. His talk was having the opposite effect he had hoped. He stood and placed his hands on her shoulders. "If you cannot stop completely, can you at least tone it down?"

The comment brought Justina to laughter. An unexpected laughter. Fabricius couldn't help but join in.

Justina turned to face her brother. "I will hold my tongue and play nice. I understand it is slaves that took Lucilius' parents' lives, and I'm sure that Lucilius' hatred toward slaves in general has grown as a result. I will do this for you, brother. But only you."

Fabricius smiled. "Thank you."

"But I will want a favor in return."

His smile wavered. "Of course, if it is within my power."

Justina sat back down, and Fabricius sat next to her. "I have changed my mind, please tell me about your patrol today and the slaves you encountered."

The request was not what he had hoped for. "Are you sure you want to hear it? Should we not just talk about today's sparring match? I heard it was eventful."

Justina nodded. His attempt to change the subject had failed.

"Very well. I can see I will get no peace from you until I tell you the story. There were four of them huddled under the bridge heading out of Rome. Two were cowering like scared pups and the other two, clearly the leaders, were vicious, like rabid dogs. Those two were dispatched quickly, one at the scene and the other a short time later at the hands of Caesar. The remaining two have been stretched onto crosses and will join their coconspirators in Tartarus soon."

"Caesar killed one of them?"

"Yes, when they were presented to him. I heard news from Brutus before he took leave."

"Does he have the right to do so?"

"Caesar has the right to do as he wishes," Fabricius said. "He is not questioned on what he can and cannot do. He just does and Rome accepts."

Justina paused for a moment, taking in the account. "How was the first slave killed? Caesar was not at the bridge."

"No, Caesar was not there. It was our patrol that was responsible for the first death." Fabricius wasn't happy with the direction her questions were taking. He was sorry he had mentioned it to her in the first place. There was only one question left to ask, and it was the one question he wanted more than anything not to answer. He tried to will her not to ask it, but he knew it was coming anyway.

"At who's hand did the slave die?"

Fabricius looked down and was silent for the longest time, then suddenly stood. "I must prepare for dinner," he said, his posture more a soldier than a brother. "Please remember what we spoke of regarding Lucilius."

He opened the door to leave. Justina sat in silence. When he was halfway out the door, he stopped. "Well played today besting Herminius I hear," he said without looking back in the room. "Clearly, he has no place on the battlefield. Fortunately, he is a natural born talker. He may yet make a great senator."

Justina was silent.

"What are we to do with you, sister? You seem to refuse to fit into any established role."

"Why must one fit into a role, brother? What good has that done anyone?"

Fabricius looked down and shook his head. "That dress suits you," he said and slipped out of the room, shutting the door behind him.

❀

*J*ustina sat quite a while in silence, then she stood and fixed her robes in preparation for dinner. "One day, my name will be known to Caesar himself," she whispered. "The last thing any man who challenges me will feel is the sting of my sword."

CHAPTER 8

MARCH 6, 55 BC

*T*he slave hadn't seen him following. He had been instructed to wait in the entryway, but he was Caesar, and he waited for no one, especially when asked to do so by a slave. He could hear Crassus as he approached the dining room, still undetected.

"Try the sauce, Tertulla," Crassus said to his wife. "Its sweetness is derived from the honey of Egyptian bees. It arrived this very morning."

Before his wife could answer, the slave entered the room. "Dominus, Caesar bids an audience…" The words had no sooner left the slave's mouth when Caesar strode into the room from behind him. As he passed the terrified man, he smiled.

Crassus waved the slave on. "Hail the bull who rushes in with matters far too urgent to observe decorum," Crassus said without standing. "Apologies for not having set a plate for you at our table, Caesar, but I do not recall inviting you to dinner. I was expecting you a bit later."

"You invited me, and I have come," Caesar said, studying the room. Marcus Licinius Crassus was a wealthy man, a very wealthy man. In fact, he was likely the wealthiest man in all of Rome. Like all good Romans, Crassus flaunted his wealth. It was apparent in every part of his life, but no more so than in his magnificent home. Stepping into Crassus' domus was like stepping into an emperor's palace. The spacious house surrounded a grand atrium, filled with all manner of plants, flowers, and olive trees. Entrance to the home was gained by passing through a large peristylum, complete with a fountain, in the center of which stood a life-size marble statue of Venus, the Goddess of love, sex, beauty, fertility, and victory, her blond locks flowing in the wind.

A marble bust of Crassus himself, clearly from his younger days, greeted guests. Just above the bust was a relief featuring the Greek hero Meleager attacking a boar with a spear while Artemis, the Goddess of hunting and wild animals, looked on. As was common at the time, Meleager was depicted nude. The walls of Crassus' house were decorated with colored plaster and the floors adorned with intricate bright-colored mosaics depicting birds, animals, gods, and, of course, people. Crassus even had himself portrayed in battle. A stunning victory over the slave king Spartacus. Dozens of sculptures, mainly of nude women, or men manhandling nude women, filled the great hallway.

"Besides," Caesar continued, "I have matters I wish to discuss with you before your house fills with eager ears and rampant tongues too quick to spill lies. I'm sure your family has had their fill of food."

"You wish to discuss Pompey then," Crassus said.

Caesar was not pleased that Crassus had said the name aloud. "Yes, Crassus," he said with a glare, "I wish to discuss Pompey."

He could tell by Crassus' face that it was best to stop all talk of Pompey until his family left the dining area. He waited as Crassus motioned for all to leave, then took a seat at the opposite end of the table. The room smelled of peacock and ostrich. All manner of apples, oranges, pineapples, and mangos filled bowls placed strategically around the table. Smaller bowls held dates and nuts. Goblets were filled with wine.

"Please, go on," Crassus said.

"I pray we are of the same mind. That we share the same intentions, and that I may openly speak with confidence."

Crassus took a sip of wine without offering Caesar a glass, paused, and then answered. "It goes without saying that I share your thoughts on a great many things, Caesar. You may speak freely with me, but it is best you do so only when we are in private. You must be mindful when Pompey is around. His army is a viable match for your own. The two of you may be divorced in aspirations, but you are married in the eyes of the senate and the people of Rome. That is what gives the Triumvirate our power." Crassus took another drink. "It would be wise to hold back your disdain for the man, certainly the more visible part."

"What have I to fear from the senate? Those gargantuan lumps are too busy having orgies and living their sumptuous lifestyles." Caesar lifted an apple from the table, smelled it, and then placed it back in the bowl. "A lifestyle which I graciously provide them and will continue doing so until I rightfully lead Rome, as Emperor." He reached for a different piece of fruit. "As far as the people are concerned, they bow to me. They worship Caesar."

Crassus stood and walked to the other end of the table, taking a seat next to Caesar. "I caution you," he said and leaned into Caesar, his tone much softer. "Share your thoughts openly, but only with me and none other. The walls, even these walls, will echo your intentions, and if those intentions should make their way into Pompey's ears, it would make things," Crassus paused, "let's just say complicated. Like it or not, Caesar, the senate is our ally. Whether that allegiance is gained by respect or fear, it matters little. You must treat them as allies, play the role. Pompey has significant influence in the senate. The end will justify the means."

"Here we are, Crassus, almost two decades from your defeat of the great Spartacus and yet you still credit another. Pompey has continued to rise because of false tales. You, yourself have injected your support into those tales." He leaned forward until he was face-to-face with the man. "At what point do we show Rome who he truly is?"

Crassus looked down, then stood and went back to the other end of the table. "Pompey was not completely void of due credit for our victory over the rebel king. Spartacus raised an army 70,000 strong. He was a formidable opponent even for a leader like myself. Pompey's assistance, although brief, did end the uprising."

Caesar returned the fruit to its bowl. "You needn't worry, Crassus. I am no child. I know what is expected of me and will play my role with the senate. I will also coddle your puppet, Pompey, for now. But when the time comes to dispose of good Pompey, I will do so with as much regard as the straw that wipes my ass."

For the second time that evening, the house slave announcing a visitor interrupted Crassus. "Pompey to see you, Dominus." Only this time, the visitor didn't immediately follow the announcement.

"Show him in," Crassus said and stood. He tried to look noble, but Caesar could see the sweat beginning to form on his brow.

Gnaeus Pompeius Magnus, known simply as Pompey, was younger than Crassus, but older than Caesar, and while he commanded a large, well-respected army, he looked more like a self-indulging senator these days than a seasoned warrior. His short but curly hair was combed forward in the Roman style and he wore a muted tunic, covered by a leather breast plate dyed yellow, emblazoned with his crest, and draped with a bright red robe. When he entered the room, he looked first at Crassus, then eyed Caesar sitting in the chair.

"Good evening, Crassus," Pompey said, passing Caesar to offer his hand. "It would appear I am late."

"Nonsense, good Pompey," Crassus said taking his hand. "Your timing, as usual, is perfect. Caesar himself arrived only moments ago."

Pompey smiled broadly, but his face betrayed his thoughts. "Good Caesar," he said, offering his hand. "Or should that be Hail, Caesar? I do hope your timing coincided with dessert?"

Caesar accepted Pompey's hand without bothering to stand. "Hail, Caesar?" he asked. "Well spoken, Pompey, but a simple curtsy will suffice. And I missed dessert, though I'm certain one of the slaves here can bring you something if emaciation has you wretched." He dropped his gaze to Pompey's expanding midriff.

Pompey offered Caesar a forced smile but did not release his hand. Instead, he tightened his grip. He had powerful forearms, and while his middle may have expanded with age, the steel in his arms, forged by sword in hand, had not lessened over the years. The grip caught Caesar off guard, and he adjusted his position. Pompey noticed and seemed pleased. But Caesar was no soft politician. His grip had been tested in battle as well, and he had never once had his gladius knocked free from his hand. Both men worked to squeeze the other into submission, eyes locked, each reluctant to be the first to let go.

Crassus spoke to break the tension. "Shall we all take a seat and discuss the business at hand?" he asked, moving back to his original seat. "Pompey, please, take a seat here by me."

Pompey's eyes were slits and his smile tight. It looked as if he was about to take a step toward Caesar when he suddenly chuckled slightly and released his grip. He walked slowly and deliberately to Crassus, then took a seat. But he wasn't done.

"What is the name of that woman of yours?" Pompey asked Caesar. "The one who attends to all your boyish needs?" Crassus shot Pompey a disapproving look, but it had no effect. "Servilia, isn't it? As I recall, I killed her husband in battle many years ago but never had intentions on someone so threadbare to take his place."

Caesar grinned. If Pompey wanted to play games, he was happy to oblige. "You would be surprised at Servilia's talents. The finest and most experienced whores in all of Rome have never satisfied a man as much as she." He paused. "That is, for those who prefer a woman's touch, of course." He sat back in the chair and lifted one leg onto the other, purposely showing Pompey the bottom of his shoe. The offence was noted. "Of course, her best talent is keeping me from bedding slaves, as is the custom, I understand, with others." He put his foot back down and leaned forward. "Oh wait, did I not hear that you, Pompey, favor the company of slaves? The same slaves who murder good Roman citizens."

"Slaves serve a need without entanglement," Pompey replied. "They have neither voice nor agenda. The same cannot be said for Roman whores."

"The gods be dammed!" Crassus yelled out. "You two are like a couple of cackling fish mongers debating the price of the day's catch. Be still, both of you! If you recall, we have business. The reason for our attendance here this day."

His words cut through the thickness that filled the room, drawing the attention of both Pompey and Caesar. "Take heed and keep your minds to the task at hand," he continued, "There are many whose land and people we've conquered that would take revenge should we forget ourselves and become comfortable. Caesar, your quick handling of the slaves who killed two nights past sends a good message, one I hope will echo throughout Rome. Displaying those who disobey their masters in the market place tomorrow will go far. And Pompey, I pray the senate will be made aware of how quickly and effectively the situation was handled."

The two military men nodded their heads in agreement. Crassus continued, "Do you recall some fifteen years ago when we met at this same location? The three of us bonding together so no force in the Empire could oppose us. Strong as a fist to rule as we choose."

Caesar remembered the meeting well. The rebel uprising had just ended, and it was agreed that Pompey and Crassus would be held up as heroes of the battle, though Crassus to a much lesser scale. For his part, Caesar had been leading conquests, expanding the Roman Empire. The three men agreed that day to work together, forming the Triumvirate, for the mutual benefit of Rome, or at least, that's what they told each other. In reality, Caesar saw it as a stepping-stone to the empire he was destined to rule. There was only one man who stood in his way.

"This walk down memory lane is nice, Crassus," Caesar said. "But what are you getting at? If you have a point to make, then make it."

"With both of your various concerns in Rome," Crassus replied, "I propose to take position of Legatus once again, as we expand our interests abroad, and lead an army to those means."

Caesar laughed hard. Pompey joined him. Crassus frowned.

"You? The richest cock in Rome, want to lead the charge?" Caesar said. "I would think a man of your station, and years, would rather enjoy the fruits of your past glories and not muddy yourself in the trenches. What have you to gain by such an action?"

Crassus' eyes drew flat, and his posture stiffened.

"I have to stand with Caesar on this and question motives, Crassus," Pompey said. "Your sage counsel and wealth have brought Rome the world. War is an ugly thing, as you well know. Surely your battle with the slave king Spartacus hastened that realization. You have achieved by hand, or by proxy, a great many victories. It has come time for you to sit back and enjoy the spoils."

Crassus had celebrated his sixth decade of life and yet, did not have the body of a man befitting his age. While wealth often brought with it portly stomachs carried on weak limbs, Crassus had not let wealth diminish his physical stature. Still, this was unexpected. Crassus wasn't just posturing, this was something he truly desired. Glory in campaign. Caesar understood the desire and need to fulfill the thirst that can only be quenched in battle. He also knew when and when not to press an advantage.

"Counting coins brings little solace to a heart intent on the fight," Caesar said. Though he addressed Crassus, the comment was meant for Pompey. "The glory of battle is exhilarating. It keeps one youthful. I understand your need, Crassus, as just yesterday morning I myself tasted blood. But, Pompey is right on this."

"I hear what you both are saying and shall take your words under advisement," said Crassus. He was obviously disappointed and did little to hide it. But business had to be done. "For now, shall we simply enter into an agreement." He stood. "Your pledge to keep close the senate and the people while maintaining a keen eye on the prosperous future of Rome? Agree and I will continue to pour my wealth and influence upon you both."

Pompey stood and took Crassus' hand in agreement. When Caesar stood, Pompey flamboyantly curtseyed, then walked past him without offering his hand. "I shall take my leave, Crassus, so that Caesar may enjoy his dessert." He turned to Caesar. "Watch for the seeds, good Caesar, we wouldn't want you to choke."

After Pompey left the room, Crassus walked to the other end of the table. "You must watch more closely what you say to that man," he warned. "The two of you are insufferable, and I fear the consequences your words will bring."

Caesar watched Pompey depart, then suddenly turned to Crassus. "Your wealth may have aided in my rise, Crassus, but the people of Rome love Caesar, with or without your money. It would do you well to keep that thought close as you enjoy the

60

prosperity brought from being associated with the Emperor. I will continue to focus on Rome as you wish, but only because that is my focus, not because you think you have right to command it." He paused, then returned his gaze to the exit. After a moment he continued, "I loathe that man, but I will endure his insolence until the time when there is no longer any benefit to our association."

CHAPTER 9

*a*ntonia was late, and she knew it. They would all be preparing the evening meal by now and Cato would be wondering where she was. If the gods were on her side, she would be able to slip in unnoticed. She could jump right in to her duties, and Cato would not be the wiser. Unfortunately, the gods cared little about slaves, and instead of sneaking in undetected, she met Cato, arms folded, waiting for her arrival.

"You continue to extend privilege beyond your station, Antonia," he said looking down at the young slave. "Have we not already spoken of this?"

"I was called by Justina," Antonia replied, placing an emphasis on her master's name. "Perhaps you should keep close thoughts of your own station and take less regard for mine, old man." Cato may have been the head of the slaves, but he was an old man with old ideas, and Antonia was not about to stand there and listen to them. She tried to walk by him, but Cato put his arm out to stop her.

"Your care is but for your own regard, Antonia. Your fraternizing is much too provocative, especially after the last few days' events. You bring attention not only to yourself, but to the entire household."

"It is only these walls and your constant scolding that keep me shackled to the reality of my station." She sent Cato a glare that only a teenager could muster. "Outside these quarters, Justina and I have nurtured a sisterhood. That is something your kind could never understand."

"It is solely for your own good that I tether you to reality, Antonia," Cato said, unfolding his arms. "Justina is not your sister, she is your master, your Domina. I too have a rapport with one in this house, someone who confides in me. But I am continually aware that he is my master and it is his will that determines my life. Being old may have taken my hair, but it has also afforded me a perspective of many years. I have seen how quickly a relationship can change from one of camaraderie to one of a dog lying at her master's feet."

She was not a dog, and she knew Justina would never treat her that way. Cato did not understand. His taste of freedom was brief, possibly bitter. Perhaps he'd been a slave so long, he no longer knew how to be a free man. Why he gave it up so quickly, so willingly.

"Tell me, Cato," she said, "was the taste of freedom so bitter that you preferred the life of a dog instead? For how many years have you been owned? Do you even remember?"

"I have served this family well and with honor for nearly seventeen years," Cato answered. He refolded his arms and stood a bit more erect.

Antonia shook her head. Cato was an anomaly. She didn't understand how he could be so proud of serving a house as a slave, especially having once been free. "Why Cato? Why would anyone ever give up freedom once the taste has crossed their lips? I do not understand how a free man could possibly choose the life of a slave? Were you captured in battle? Were you devoid of property?"

"I neither owned land nor was captured in war, Antonia. My reasons for being here are my own, and you would be wise not to project your own desires onto another's way of thinking. It is a commitment I have chosen and I am honored to fulfill. Something I am sure you would not, or could not, understand."

Cato was right about that. She did not understand. All she felt was sorry for him. "I was born into slavery," she said. "Both my parents were slaves under this very roof. But I ache for freedom. I don't know how you cannot. I may have been treated with kindness in this house and provided for after my parents passed, but even though they regarded this house as their home, I long for something more."

"It is a longing that will bear only bitter fruit, I'm afraid."

"If you cannot understand my desires, then at least consider my role. I am forever beholden to Justina. I trust her to remind me if I were to take liberties with my station. As far as she is concerned, this is my house as well."

"Then surely disappointment is your fate, girl. Your *brother* Fabricius killed a slave this very week."

The news was unexpected, and it hit Antonia hard. She stepped back and cupped her hands to her mouth. "No," she said shaking her head. "It can't be true."

"Fabricius is a soldier, Antonia. He obeys a higher order, one that has little regard for the life, or desires, of a slave." Antonia continued to shake her head as Cato pressed on. "Open your eyes, Antonia, and understand that, lest for the grace of the gods, we will all befall a fate similar to those who hang on the cross. And now, we share a roof with the son of the slain parents."

Antonia wanted to hear none of it. How many nights she had dreamed of Fabricius' gentle hands caressing her arms, her thighs...her breasts. "Fabricius would never lay sword nor hand upon me," she said without thinking. "His touch would be welcome with open heart, and I believe he feels the same."

Cato frowned. "If that were the case, he could take you whenever he wanted, as is his right. He may be a gentleman, but he is still Roman. Those dreams need be replaced with reality."

Antonia was unable to hide her shock.

Cato looked down at her. There was pity in his eyes. He placed a hand on her arm. "I fear for you, Antonia. Still, my advice and guidance is here to help if you choose to take it. I pray you will strive to make wiser choices. If the day comes when you are shown real Roman law for slaves, I will not be able to help you. Now, wash up and help prepare dinner for our masters."

CHAPTER 10

*D*inner would not be enjoyable this evening. Not dressed as she was. It wasn't bad enough Lucilius was staying with them, but now she was forced to wear these silly robes and decorate herself with feathers and jewels. It was embarrassing. Still, Justina didn't want to upset her mother so she did as she was told and transformed herself into a "proper Roman woman."

Justina was the last to arrive, being in no hurry to come to dinner. By the glare she received as she took her seat, her mother was not pleased by her tardiness. It didn't help that she had to sit beside her. At least having Fabricius on her other side would help balance things a bit. Herminius, who was seated across from Alba, smiled at his sister. She smiled back, but her mood changed when she saw Atilius and Lucilius next to him. Sitting at the head of the table was Livius. He raised his eyebrows at his daughter, then smiled when she mouthed an apology.

Cato and another house slave stood in opposing corners as other slaves brought out the main entrée of boar, along with bowls of fruit, nuts, bread, and jugs of wine. Everyone began to eat. Everyone that is, except Lucilius. He seemed to have no appetite but was looking down, moving the food around his plate. Alba noticed. "Is all well, Lucilius?"

Lucilius looked up at Alba. "Yes, of course. It is just that, well, family dinners at my house were seldom shared by all of us. This is a genuine pleasure, and I am humbled to be a part of it. Blessings to all who dine here."

"You are kind, dear Lucilius. But it is we who are honored to have you," Alba said and gave him a motherly smile.

Justina was touched at Lucilius' show of emotion. She couldn't image what it must have been like to find your parents slaughtered, to arrive home and find their butchered bodies. Despite herself, her heart went out to him. That is, until she saw the distasteful face he made when a slave bent by him to place a bowl of fruit on the table.

Her father must have noticed it too. "Until the day comes when you can stand on your own," Livius said, drawing Lucilius' attention, "we are steadfast in seeing to your comfort and sustenance."

Lucilius smiled shyly, then turned unexpectedly and addressed Justina. "Your bosom must swell with pride sitting next to a man who embodies the protections of Rome." Justina ignored Lucilius, but it did not stop him. "It was a swift and true thrust that avenged my parents," he said to Fabricius, "spilling the blood of miscreants. This is the reason I joined the Roman army," he turned to Atilius, "and look forward to Atilius' commitment to arms in the near future."

Atilius smiled brightly. Justina was quickly losing her appetite as well.

"Fabricius did as he was commanded," Livius added. "Which is all that can be asked of a soldier."

"Indeed!" said Lucilius. "But it begs the question why we would even allow slaves to exist in the first place? In my house, slaves will be shackled. Unchained only to do as I command."

Justina's face turned as red as the pomegranates in the bowl in front of her. Fabricius put his hand on her leg and squeezed it. The touch startled her and brought her attention away from the vile coming from their guest's mouth. She looked up at her brother, who returned her glance with pleading eyes.

Herminius spoke. "We thank the gods for watching over our brother and placing him safely within our walls, Lucilius. And it seems that Justina is destined to follow in his, yours, and Atilius' footsteps. She quickly bested me in our last sparring session."

"Yes, Justina will be quite the warrior, without man or mission," Atilius jumped in. "Living here, I'm sure, until the day she finally succumbs to foolish goals that will never come to be, or chooses the life of a Vestal Virgin."

The look Justina flashed Atilius would have made the demons in Tartarus cower. Fabricius squeezed her leg a second time, only on this occasion, it did not have the same effect. "Oh dear brother," she said to Atilius, "better it would be to die alone for a just cause than to be unworthy of companionship. Lucky for you, there will always be slaves to satisfy your uncontrollable lust. And if they are gone, there is always your own hand."

"Justina!" Alba yelled.

Herminius spit out his food.

"Such talk is unbecoming of a proper Roman woman." Alba continued, "Sometimes I think it would be better if your tongue was snatched from your mouth. I'm sure a full day of chores tomorrow will slow that tongue of yours."

Atilius smiled.

Justina had crossed the line, and she knew it. She looked down at her plate and then up at Fabricius who was shaking his head.

"You could learn a great deal from your brothers, Justina," her father spoke up. "Fabricius does as commanded and has attained a centurion rank faster than most. Although I do believe I was a year younger when I got that title," Livius smiled at Fabricius. "Herminius' command of words far out favors swordplay. Rome does well having both types of men. One must learn when to use the sword and when to use the tongue."

"Your father speaks the truth, Justina," Alba said. "Rome has legions of soldiers. It has no need for your sword. The day is not long away to introduce you officially to society and with the gods help, find a suitable man. I do not see any currency in favoring the sword or holding close confidence in slaves. Men would find that unbecoming of a proper Roman woman."

There was that phrase again.

Lucilius jumped in, seemingly unable to resist. "Some yet find assurance with their slaves and that favoritism is alarming," he said. "I find it best to shackle them tightly. Unless, of course, it hinders their service."

Just then, the second course was brought in, and the room grew quiet. Justina sat still, trying to focus on the dish in front of her. Alba watched the motions of the slaves. Justina knew she was running a checklist in her head, making sure every task was completed as expected. Livius looked over at his daughter. Their eyes meet briefly. His face was not one of anger but of confusion. She imagined he was wondering what to do with her.

Atilius did little to hide a smug grin. But his smile was quickly dispatched when his eyes were met by Fabricius. Lucilius was not paying attention to the family at all. Instead, he stared at the slaves, intently watching every move each one made. When a female slave placed a dish in front of him, his body tightened, and he involuntarily pulled away.

"Is all well?" Livius asked.

Lucilius was wide-eyed. "Apologies," he said, "but the sight of slaves has made me uneasy. May I ask pardon and retire to my room?"

"Lucilius is correct," Atilius added. "Too many slaves have extended their welcome beyond reproach. If it was not for our centurion, my prowess with a gladius, even Justina's weak abilities, thoughts of escape could likely fancy the desires of the slaves within these very walls. Father, you were once a soldier. Do I not speak the truth when I say we would slaughter these ingrates before they even considered drawing a knife or sword against us? Would it not be best to keep them chained, as most Romans do?"

This was getting out of hand. While she did not agree with it, Justina could certainly understand Lucilius' apprehension toward slaves. However, Atilius was simply displaying bravado in the sight of a friend. Justina looked to her father, willing him to speak up, to do something.

Atilius' words had apparently done the trick. "Perhaps it's best if you accompany Lucilius to his room, Atilius," Livius said in the voice of a commander. "It would appear you have become over-agitated from the week's events. Take time to clear your head."

Atilius turned to his mother looking for comfort but received none. It was Justina's turn to flash the smug smile. As she hoped, it infuriated Atilius. He stood up sharply, forcing his chair back-ward. Livius sent him a warning glare.

Lucilius, placed his hand on Atilius' arm. "Apologies, Livius," he said. "Atilius and I will take our leave."

Livius nodded, but his face remained hard.

Fabricius watched as the two men left. "Perhaps a tug on the leash of both Lucilius and Atilius will hold them at bay before they rush to error, father. Cato is a trusted slave who watches over this house. Neither he, nor any of the others have given us reason not to trust their actions. Antonia tends to Justina more in the manner of a sister than a slave."

Alba slammed her fork down onto her plate so hard that it made Justina jump.

"Never say that again, Fabricius," Alba bellowed. "A slave will never be a relation to any in our family."

Livius ignored his wife and spoke to his son. "I foresee a furtive plot brewing between those two. I will ask Cato to keep a close watch over them. They will avoid initiating a fight with him, regardless of their personal convictions." He addressed the rest of the family. "That being said, if any of you notice anything disconcerting, make haste in reporting it to me." He then turned to Alba. "I am still the head of this household," he said purposefully, "and until something changes, my word, my will."

With the sting of his mother's words still fresh, Justina leaned into Fabricius. "You seem more concerned about slaves than I," she whispered, "yet you kill them on command."

"Do us all a favor, sister, and fill your mouth with bread, so that it may prevent you from running it so," he said back, louder and stronger than the whisper he received. "Such a trait may make you more appealing in your search for a man."

Now everyone at the table was angry.

CHAPTER 11

*W*hen Braccius entered the room, Caesar was sitting at his desk, surrounded by parchment. "Hail, Caesar!" he said and slammed his fist against his metal chest plate before extending it outward.

Caesar looked up. "Yes Braccius, come in."

Braccius walked over to the desk and stood at attention, waiting to be addressed. He was still in uniform, gladius by his side, but without his helmet. This was not a place he liked or wanted to be. In fact, he could already feel the sweat forming in the palms of his hands and backs of his knees. His pits would be next. Braccius was much more comfortable in front of his troops or on the field of battle.

Caesar reviewed several documents, one at a time. He seemed to be in no hurry to speak to Braccius. It did little to relieve Braccius' apprehension. As he stood there, he ran through everything he had done that Caesar could have discovered. By the time Caesar turned his attention to his Legatus, Braccius was floating in sweat.

"I have inquiry about a certain centurion," Caesar said.

"I take pride in knowing all men under my command, Caesar,

but I would need you to be a bit more specific. Of whom do you speak?"

"One involved in a recent encounter. The centurion you were on patrol with earlier this week. He stood by your side when you captured the four slaves."

Braccius knew immediately of whom Caesar spoke. "That centurion's name is Fabricius."

"Tell me of him."

"He's a good man." Braccius said, trying his best not to act unnerved. He wasn't sure why Caesar wanted to know about Fabricius, why his name was coming up now, but he decided it was best to show the man in the best light. "He has risen quickly and is most astute. He comes well reared from a noble family and has served Rome faithfully for seven years. He is evolving as a leader and is quick on his feet, but follows orders well and is quite skilled with a sword."

Caesar returned to his documents, moving them from one position on his desk to the next, looking at each only briefly. Braccius was left to wonder about the reason behind the inquiry. Then Caesar spoke unexpectedly. "Can he best you?"

Braccius smiled and almost chuckled. "We have sparred some. He has failed as of yet to best me, though he continues to improve."

"I see," Caesar said and looked once again to his papers.

Braccius took a deep breath. "If I may inquire Caesar, Fabricius is a loyal soldier to Rome. Does a concern exist?"

Caesar took his time before answering. "Most likely not. Though tales of his slave killing seem somewhat exaggerated. It had the mark of a more skilled swordsman." He stood up, leaned on his desk and locked eyes with Braccius. "Someone of a higher rank."

It was becoming very clear that Braccius had made a mistake when he ordered his centurion to take responsibility for killing the slave at the aqueduct. "Apologies, Caesar. It was indeed my sword that parted the dog from his earthly bonds. It was, I'm afraid, a task of simple pleasure, much as I saw in your own eyes when you did the same that afternoon."

Caesar walked over to Braccius and placed an arm around his shoulder. Braccius stiffened. "Relax, my friend," Caesar said and patted him on his chest. "Your loyalty is without question. You, and your sword, have served me well over the years. What you do on patrol is of little concern to me." Braccius let out an audible breath.

Caesar removed his arm and returned to the other side of his desk. "However, ignoble boasting for a task not performed does give me pause." Braccius' relief was cut short, and he stiffened a second time. Caesar continued, "Tell me, this Fabra…"

"Fabricius."

"Fabricius," he repeated. "Is he a braggart?"

"It is not a trait I have noticed in him. I would be surprised to hear he made such claims to other than as I had commanded."

Caesar stood in front of his chair and returned his attention to the parchment before him. "Tell me of his family. Who are they? Do you know them? More importantly, have I heard of them?"

"Fabricius is of house Livius, a most favored butcher of Rome."

Caesar suddenly looked up. "This centurion's father is Livius? I know this name."

"I am not surprised, Caesar. Livius was once a soldier himself under Pompey's rule. He often shares the best cuts for the legion. I doubt though that his meats have made their way to the senate or your plates."

Caesar lifted his head. Though he gazed forward, his eyes were clearly seeing the past. He stayed there for a while, then finally spoke. "Yes, I know this name. Livius. He once held the heart of Servilia."

"That must have been a long time ago, Caesar. He is married with four children, the oldest being Fabricius, who is well into his twenties. I'm certain he has no claim on Servilia."

Caesar was suddenly and harshly brought back to the present. "You think I am concerned with a past affair?" he barked. "When Caesar beds a woman, they lose all thoughts of any other."

"Apologies Caesar," Braccius said and bowed his head.

Caesar seemed to return to his thoughts. "Yet, there does seem to be some crossing of destiny between this family and your soon-to-be emperor. Something that may be worth querying."

"What would you have me do, Caesar?"

Caesar returned his attention directly to Braccius. "Arrange an audience with this butcher, and I will determine where his true allegiance lies."

"As you command. I will arrange a meeting this coming week." Braccius saluted and exited the room, leaving Caesar to his thoughts.

🌸

*C*aesar rubbed his chin, looked down at the parchment in front of him, then took his seat. Though he was first a warrior, his time with the senate had taught him the ways of a politician, and the one thing he had learned was to take advantage of opportunities that were laid before him. He couldn't help but feel that one such opportunity had just occurred.

CHAPTER 12

*J*ustina swiped the wooden gladius hard through the air, pulling it down in a cutting motion across her body. She raised it again and duplicated the motion in the opposite direction, then repeated the action again and again, pushing out a large breath of air with each swipe.

The maroon dress lay draped unceremoniously over the end of her bed, the jewels scattered on her dressing table. It had not been a good day. Though it started out well, it had gone downhill quickly. Dinner had been ruined, and now she faced a full day of chores on the morrow. Even Fabricius was mad at her. She couldn't blame him, though; she had promised to hold her tongue. *Atilius makes it so hard.* Now Justina was ending the day as it had begun, with practice sword in hand, only this time, she was in her undergarments.

The lightest of knocks came on the door. It was so light, she almost didn't hear it. She put down the sword, slipped on a cover, and went to the door. Antonia was on the other side.

"Come in," Justina said with a smile. Antonia was always a welcome sight, but more so after the day she had.

"I will have to suffer Cato's scolding if I'm discovered," Antonia whispered. She looked over her shoulder as she entered the room. "Put your mind at ease." Justina closed the door behind her. "I will make it quite clear to Cato that your company is always welcome regardless of what mother says, or time of hour."

Antonia stepped inside and stood next to the bed. She rubbed her hand up and down her arm, looking more at the floor than at Justina.

"What occupies your mind so?" Justina asked.

"I lay awake with many questions and thoughts," Antonia started, but then paused. Her gaze remained on the floor. Antonia's trepidation was evident, but it was certainly understandable. If her day was anything like Justina's, Antonia would need to get it out. Justina decided to remain quiet and give her all the time she needed. After a few moments, Antonia looked up. "I know this is imposing, but I had to act upon my impulse."

"Come," Justina said. "Sit. Tell me what vexes you at this hour." She led Antonia to the bed. With everything going on in the house this day, a talk would do them both good.

"I know I serve this house, but my thoughts continually turn to having your company," Antonia explained. She looked down at her lap before continuing, "Cato is forever cautioning me to keep my place, my station, but something inside me speaks louder."

"Cato has good intentions for your safety. The death of Lucilius' parents is ever present in every mind. Many people are on edge, and the situation is made even more unbearable by that brute living under our roof." She took both of Antonia's hands in hers. "You needn't worry, Antonia, I never think of you as slave. You are sister to me."

Antonia looked up and smiled. "I feel the same way about you, Justina. I dream of a time when I can travel this country with you, not as your slave, but as your equal."

Justina went to hug her friend but Antonia's embrace was hesitant. Justina pulled back. "I fear this is not all you have on your mind."

Antonia dropped her gaze.

"Go on," Justina said and moved a strand of Antonia's hair behind her ear. "You can speak freely here."

Antonia smiled and nodded. "I wonder, did it bring you sorrow to hear of Fabricius killing a slave?"

Justina knew what her friend wanted to hear. It was understandable. If Justina had been a slave, she would be worried as well. It was one thing to hear about the death of a slave, quite another to have the man responsible for that death living under the same roof.

"I worry for my brother," Justina said and squeezed Antonia's hands. "I cannot explain the disparity between one person being born a Roman and another a slave. I only wish I knew how Lucilius' family treated their slaves. If that treatment drove them to such desperation." Justina placed a hand on Antonia's chin and raised it until they were eye to eye. "Fabricius has always strived to treat you fairly, and he seems to truly care for your wellbeing. Yet, he is a Roman soldier, and as such is honor-bound by duty. As far as Roman law is concerned, his response was just, in light of the crime that was committed."

Antonia returned her gaze to her lap. It probably wasn't the response she had hoped to hear, but it was the only one Justina was able to give her.

"Your brother is strong and noble," Antonia said. "He is most adept at caring for himself, and we all feel better with his presence." Despite herself, Antonia blushed.

Justina noticed.

"Antonia, your cheeks turned red."

"It is very hot in here," she replied and brought her hands to her face.

"Hot with desire, I'd wager," Justina joked with a smile. "I can't blame you, though. He is something to look at."

"Much better than Atilius." The two girls laughed.

The reverie was suddenly broken when the door burst open. There stood Atilius with Lucilius by his side. Startled, Antonia screamed out. Justina was more angry than surprised.

"What are you doing, Atilius?" she yelled at her brother. "How dare you enter my bedchamber without announcement or invitation!"

Atilius strode into the room and picked up the wooden gladius Justina had left on the bed. He took a couple of wild practice swings, then eyed the blade before swinging the sword once again. His movements were disjointed, as if he was not in complete control of his limbs.

Justina stood and faced her intruders. A familiar odor assaulted her senses. "You reek of wine," she said and pointed to the door. "Get out!"

Atilius ignored his sister's command. "Although we have no blood between us, Justina," he bent forward and pointed the gladius at her face, "and if not for my father, you might just be a common slave." Atilius had trouble keeping the sword steady as he spoke. But he managed to get himself to stand erect, at least for a moment, as he continued, "I still must demand that as a member of this household, you act as a lady and divorce yourself from the notion that befriending slaves is the Roman way."

"What I do is my concern, and my concern alone, brother. And my birth father, a Legatus in the Roman Army, would have me far removed from being a slave. Me being your sister can only serve to promote your own station with the ladies."

Antonia chuckled but quickly covered her mouth.

Atilius turned to Antonia and almost fell forward. "You find this funny, slave?"

"Apologies Dominus," Antonia said with bravado. "But it would seem you are wasting time playing with a wooden sword. Would it not be more satisfying playing with each other's swords?"

79

Justina turned quickly to Antonia, eyes wide. Antonia was sitting erect on the bed, smiling broadly. This was not good. Having two drunken men in the room was not the time to hurl insults delivered by a slave, and Justina knew it. She tried to snatch the sword from Atilius' grasp, but he pulled it away before she could get a good grip. As Atilius turned to face her, Lucilius crossed the room toward Antonia.

"Tomorrow at dawn, we will watch your kind take their last breath as they hang on the cross," Lucilius said through slurred speech. "Of course, you, slave, will be cleaning up my shit, but your girlfriend will behave as a proper Roman and join us."

Justina made a move toward Antonia, but Atilius, suddenly clear of action, cut off her only path to the bed. She glanced at Antonia, trying to get her attention, but Antonia wasn't looking at her. She was focused on Lucilius, defiantly facing their intruders. She was not understanding the situation. Not understanding the danger that was present. With her only path cut off, Justina tried another tactic. "While you may be living under this roof, Lucilius, you are not in position to dictate my actions. My mother has already reserved my morning with chores. Apologies, but I will be unable to join you in the task of hurling rocks at helpless slaves."

Atilius suddenly dropped the sword and lunged at his sister. Before she could react, he got himself behind her and took her in a chokehold, twisting her arm behind her back.

Antonia gasped and pulled her legs up onto the bed, binding them with her arms. The danger had just turned real. While Atilius and Justina had matched swords in the sparring room, this was the first time he had attacked her physically. Caught off guard, Justina struggled to call out to Antonia, to tell her to run, but Atilius was holding her far too tight and when she tried to speak, he tightened his hold on her neck.

Lucilius bent down and picked up the fallen sword. "I will not challenge your mother's wishes for your morning plans," he said and flipped the weapon to hold it by the blade. "However, the afternoon will see the three of us to the town square."

Justina fought to free herself but couldn't break Atilius' grasp. The blood was rushing from her face, and she could feel herself growing faint when Atilius suddenly loosened his hold on her neck.

"You better agree to go, Justina," he said. "If you know what's good for you."

Justina sucked in a great breath, then called out to Antonia, but before she could form the words, Atilius reapplied his hold, again cutting off her air.

"Agree!" he repeated and slightly released the pressure on her neck.

Justina barely got a breath in. "No!" she spat out. "Antonia run!"

Her breath was stolen once again.

"Oh, you will go," Lucilius said, then jumped to the bed. Before Antonia could react, Lucilius had her by the wrist and pulled her to the ground. Unable to catch herself, she fell to her knees. Lucilius slammed the hilt of the wooden sword across her back. Antonia screamed out in pain.

Atilius laughed.

Justina could feel his grip loosen. She slid a hand under his arm, creating a buffer to her neck. The act allowed her to regain her breath. While both Lucilius and Atilius concentrated on Antonia, Justina lifted her leg high and slammed her heel down on top of her brother's foot. He yelled out. Justina took advantage of his distraction and pushed him hard against the wall. His grip slipped, but before she could get herself turned around, Atilius regained his grip on her arm and cranked it hard behind her back. Pain shot up through her shoulders.

"She almost bested you," Lucilius said.

Atilius tightened his grip. Justina's arm began to tingle.

With Antonia still kneeling, Lucilius raised his arm high in the air and prepared to strike another blow. "If you want this to stop, you need just agree to join us tomorrow," he said to Justina, then hit Antonia a second time. She cried out.

"Leave her alone, you son of a jackal!" Justina screamed as she fought in vain to get free. "You will pay for this! Both of you! I swear!"

Lucilius laughed and hit Antonia a third time. The blow broke her skin, and the wound began to bleed. Antonia sobbed heavily.

"Stop! Stop!" Justina cried. The fight fell from her, and she started to sob. With little choice left, she gave in. "I'll go," she agreed. "Just leave her alone."

Atilius pushed Justina away. She rushed to Antonia and threw her arms around her back.

"A full week has not yet passed since I lost my parents to these slaves, and I will not let a similar fate befall this house," Lucilius said, still holding the sword. Justina looked up at him with tears flowing. "They will learn we are their masters," he continued, "with the sting of a beating for their insolence. Perhaps such an action may do you some good as well, Justina."

He raised the sword, and Justina put her arm up to block the impending blow. But it never came. Instead, Lucilius threw the sword on the bed and joined Atilius at the door. It bounced and landed hard on the floor. "Don't stay up too late," Lucilius said. "You have your chores to complete so we may get to the square. And not a word of what just transpired or I will have little choice but to let your mother know it was the slave who attacked us."

The two assailants slapped each other on the back as they left the room.

Justina turned her attention to Antonia. She was on her knees sobbing. The wound on her back bled, through her tunic, and Justina dared not touch it. She would have to get Antonia to the Medicus, but had no idea what to say to him. She bent over and kissed Antonia on the shoulder.

Antonia looked up, and Justina could see the disappointment

in her eyes. "Apologies," Justina said. "I truly never thought they would hurt either of us." Without a word, Antonia rose and ran from the room. Justina called after her, but Antonia did not turn back.

Justina sat motionless on the floor, the wooden sword only inches away. After a while, she rose and took it in her hand, eyeing the blood still gleaming in the candlelight. She began swinging it with wild abandon, trying to free the head of some unseen opponent from its body. As the swings grew stronger and more forceful, she finally cried out and flung the weapon across the room. For a moment, she simply stood there. Then she threw herself on the bed and sobbed until she found sleep.

CHAPTER 13

MARCH 7, 55 BC

*I*t was hot. Miserably hot. Justina would rather have been anywhere else in the world than here. Atilius and Lucilius were light of step, teasing each other as they made their way through the forum. While Atilius took in the sights, his friend was of sole purpose—find the crosses on which the murderers hung. Justina stayed several steps behind, just ahead of Cato and the Medicus. She found no joy in the day's events.

While Lucilius continued forward, Atilius slowed his pace until he was even with his sister. "Are you not excited to see the just punishment that awaits slaves who turn against their masters?"

Justina's gaze remained straight ahead. "I am here solely because you forced my hand. It is not something I look forward to or want to see."

"It will do you good to witness the results of treachery," Atilius said forcefully. "Perhaps it will help you understand the line between Romans and those destined to serve Romans."

Justina shot her brother a stern look. She understood well the purpose of this public display of torture. Caesar wanted to ensure the citizens of Rome knew he had captured these slaves and dispatched their punishment quickly. He also wanted to send a message to anyone who might be contemplating a similar crime. But in Justina's eyes, watching people suffer and die on an instrument of torture was cruel, and anyone who would display such brutality in public was nothing but a monster.

Atilius pressed. "You should honor Lucilius by casting a rock. It will do much to show your support for the people who raised you and call you family."

"I will throw no rock at a helpless person. It is bad enough I am forced to watch you gain some kind of perverse enjoyment from this. It is not something you can make me do."

"You need not worry, Justina. Your protector Cato will deliver you from evil. Apparently, father does not trust you in our company alone."

"Your father charged me to keep Justina close," Cato said. He looked past Atilius toward the market, "lest your exuberance causes the situation to sour." He turned his attention to Atilius. "He was worried you may run off instead of protecting her."

Before Atilius could offer a response, Lucilius yelled out. "There! Those who have defiled my house and killed my parents!"

As Atilius ran after his friend, Justina slowed her pace even more, allowing the sounds and scents of the forum to fill her senses. Justina had been to the forum on many occasions. Alba typically sent her with Cato and a long list. At times, the Medicus would join them. This was one such occasion.

The Medicus had a name, but Justina didn't know it. He was responsible for the health of the family and had always gone by the name of his profession, which was tradition. Though he wore the tunic of a slave, the Medicus was treated with much more reverence and was typically allowed to come and go as he pleased. He was an elderly man whose age showed both in his face and in the flowing grey of his hair. He moved with a slight limp and always seemed to be looking for something. He was a master of herbs, happy to reveal the secrets locked inside each one. Justina would sit for hours and listen.

Today, the Medicus was looking for a specific herb, the calendula flower. "It calms skin irritations and helps with bug bites," he had told her. He showed her how the bright yellow petals were heated in water, wrapped in a light cloth, and then applied to the skin. He would even ground up the versatile flower, mix it with olive oil, and add it to Alba's nightly skin treatment. She was amazed at how one little flower could do so much.

Justina enjoyed the forum. There was a certain excitement in hearing the merchants call out their wares. Almost anything could be found at Rome's forum: bread, meat, fruit, fish, spices, wine, even clothing. Other things too, if you knew where to look. The market was filled with the most amazing odors. Cooked meats flavored with exotic spices all meant to whet the pallet and tempt the nose. Scents that could only be experienced in Rome.

The market was filled with people, mostly the middle and lower class, and, of course, slaves. Everyone wanted the best price, but bartering was a delicate dance. Buyers offered prices. Merchants first feigned offense, then countered with a price of their own. The volley would continue back and forth until a price agreeable to both was found. Smart buyers knew when to press forward and when to take the price offered. Patience was the key.

As Justina watched a merchant engaged with a customer, Cato came up behind her. "Shall we stay here, Domina, and let the boys attend to their folly?"

She wanted to say yes, wanted to remain in the forum, avoiding the sight that awaited her, but her mind went to Antonia, and she knew she had to go. There was no choice. "No," she said reluctantly. "We'd better go."

*T*he boys forgot all about Justina, Cato, and the Medicus in their haste to get to the crosses. When they arrived, they were met with a gruesome sight. Crucifixion was not a type of punishment in Rome, but rather a method of torture that was particularly cruel. That was the scene when the two boys arrived. Both Domitius and Camilla hung from crosses, their arms bound with large, strong cords. Domitius was positioned with his spread arms forced over the backside of the cross. He was bound at both wrists. This position was a favorite of the Romans, because of the severe pain it caused to the shoulder joints. His chest was bare except for marks where his tormentor's whip broke through the flesh. His legs had been placed on either side of the vertical pole and nailed in place, the anklebone shattering as the crude metal was hammered through his legs into the wood. His wife Camilla was to his right. Her ankles were also nailed to the cross, but her arms had been bound to the front of the horizontal member. This position was little better than his. While it did not cause severe pain to the shoulders, it did force all her weight to fall on shattered ankles.

Rocks were stacked on the ground a short distance in front of the crosses, placed there to be cast at those who were hanging. Their only purpose was to increase the pain the sufferers bore. Atilius bent down and immediately picked up a stone, waiting for his friend to do the same, but Lucilius just stood there. The events of the past week rushed through his head.

As soon as he walked into the house, he knew something was wrong. It was simply too quiet. He rushed up the stairs to his parents' bedroom. The door was open, but he didn't go in. Not at first. He knew what awaited him, but he didn't want to face it, didn't want to make it real. There was stillness in the room, and it seemed much colder than normal. With his heart pounding, he took a deep breath, got up his courage, and rushed into the room. The horror of the sight stopped him in his tracks. He had been a soldier long enough to know a battle had taken place. A brutal battle.

He rushed to his mother's side. Her skull was almost split in two, the surprised look still frozen on her face. It was more than he could bare. He fell to his knees at the side of the bed, his stomach twisted inside him. It came upon him so quickly, he didn't expect it, couldn't stop it. He turned from the bed and vomited violently.

Afterward, he sat on the bed beside his mother, cradling her head in his hands, pulling her against him. It was a pain he had never experienced. When he finally left the room, he headed to the slave's chambers. Each one was empty, and it was then that he knew what had happened. It was then that the emptiness inside him was replaced with an all-consuming rage.

Atilius hit his arm with a rock. The action brought him back to the present. "Here," he said. "Aim well, brother."

Lucilius looked at the stone for what seemed an eternity, then his eyes hardened. He took the rock, pulled his arm back, and flung it at Domitius. The stone hit its mark, landing with a dull thud, then dropped straight to the ground. Domitius didn't move. There was no reaction of any kind.

"The gods piss on me again, depriving me of just reprisal!"

"The woman still writhes on her cross," said Atilius. "Better to find your reprisal there, brother." He reached down and handed Lucilius a second stone. "Make this stone find its mark and send her to Tartarus with her confederates."

Lucilius did not hesitate this time. He cast the rock even harder than before.

❀

*T*he pain was beyond what she had ever thought she could endure. Why had she agreed to go? To run away? Their treatment hadn't really been that bad. Why hadn't they just slipped away in the curtain of night? The sun was relentless. It baked her skin and dried her lips to the point of cracking. How she longed for water. The moisture coming from her eyes had been a slight relief, but she had long ago lost the ability to form tears.

When the nails were driven through her ankles, she had passed out. When she finally awoke, her arms felt as though they had been pulled from their sockets. She tried to straighten her legs to relieve her tired arms, but was met with an immediate pain so intense, so harsh, it forced her to cry out. The Roman soldier had laughed at her misery. She had forced her weight onto her broken feet as much as she could, but all she managed to do was prolong the agony. *There are no gods*, she thought to herself. For if there were, they would have taken her long ago. Taken her like they had her husband.

The stone collided hard against her chest. She winced from the pain with a low gasp. While she wasn't able to lift her head, she could still see a bit in front of her. Her dry eyes burned, and her vision was blurry, yet she was able make out two men, no boys, standing at the pile of rocks. She heard one of them shriek with joy. She tried to focus on her two tormenters. One was shorter than the other. He was the one laughing. The other seemed more sad than angry.

It was at that moment she recognized the boy. *No*, she thought to herself. It couldn't be. It couldn't be Lucilius. She began to sob. The sound unmistakable, even if her eyes remained dry.

"The wretch sees me!" she heard him say. "She recognizes her tormenter!"

The other one, the shorter one, picked up a stone and prepared to launch it at her. It didn't matter. She deserved their torment. But as he cocked his arm, it looked to her as if Lucilius stopped him. He did stop him.

"Pause a moment, brother. I would like her last few breaths spent with confession of motive. Then have your way with her."

Yes. Yes, she thought, *come closer. Let me clear my conscience.* Lucilius came to the foot of the cross, just below her. His eyes wanted answers. She sobbed, the grief stronger than the pain.

"Why have you taken my parents from me?" he spit out. "I've never witnessed you beaten or mistreated. You have been in my house as long as I can remember." His tone was more determined than angry.

She could feel the life ebbing away, but she refused to go. Perhaps there were gods after all. Perhaps that was why they had prolonged her suffering, why she had been tasked with enduring this unimaginable pain. Perhaps the gods had decided to allow her to rid herself of the guilt that racked her more than the cross ever could.

She tried to form the word, but her screams had long ago taken her voice. Her cracked lips were as dry as her throat, and they sent sharp pains when she moved them. Still, she pressed on. She needed to say the name.

"Speak, traitor!" Lucilius yelled.

"Mah," she finally found her voice. It was soft, barely a voice at all. She could see Lucilius trying to get himself as close to her as possible.

"What?" he asked. "What is it you are saying?"

"Mah...rone...ah," she managed to get out. "Mah...rone...ah," she repeated.

❦

*L*ucilius stood there, not knowing what to do. The slave had said the name and in an instant, he knew what had transpired in his house that night. He knew who had killed. More importantly, he knew who had not. The woman, more dead than alive, on the cross in front of him may have run away, but she had not caused the death of his parents. He had been robbed of his revenge. Fabricius had taken Glacious and someone else had taken Marona. He had nothing. There was none left. He turned and walked back to Atilius.

"Send her to Tartarus, brother," Lucilius said, "and have her darken my life no more."

Atilius wasted no time in picking up a stone and launching it at the woman. It hit her hard in the shoulder. He turned to celebrate the throw with Lucilius, but his friend had already walked away.

"Look, she still lives," Atilius called out. "Have we not come for sport and function?" Lucilius kept walking. "Lucilius!" he yelled out, to no avail. Atilius turned back and picked up another rock. He pulled back his arm ready to cast, then looked back at Lucilius. He turned to Camilla. Her head was drooped and her breathing shallow, too shallow. He dropped the rock and ran to catch his friend.

🌸

*L*ucilius was standing at the cross when Justina arrived with Cato and the Medicus. She watched his head drop, then he walk away without looking back. "I don't understand," she said to Cato. "What matter of conscience befell him? Could it be a fleeting moment of humanity? They cajole and threaten to have us here with them, and then leave absent resolution."

Cato looked hard at the woman on the cross, her face reflecting the torture her body was experiencing. "Their desires change as the wind, Domina, without conviction or purpose," he said turning his attention to Justina. "Perhaps he discovered something unexpected. Perhaps the slave on the cross was not the murderer he had hoped." He looked back at the dying woman. "Perhaps that knowledge robbed him of his desire for revenge."

What a strange thing to say, Justina thought. "Look upon her,

Cato. Do you believe she ever possessed malice? She looks far too kind for that type of action."

"It matters not, Domina. Roman law dictates that all slaves in the household share the same treatment for egregious acts against their masters."

Justina turned to Cato. "If she played no part in the crime, how is it honorable to punish an innocent, void of wrongdoing, for the capricious actions of another? Does this not curse Rome and all we hold dear?"

"It serves as a useful deterrent," Cato explained. "One slave may plan and scheme, but if that plan is shared with another, the second slave may confide in his master the plot and save his own life and the rest of the house. This is the way of Rome, Domina, and it is best not to question Rome's provenance, lest a similar fate befall the asker."

Justina turned back to the poor woman on the cross. She found herself unable to turn away, and before she realized it, she was walking forward. It was a gruesome sight. What pain she must have endured.

"She has passed, and I have done as my master requested," Cato said. "Let us gather the items for the Medicus and return home." But Justina kept moving forward, transfixed. Cato stepped closer. "Let us go, Domina," he said a bit louder.

"I have many items to get, Domina," the Medicus added. "It would be best if we stuck to our task."

"Just a moment," Justina replied. She stood at the foot of the cross and looked up at the woman nailed there. It was at that exact moment that the slave opened her eyes.

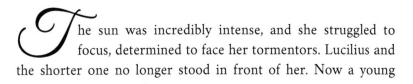

*T*he sun was incredibly intense, and she struggled to focus, determined to face her tormentors. Lucilius and the shorter one no longer stood in front of her. Now a young woman was slowly approaching. There was curiousness in her face, a desire for understanding. She was staring intently, as if there was some sort of secret to discover, as if looking into Camilla's eyes would unlock a hidden door.

She was beautiful, with dark hair and bronze skin that seemed to glisten in the sun. In fact, there was an aura of light surrounding her. The young woman was so close, she could easily touch Camilla's legs, if she dared. But she did not. Her eyes were fierce, but kind, and they reminded Camilla of another time, another place, so many years past.

Holding the baby in her arms, wrapped in a blanket, Camilla remembered how full of life the child was—how full of potential. Potential that could never be realized unless her path was diverted from its current course. That is what the man standing in front of them had said, when he handed the baby to Camilla. The man with fierce, kind eyes. The man who had brought them freedom.

They had made a promise to protect. Though it cost them their newfound freedom, it was a promise they all eagerly accepted. But it was a hard promise, one that eventually cost her and her husband their lives.

A dark man stood behind the young woman. He too was looking up at her, but his face was not filled with a desire to understand. No, his face was...

"Cato," she thought she heard the young woman call him. "Something troubles you."

"Apologies, Domina." he said. "It is nothing with which to concern yourself."

Was she hallucinating? Did the girl just call him Cato? And didn't he call her "Domina," which could mean only one thing.

She strained her eyes to look at the man. It was Cato and the Medicus who stood next to him. Her mind went back to a time, some seventeen years ago, when they were all together in another place. Standing in front of the man who had won their freedom.

"Romans value a worthy Medicus," the man told them. "Your leave will assure your future and that of my daughter. Travel safe."

Cato stepped forward. "I shall accompany them on their journey to ensure they make it to Rome," he told the man. "I pledge to watch over your daughter."

"Do you understand what you are saying? I will need you in battle, Cato."

"You have made sacrifices to grant our freedom that can never be repaid," Cato replied. "I hope this small gesture will show you what you have done for thousands of slaves."

The man reached out and took Cato's forearm.

"We shall seek a noble Roman family in need of a Medicus and wanting for a daughter to call their own," Cato said. "I will offer this family my services for the time it takes to raise Justina."

The four of them and the baby had headed to Rome but were forced to split up along the way. Fearing they would be easy to spot as a group, Cato suggested they disband. She had tried to get Cato to allow her and Domitius to take the child. "We will look like a couple with a baby," she had told him, but Cato wanted nothing of it.

"I am most suited to protect her, and I will not let her out of my sight," he told them. "The Medicus and I will head to Rome with the child."

That was the end of it. Camilla and Domitius had eventually been captured and resold into slavery. Over the years, they lost track of both Cato and the Medicus, landing in a house that hadn't worked out so well for them.

And now, just as the life was about to leave her, she had found them once again. Cato and the Medicus standing here could only mean one thing. The young woman in front of her was the baby she had sworn to protect so long ago. The surprise and joy gave her the strength to form words.

"You made it," she whispered to the young woman standing below her. "By the gods, you made it."

Her words were not as strong as she had hoped, and Camilla wasn't sure they had even been heard. Then she saw Cato place his hand on the girl's shoulder. "Let us go, Domina," he said. There was urgency in his voice. "The market and the Medicus await." She watched as Cato turned from the cross, hoping the young woman would not follow. She did not.

"Wait, the woman speaks."

Camilla tried to smile. The girl had heard her make a sound, even if the words had not been clear. She knew she had one chance. One chance to gather enough strength. One chance to let this girl know she had fulfilled her promise.

"She babbles nonsense, Domina," Cato said. "The poor woman has succumbed to the throes of death and is delirious with suffering. Let her pass without interference."

No! Cato, no! she thought to herself. *Do not take this child from me! Do not have me lose this chance.* She had to speak. Had to make herself heard this time.

"You made it," she said, suddenly strong of voice. Cato had heard her, and when he turned to face her, she spoke again, "I thought only my husband and I had made it safely once our paths separated."

The young woman seemed confused, but why? Had not Cato informed her of her past? "She seems to be talking to you, Cato," the young woman said. "Am I mistaken?"

Cato looked up at her. "She resides in the throes of delirium" he said, then to the young woman, "Let us go. We have tasks to complete and can no longer afford wasted time with the babbling of the suffering and dying." Cato took hold of the young woman's arm and attempted to lead her away.

Had Cato not told her of her past? Of her future? Of her destiny? Why was Cato hiding this from the girl? As her body weakened, her resolve grew strong. Maybe Cato wouldn't tell her, but he couldn't stop her from doing it.

"Sparta," she tried to yell, but her voice was too week. Cato had succeeded in getting the girl to walk with him. She tried again but was unable to get the entire name out, only managing a weak "Sparta." The girl was walking away now, taking with her Camilla's last chance. She could not let that happen. From somewhere deep inside her, she found one last bit of strength and yelled out "Spartacus. Spartacus! Spartacus!"

It was marvelous. She saw the young woman turn in a flash. "Spartacus?" she questioned Cato. "Does she mean the slave leader?"

But Cato was smart and quick. "Many on the cross chant his name before death," she heard him say. "It is their last taunt for any Romans listening. Let us take our leave, Domina. No reason for your memories to embrace this tragedy."

She saw the two of them turn again and knew she had failed. There was nothing she could say. Nothing that would make the young girl turn. With every last bit of life within her, she yelled out the only thing she could think of that would make the girl understand. The only thing she had left to say.

"Just... Just... Justina. Justina! JUSTINA!"

Cato and the girl both turned to face her at the same time. With her last bit of sight, she saw the shock on their faces. She watched as Cato's shock turned to anger. And as the life finally ebbed from inside her, as the gods came to take her to Tartarus, she saw the girl looking up at Cato, those fierce eyes demanding an answer, and she knew in that moment, that Cato hadn't thought to change the girl's name.

CHAPTER 14

MARCH 8, 55 BC

*T*here was no chance of sleeping. The day's events would give him no peace, for they had made no sense. All he and Lucilius had spoken of the day before was the chance to avenge the death of Lucilius' parents, to hasten the two murderers' trip to Tartarus. Atilius had looked forward to it, was eager for it to happen. But it hadn't. In his mind, the scene played out over and over again; Lucilius walked up to the slave and then passed him without casting a stone. There was no reason Atilius could conceive that would account for Lucilius' reaction, for his refusal to act, for his cowardice. For most of the night, he had been staring at the ceiling, but now he was staring directly at Lucilius who slept in the bed next to him, willing him to wake.

Whether it was Atilius' will or the light of day, Lucilius awoke, and clearing his eyes, saw his friend in the next bed. "My brother," he said resting himself on his elbow. "Why do you stare with such intent?"

Atilius didn't answer. Instead, he rolled on his back and returned his gaze to the ceiling.

"Am I that easy on your eyes this early in the morning?" Atilius remained silent staring at the ceiling.

"Speak, brother."

Atilius stayed silent a bit longer, but eventually spoke. "I have yet to find rest from yesterday's proceedings."

"What has kept your eyes from slumber?" Lucilius asked. "Was my snoring too loud? Do I have a smell I am unaware of?"

It was obvious Lucilius was trying to lighten the mood, but Atilius would have none of it. "I do not know how to approach this subject without insult."

"Speak your mind, brother. Tell me what vexes you at this early hour."

Atilius took a deep breath, paused, and then spoke. "We had but one goal yesterday and that was to punish the people responsible for killing your parents, two innocent Romans, good people," Atilius said, still on his back. "And yet, when the opportunity arrived, you walk away before the mission is complete."

Lucilius sat up in his bed, and Atilius turned to him.

"You got up close to the whore on the cross. I saw her lips move. What could have spewed forth from that demon to make your hatred take a turn? What lies could she have mumbled to spare another rock being thrown with intent? You are my brother, Lucilius. You are a Roman soldier."

Lucilius grew stern. "I need not you to remind me of my place," he barked. It was not the response Atilius had expected. "I know I am a Roman solider. And yes, those on the cross played a role in my parent's death." Lucilius looked down and softened his tone. "Yet I knew this slave, Camilla, for almost my entire life. Slaves are dogs, yet this one was always fair to me. I don't believe she deserved such punishment." He hesitated. "There is no way her hand delivered the final blow to either of my parents. It was not her nature."

"Nature?" Atilius yelled out, suddenly sitting upright. "Slaves are indeed dogs, and all dogs have it in their nature to do evil. You do not know who delivered the final blow to your parents. All you can do is celebrate the knowledge that they are in the afterlife, serving your parents now, hopefully chained and beaten."

"It only matters that justice has been served and Rome is better off for it," Lucilius said dismissively. "I must ready myself for leave. I have patrol today."

Atilius watched as Lucilius stood and dressed for the day's duties. This was not the Lucilius he had come to know, not the Lucilius bent on revenge. He still did not understand what had caused yesterday's change in attitude, but he was determined to get to the root of it.

"You have suffered a great tragedy," Atilius said. He swung his legs to the side of the bed, then stood. "You have the opportunity to avenge such a tragedy. I saw how easily you beat a slave in this house without thought or remorse. Yet when faced with the slave responsible, whether directly or not, you pause your actions." Atilius moved across the room to Lucilius and stood before him, confident in his bravado. "Why the moment of weakness?"

Lucilius shoved the younger, lighter Atilius backward, causing him to stumble. Before Atilius could gain his footing, Lucilius pressed forward. "You think I showed mercy to the woman?" he yelled. "Killing her with a stone and sending her off to the afterlife would be more merciful than to let her suffer on the cross. Who are you to judge me, boy? You are not even in the military."

Atilius was caught off-guard and was now almost cowering as Lucilius hovered over him. "I am a Roman solider, don't you ever forget that," he bellowed, spit flying from the corners of his mouth. "If I choose to beat a slave, I will do so!" Lucilius looked down at his wide-eyed young friend, the fear evident. He took a step back and allowed Atilius to stand.

"We are Romans," he continued in softer tones. "We do not question our way of life. We do as we are told. The few things in this life that we control on our own, will be ours to choose. Whether I want to throw a stone or not, is my choice, not yours, not Rome's." He took hold of his gladius and armor and headed to the door. He paused with his back to the room, lowered his head, and then left without another word.

It didn't matter, Atilius had already turned away. He didn't want Lucilius to see the tears beginning to well.

CHAPTER 15

*B*rutus was sitting by himself, nursing a glass of wine, when Servilia entered the dining area. She was wearing a bright red silk robe that was, for the most part, transparent. Brutus did not smile or look up when his mother passed. That meant only one thing—he was brooding. Her only son enjoyed brooding, and he was good at it. If a living could be had by brooding, her son would have more coin than he knew what to do with. He came by it naturally though; his father was a brooder as well. Not quite as good as his son, but a contender nonetheless.

"Good morning," Servilia said with a smile. She walked over and kissed her son on the forehead.

Brutus finally looked up at his mother. "Good morning?" he questioned. "The sun is nearly completely above us. What causes such a late awakening?"

Though Servilia loved her son, he worried a little too much about his mother's activities for her taste. But she knew how to handle that. "Well, son, if you must know, playing with Caesar last eve tired me greatly. He had the energy of a tiger and the evening lasted much longer than expected. Seeing him twice this week was a treat for your mother. I needed a few extra hours to find slumber." Servilia lifted a glass toward the female slave who entered the room. "I'm not sure how this is any of your concern or business for that matter."

Brutus returned to his brooding, concentrating on the contents of his own glass.

The slave poured Servilia the calda she had just made—a mixture of warm water, seasonings, and wine. The spices filled the room like a satchel of potpourri. Servilia took the time to breathe in the scents before taking a sip. "Now, this is how my son should be greeting his mother. Not with questions about my sleeping habits." She motioned for the slave to put down the ewer and leave, then walked over to the chair adjacent to Brutus and sat, crossing her legs.

She looked over at her son. He was the greatest—perhaps the only great thing—she had accomplished in her life. He had grown to be a fine young man. Servilia was immensely proud of him.

Even so, it was hard sometimes for Servilia to see him as a man. He would always be her little boy, her little chubby man. After Brutus the Elder was killed, he was all she had. Those were rough times. Society was not always accepting of single mothers. If your husband died in battle, you were simply expected to find another. It's not that she didn't have offers, they just weren't the right offers from the right men...or man.

"I have much to discuss with you," Brutus said.

"Yes. That would seem obvious."

Brutus let the comment pass. "After all these many moons at Caesar's side," he continued, "Do you trust him? Do you believe the words that spew from his mouth?"

"I'm barely awake and these are the questions I start my day with?" Servilia took another sip of calda, purposely taking her time. Brutus had made his opinions of her current relationship clear on many occasions, and, quite frankly, she wasn't in the mood to hear them again this day. Brutus would have to wait for her response. "Why would I not have trust in him?" she finally said. "Regardless of how you view my arrangement with Caesar, there isn't anyone I could bed with higher title."

"Yes mother, you make a son proud," Brutus said. "Truth be told, Crassus would be a better title. And someone more your speed."

"That old brute?" Servilia said with a chuckle. "Sure, his money would be a fun ride, but I do not believe his cock would provide the same pleasure."

Brutus sent his mother a disgusted glare. She smiled.

"Why are you suddenly worried about my relationship with Caesar?" she asked, sitting back in her chair. "He makes sure I do not go without," she paused and brought the glass to her lips. "Thus, you do not go without." She looked over the rim at her son, then took a sip. "He also gives you assignment on occasion."

Brutus sat forward in his chair. "You would be wise not to mistake his scraps for generosity. And as far as my well-being, he is barely responsible for such."

"Do you prefer I find someone who cannot afford us this nice house, a few slaves, and all the food and wine we can consume?"

"I prefer you weigh your trust in the man, and his trust in you."

Servilia paused for reflection. Brutus could be surly, but he did always have her best interests at heart. He loved his mother, and she loved him. She took another sip. "Caesar does not share important military secrets with me, if that is your concern. He shares only his bed. I believe our relationship, or whatever people may refer to it as, has a bond of trust. So, yes, dear son, I do trust the man."

The two remained silent, sipping wine, looking at everything but each other. After several glasses, Brutus finally spoke. "Do you remember the promise you made to me when I was a young boy? I had just seen eight birthdays when my father, the man you loved, was taken from us and sent to the afterlife. You do recall him? Do you recall what you swore to me?"

Servilia knew the promise of which her son spoke. His father,

Marcus Junius Brutus the Elder was a soldier, a descendent of Lucius Junius Brutus, the man who overthrew Tarquin the Proud and established the Roman Republic. He challenged Pompey in the great battle following the death of the dictator Lucius Cornelius Sulla. While he fought bravely against Pompey and his army, his own forces turned against him and he was left with no choice but to surrender. Pompey's legion of horsemen escorted him to Regium Lepidi, a small town upon the Po, where he was granted retirement. Exile was the better word for it. Servilia and Brutus were to join him, but her husband was there for but one day when he was murdered by a henchman sent by Pompey.

Servilia evaded the answer. "Over the years, many foolish words have spewed out of my own mouth. Please son, enlighten me."

"You said one day we would have our vengeance. We would make the man responsible for taking my father, your husband, pay for his betrayal."

"I remember," Servilia said. Her eyes hardened, and she grew suddenly stiff.

"Now you are in prime position to make this happen. Your word, your influence, your actions, can end that man's life. I need you to follow through on your promise."

It was Servilia's turn to examine the inside of her glass. She swilled the liquid, then took another sip. "If that is what keeps my son up at night and tears away at him some twenty-plus years later," she said lightly, "then, my sweet son, I will do what I can to fulfill that promise." She stood, crossed over to Brutus, and kissed him on the forehead. "Now, can we eat?"

"One other thing," Brutus said. Servilia rolled her eyes, but not so he could see. "Caesar mentioned that a soldier friend of mine, while on patrol, didn't kill a rebel slave but was given credit for it. I trust this soldier. Would Caesar speak falsely about this incident?"

"To what gain?" Servilia asked, doing little to conceal her

annoyance. "Caesar takes credit for many things he may have little or nothing to do with, but a simple soldier killing or not killing a slave, he would not make up. There are far more important things to lie about in his life. Now come, let's eat."

Brutus massaged his chin and looked down to the floor. Eventually he spoke, "I go to see my friend Herminius today." He looked up at his mother. "We are meeting in the town square. I hope you will be fine laying around here, eating, drinking," with a pause, "sleeping."

Just then, a knock came on the front door. Moments later, a slave arrived with a message he handed to Servilia. She opened the note, and a slow smile formed on her face. Brutus watched her the entire time. "What is it?" he finally asked.

"Oh great Jupiter, I thought today was going to be a bore," Servilia said, waving the note. "Looks like the great Caesar misses me already. He's requesting my company this very afternoon." She folded the note and tucked it into her robe. Then she kissed Brutus a third time on the forehead. "I best ready myself," she said and left Brutus sitting in his chair.

CHAPTER 16

*S*he couldn't get the image of the woman out of her head, or the name she had spoken. It played in her mind over and over again. "Justina. Justina! JUSTINA!" Cato had a justification for the woman yelling out the name Spartacus, but he was unable to explain this one away. And that was not all. "You made it," the woman had said, and she was looking directly at Cato. At the time, Justina had written it off as the delirium of a dying woman, but now she was not so sure. There was no way the slave could have known her name, unless she had known Cato, but why would he lie about that?

Lost in her thoughts, Justina didn't notice Atilius enter the dining room. He took the chair across from her and sat quietly. Antonia also entered the room with plates of food.

"How's the back?" Atilius asked with a smile looking at Antonia.

It was only then that Justina realized she was not alone. She glared at Atilius, then turned to Antonia. There was sadness in her eyes. Her hand shook as she placed the dish on the table before Atilius. She was not wearing her usual tunic, the one that left exposed a portion of her back and chest. On this day, she was wearing a fuller piece, one that covered her bruises. She placed the other plate in front of Justina without looking at her.

Cato was standing in the back of the room as well. He stepped forward to the dining table. Antonia glanced up at him, then quickly lowered her head. His eyes narrowed. "Will there be anything else, Domina?"

Justina looked at Cato for several seconds before answering. He did not move his gaze from her, did not flinch. His eyes gave nothing away. "No," she finally said. "This will be fine."

Cato nodded, then motioned for Antonia to follow as he left the room. Once the two were gone, Justina addressed Atilius, "So brother, what happened to your boyfriend yesterday? He's quick to hit innocent slaves yet won't throw rocks at the ones who killed his parents?"

"Watch your tongue, Justina," Atilius snapped. Her words had struck a chord. "You know not of what you speak. Lucilius threw a rock, and his aim was true."

"Yes," Justina said. "At one who had already passed from this life. But the one who yet lived, at that one, he threw no stone. This is your idol?"

Atilius' eyes hardened. "Because you are a woman, I would not expect you to understand. You know nothing about the ways of men. Why would Lucilius bring an end so quickly to the suffering of the damned? Better to let her linger on the cross than find a quick demise."

Justina chuckled as she took a bite of food. "That may be what you choose to believe, but I saw his face as he walked away. Your mighty hero was just shy of crying for that slave. And yet, he will beat Antonia just to have audience watch his sorrow?"

"Lucilius does as he chooses. It would be wise for you to remember that."

A knock came on the front door. Cato left the dining room to answer it. At the same moment, Alba entered the room and awaited Cato's return. When he came back, he had a note. "Domina," he said as he handed it to her. She took the parchment, then dismissed him.

The note bore the unmistakable seal of Caesar. Alba called to Livius as she walked toward the dining table. "You have a note," she said. When Livius entered the room, Alba handed him the note.

"What is this?" he asked.

"Something from Caesar," she said. "You'd better open it."

Atilius turned in his seat to face his father. Livius took the note from his wife and broke the seal. He read the parchment but was visibly confused by its contents.

"What is it?" Alba asked.

"A request to meet Caesar. For this afternoon."

"What could Caesar possibly want from us?" Alba asked.

"Perhaps he has heard of the great meats I put out and wants an event catered," Livius said with a smile.

"That would be amazing!" Alba replied with a huge smile on her face. "We would be the talk of the town. All of our hard work and now this reward."

"There is but one way to discover the meaning of this request," Livius said. "I must ready myself. It would not be wise to be late for this meeting."

Livius left the room. Alba rushed to follow.

Atilius turned to face Justina. "You see, my father is finally getting the recognition he deserves."

"Your father?" Justina repeated. "I live in this house too, yet all my life you have refused to call me sister, refused to acknowledge my part in this family."

"I will call you sister when you act as a sister should," Atilius said.

It was all Justina could do not to throw her plate of food at Atilius. "Now that Lucilius is on patrol for the day, why don't you and I finish what you started in my room? Meet me in the sparring area later today. Then you can start calling me master instead of Justina."

Atilius laughed. "Your little friend took a nice beating the other night. Now, you want the same done to you?" he said with a smile. "I welcome the chance, Justina. And when you cry again, like you did the other night, you will finally understand that you are a girl. There is no place for you in battle. Your place is behind your husband, pregnant, fulfilling his every need." Atilius stood and shoved the plate of food across the table. "Have your slave girlfriend tend to my plate. My appetite has left me."

CHAPTER 17

*A*ntonia was still cleaning the dishes when Cato walked into the preparation room. He dumped the food from Atilius' plate and motioned for the other slaves to leave. "Show me your back," he said to Antonia when they were alone. When she hesitated, he barked. "Now!"

Antonia turned her back to Cato and removed the top of her tunic. The welts from the wooden sword were still present. Correction of slaves was common in any house, but no one in house Livius had ever resorted to violence. Cato clenched his fist at the sight.

"Who did this?" he demanded, arms crossed.

"Does it matter?" Antonia asked and pulled up her tunic to cover her back.

"This family does not believe in violence toward slaves," Cato said, urgency in his voice. "I need to know who did this. Not just for you, but for all the slaves in this house."

Antonia looked down. "I have been warned not to speak of it," she said weakly. "I do not wish a repeat of the incident."

Cato pressed. "Was it Dominus?"

"Of course not," Antonia said forcefully. "He has never laid hand to me."

Cato knew the culprit. There was only one person who had managed to bring unease into this household. Things were progressing just as he feared. "Everyone under Dominus' roof is responsible to Dominus. If he was not the source of this punishment, or did not allow it to be, then the person responsible must be identified and reported. Now speak! I cannot protect you if you do not tell me how this happened."

Antonia looked up abruptly. "Protect me? It is clear you cannot protect me. No one can." She returned to her chores.

"Then you condemn us all." He allowed his words to weigh on Antonia. She was obviously afraid, but she needed to understand the risk of not reporting this incident. If Lucilius was allowed to act unfettered, the attitude of the whole family could change.

"It was the new boy in the house," she finally offered. "The one whose parents were killed. He was drunk, and he came into Justina's room late two nights past."

Cato was not surprised. "What were you doing in Justina's room that late?" he questioned. "You know better. I have warned you."

Antonia turned and faced Cato. "We were just talking."

Cato stepped closer to Antonia "How many times must I tell you?" His voice rose. "You must be mindful of your role in this house. You are not Justina's sister. You are a slave! We are all slaves!"

Antonia dropped her head "I know," she said softy. "I know."

Cato took a deep breath. This was the first time Antonia showed an understanding of her station. He was sorry it had come to this, but she had been warned. His tone softened. "I will speak to Livius," he said and placed his hand on her shoulder.

"Don't!" Antonia pleaded. "That boy is crazy, and he hates slaves. I'm sure he will go away shortly and then we need not see him again. Please, Cato, I beg you. Say nothing."

Cato folded his arms once again. "I will decide what is best for all of us. Your evening liaisons with Justina have put us all in peril. Now finish your duties."

Danger had entered house Livius, and it was a danger that demanded thought before action. But before Cato could give the matter too much attention, he heard Alba calling from the dining room.

CHAPTER 18

*W*hen Alba returned, Justina was still sitting at the table. There was a time when the young woman in front of her was just a baby. Brought to her, accompanied by two slaves. Alba had her own baby at the time. A beautiful boy, her third. She had given Livius three boys and her reward was a young child forced upon her. A young child she was told to love, to bond with, and to care for.

What she was not given was a choice. Livius had not asked for, nor was she allowed to grant consent to this addition to the family. She was expected to simply accept the offering, without protest. Accept that her husband had brought into the house what she, herself, had been unable to give him. She had done what was expected of her and now this child, this young woman, seemed bent on disrupting house Livius.

Alba took a chair across from Justina and called Cato to bring her food. Justina bristled when Alba took a seat, even her smile was awkward.

"Where did your brother go?" Alba asked.

"You mean Atilius?"

"Who else would I mean?"

"Atilius," Justina repeated. "Lucilius' pawn?"

The comment fell hard on Alba. "You have a way with words that is destined to cause you great grief, Justina. A proper Roman woman does not dare say half the things that come from your mouth. I can't decide if you just do not care or if you are simply not smart enough to realize this."

Justina concentrated on the dish in front of her.

"I can tell you this," Alba continued, "You are turning eighteen in a few months, and I do not expect to see you under this roof much past that time." She took hold of her daughter's wrist and squeezed it hard. Justina glared at her mother, her eyes filled with both shock and anger. Alba met Justina's eyes. "I suggest you heed my warning and hasten your preparations for life under another's roof. How does someone who comes from such noble loins become so troublesome? I know it is not our raising of you. We have done all we can and more, and this is our reward?"

Justina kept Alba's gaze, defiant to the end. When she tried to pull her hand away, Alba tightened her grip. She had no intention of letting go. When Cato entered the room, Alba smiled, then made a grand display of releasing Justina's arm as Cato placed the plate of food in front of her. If he noticed the conflict, he made no indication of it. Instead, he stepped back slightly and waited.

"Excuse me, mother," Justina said standing. "My chores await."

Alba waived her daughter off.

"I'll take wine," she said to Cato as Justina left the room.

"As you wish, Domina," Cato replied and brought over the canter. "That is all for now," Alba said as her cup filled. "Return to your duties."

Cato bowed slightly and stepped backward. He walked over to the other side of the table and went to pick up Justina's plate. Alba stopped him.

"Leave it," she ordered.

"Domina," Cato said and left the room. Alba sat quietly and ate.

CHAPTER 19

*L*ivius had never been in a consul's house before, and as
much as he tried, he couldn't stop the sweat from bathing
his palms. The dining room he had been led to was enor-
mous. Frescos of great battles adorned the walls, reaching from
floor to ceiling. The white marble floor was filled with streaks of
quartz that ran through the rock like streams of water. One such
streak led to a dark spot near the entrance.

There was little furniture in the room other than several large
tables constructed of African Padauk. Pear wood chairs
surrounded the tables, which each held a wood bowl filled with a
type of fruit Livius could not identify. He was having a hard time
holding the drink given him when he arrived and rested it on the
edge of one of the tables.

He took a seat and began doing the breathing exercises he had
done before each battle. A man needed his head clear when he
took sword in hand. Killing another was nothing to take lightly.
Livius never did. In the heat of battle, it was easy to lose one's
head. Deep breaths helped him to concentrate. Although he
wasn't going to battle, he still needed his wits about him.

He had been sitting there for only minutes when Servilia

entered the room, followed by the same legionnaire who had previously been his escort. Her presence, unexpected as it was, startled Livius. So much so that he let out an audible gasp. His expression quickly changed from shock to a knowing smile when she barked at the legionnaire, "I can get my own drink. I know where it is."

It was clear Servilia had not seen him. Her back was to him, and she was busy pouring wine from a decanter that was resting on a small table across the room. How many years had it been, he thought to himself, and here she was, dressed in flowing robes that revealed more than they should. Typical. She looked good in red. She always looked good in red. He followed her curves across her shoulders and down her backside. She had not seemed to gain an ounce in all this time. He was still smiling when she turned.

Servilia had taken only a few steps when she finally saw him. Wide-eyed, the vision stopped her in her tracks. "Well," she said with a smile, "this is only my second cup of the day, so I cannot be without wits so early. Am I seeing who I think I am seeing?"

"Hello, Servilia," Livius said standing.

"Are you the Livius of whom my son speaks so fondly?" She walked over the table where Livius was standing and set down her drink.

"The very one," Livius said and hugged Servilia. "It has been too many moons since we last saw one another."

"That it has," Servilia said, returning the hug.

After a moment, Livius pulled back, but Servilia stayed close enough to keep her hands in his. "You have raised a fine boy," he said with a smile.

"Yes, he speaks of you frequently."

"Our friendship has been one that I cherish. And you should be quite impressed with the man you have raised, as he now works for the great Caesar."

Servilia flashed Livius a sly smile, then pulled him in close for another hug. The two embraced then took seats across the table.

"I am very pleased with the results," she said, grinning as she sipped her wine. "I have raised him almost completely on my own, his father taken from us at a young age." The comment brought a solemn tone. "How is house Livius?" she quickly asked, "I hear Alba continues to sink her tentacles into you as she did so many years ago."

The comment brought Livius to laughter. "She has been a good wife and a good mother to our four children. She keeps a good house and allows for my business to flourish. She longs for little other than my love, something that can't be said of most women I courted as a young man."

Seeing an old lover was more pleasant than Livius had expected. While he had thought of her many times during Brutus' visits, the emotions recalled in one's mind often pale compared to seeing that person in the flesh. Old ghosts were doing their dances, stripping away the layers of time. In his eyes, Servilia was once again young.

"And what of your children? What have they become?"

"My oldest is a centurion in Caesar's army," he explained. "My middle son took an advisory role last week with Pompey. My youngest is destined to become a soldier in the weeks to come. And my daughter," he paused. "Well, she dreams of armor and battle, but will be in need of taming soon enough, as her eighteenth birthday quickly approaches."

"A girl?" Servilia asked. "It would warm my soul to hear her name the same as mine. I imagine she and I have much in common." She took another sip of wine, slowly, purposefully, and continued, "As I recall, I myself needed taming many years ago, and yet, here I am, still wild as the wind."

The couple enjoyed a laugh, their eyes locked on each other. Livius took in Servilia as she brought the glass once again to her full, red lips. He recalled how much she enjoyed wine. He also recalled how much she enjoyed other things as she was drinking wine. Her perfume drifted across the table, and Livius found himself once again in his youth, gladius in hand. He was young when he saw Servilia for the first time.

She too was young. Vibrant and full of life. She was a tornado. Wild. Spinning, almost out of control. He had never seen anything like her. She was intoxicating. He pursued her. He the hunter, she the prey. She wasn't hard to catch, but she had made him think she was just the same. Servilia always had a certain aroma about her—roses and some kind of exotic spice. Strength and softness. When they made love, it was powerful. It was as if they were one person. In sync, moving together like a wave on the beach. Her breasts, her thighs, her lips. It was all coming back to him.

That is, until the deep voice brought him back. "Welcome Livius," Caesar said as he entered the room.

❀

*L*ivius was visibly jarred. It pleased Caesar. He glanced quickly at Servilia. She seemed a bit befuddled, but he knew it wouldn't take her long to recover. It was one of the things he loved about her.

"It is an honor to meet you, consul," Livius said, standing hastily.

"Yes, great Caesar, it is an honor to meet you," Servilia said sarcastically and took another sip of wine, without standing. She had recovered.

"The pleasure is mine, Livius." Caesar ignored his concubine and extended a hand to his guest. "I hear you are one of the finest butchers in all of the Republic."

Livius smiled.

"I also hear you and I have more in common than a desire for a good piece of pig." He looked specifically at Servilia. She lifted her glass as if to toast.

Livius's smile was replaced by a mouth agape.

It's not that Caesar truly thought Servilia would cheat on

him, it's just that he didn't trust coincidences and the name Livius had been coming up far too frequently as of late. He had been able to watch the pair unseen from his position in the alcove, but he mainly wanted a look at Livius. The butcher was taller than Caesar expected. Taller than he'd have liked him to be, by at least three inches. Caesar had hoped him to be a portly man, but it wasn't the case. He was a fit man with a robust chest and solid arms, peeking out from his plumb cloak. It was probably his best cloak. Caesar smiled. The butcher made nowhere near the money it would take to please a woman such as Servilia.

"Seems we have both favored Servilia at one point in our lives," Caesar said releasing Livius' hand. "She is quite the catch, would you not say?"

Caesar didn't wait for Livius' answer. Instead, he turned and walked over to the wine and poured himself a glass. He eyed Livius in the reflection of the ewer. Livius looked at Servilia for guidance but received none.

"I have not had opportunity to speak with her in many years," Livius finally offered. "But if she is the woman she was back then, you find yourself fortunate to be in her company."

"And yet, you let her go?" Caesar said over his shoulder. He took his time filling his glass, then turned to face Livius. "Was she not worthy of your loins?"

The man was befuddled. Caesar relished in Livius' discomfort. He just looked at the man, forcing an answer. Livius remained silent for a moment, then spoke, "Her desires back then, and as they appear now, were that of a higher station than butcher's wife. I have never had want to do more than make an honest living and raise my children. Servilia would have found her death in the boredom of my lifestyle."

Caesar laughed heartily. "Apparently the years have not changed her spirit then," he said and took a drink.

"You two speak as if I am not in the room," Servilia said,

sharply. "That may work for your wives, but this Roman chooses to be seen and heard."

Caesar looked at Livius as if the two of them were in trouble, then laughed again. "It is an impossibility for your voice to not be heard, Servilia. No one would dare argue that point." He turned to Livius and continued, "I pray you have been more successful at taming your wife than I have been taming this mare, Livius." He walked closer to the table. "I hope too that your influence on your children is equal to the strength Servilia commands over fair Brutus."

"My children respect their father and all still live under my roof," Livius said.

"Then what I am about to ask must stay confidential between the three of us. Are we in agreement?" Caesar waited until both Livius and Servilia agreed before continuing. "I am led to believe your son took employment under Pompey."

"It is so," Livius confirmed.

"You, yourself served under the man, didn't you? Or am I mistaken?"

"You are not mistaken. My service to Pompey was many years past."

"Good," Caesar said. "I would like to be kept informed on any rash movements that come from his camp. I know that Brutus and your family are quite close, so any knowledge can be passed onto Brutus and thus, to my waiting ears."

"You want my son to spy on Pompey?" Livius asked quickly. Caesar did not respond. "Is that wise?" Livius asked. "Aren't you and Pompey on the same side?"

"We all want what's best for Rome," Caesar explained. "Sometimes getting to that point puts us in conflict. Your son is respected enough to gain employment close to Pompey. That can be quite useful," Caesar turned his attention to Servilia. "I know that Brutus will have no problem relaying much needed information to me."

Caesar stepped closer to Livius and continued, "I hope that won't be a problem for your son." He paused, allowing Livius to weigh his options. But there weren't any. When the leader of Rome asks you to complete a task, it isn't as much a request as a command. Perhaps the butcher needed some encouragement. "You have another son, do you not?" Caesar asked. "A centurion in my army, if I recall. A noble man. He has climbed the ranks quickly. Good for him." Caesar put his hand across Livius' back. "I would hate for your loyalties to past commanders stall your son's further progression in my ranks."

The shock on Livius' face was obvious.

Caesar allowed his hand to slowly drift across Livius' back, as he walked toward Servilia. He touched her bare shoulder, took a seat next to her, and then turned to Livius. The trap had been set and the snare complete. There was little the man could do.

"I will speak with my son and see if he chooses to assist you," Livius said. "I would hope that Fabricius' skill and loyalty would not come into question. If that is all, I must take leave and attend to my meats for the day. I would hate for Romans to go hungry."

Servilia stood and hugged Livius. The hug was awkward. Livius bowed his head at Caesar then left the room. Servilia remained standing.

"Will he make this happen?" Caesar asked.

Servilia turned on her heels. "Livius is an honorable man," she snapped. "Trust me, your subtleness was not lost on him. But then it's seldom lost on anyone."

"I need you to make this happen," Caesar said and stood. He walked closer to Servilia and whispered near her ear, "It will only serve to strengthen our relationship knowing you have my best interests in mind." He kissed her on the cheek. "Now, I have work to do." He left her standing.

CHAPTER 20

*T*here were noises coming from the training room. Loud grunts and groans. When Antonia peeked in, she found Justina clothed in full battle gear, breastplate and shin guards in place. Antonia entered the room and sat quietly in the corner, watching Justina as she thrusted her wooden gladius, over and over again, at an unseen opponent. She was strong and quick, but not quite as smooth as Fabricius. Antonia had watched him many times from the shadows as he trained. His movements with sword in hand were elegant, more like a dance, than combat. His muscles rippled as his arm thrusted. His strong legs swept across the floor as he moved forward, then back, slashing and jabbing as he moved. She liked watching him.

Justina kept at it for quite some time before she finally paused. She was breathing heavily when she turned and saw Antonia. She removed her helmet and rushed to her side.

"Apologies," she said.

"For what?" Antonia asked.

"That I did not do more to protect you."

Antonia looked down and rubbed her hands together. "It is I

who should be apologizing. Cato has told me for years that slaves and masters cannot be friends. I was disillusioned."

Justina dropped her sword and took Antonia's hands in hers. "We are friends, Antonia. I've never once looked at you as a slave."

Antonia looked up at Justina. Tears were forming in her eyes. "It cannot be true," she said. "It is but an illusion."

"Cato has no right to speak for anyone but himself. Besides, he has little room to talk. Father treats him more as a confidant than a slave. I am a Roman woman and as such, am fully capable of choosing my own friends."

"But I am not a Roman woman," Antonia said.

"Not yet."

"Not ever!" The male voice came from across the room. Both Antonia and Justina turned to find Atilius in the doorway. Justina stood, picked up her sword, and stepped in front of Antonia.

"So," he said as he entered the room. "You really want to do this?"

"My gladius is ready."

"I am but weeks away from joining the Roman army and you want to test me? And to add to my disdain, you bring the cause of our grievance?"

"There seems but one way that you will accept me as your sister. My sword, your defeat, and the embarrassment that will truly follow. You best clothe yourself and prepare for battle."

Atilius chuckled. "I need only a gladius against you," he said as he walked over to the wooden swords resting on a rail. He picked up one and smiled. "This punishment will be quick."

Justina donned her helmet.

Antonia's first instinct was to run from the room, but she was frozen in place. How she wanted Justina to win, wanted it all to be true. Maybe a slave could find a life among Romans. Maybe a friendship could last. But she knew deep down inside it wasn't true. Still, she wanted nothing more than for Justina to make her brother pay.

"After I defeat you, your girlfriend will wash the blood from my sword, naked in front of me."

"I will take great pleasure in shutting that foul mouth of yours," Justina said and readied herself.

Atilius laughed and took a sudden jab at Justina. She easily blocked the shot and quickly parried, hitting Atilius hard on the back, causing him to fall. He got up, the anger evident.

"So you do want to do this for real?" He walked over to the clothing closet, pulled out a chest plate and helmet. "I was intending on simply embarrassing you," he said as he donned the equipment. "Now I'll make you pay with blood."

"All I hear are your lips flapping," Justina retorted.

Atilius raged a furious attack at Justina, coming at her without warning. It didn't surprise Antonia. A fair fight wasn't in his nature. All he ever seemed to care about was taking the advantage whenever and wherever he could. Yet Justina didn't seem caught off guard. She managed to block every thrust, easily countering his attack, at first. But then it began to change.

Atilius' attacks were relentless. He seemed to have an unlimited supply of energy, swinging his gladius with controlled abandon. His intent, it seemed, was not one of triumph, but of conquest. Justina was losing her footing. Though he had not yet managed to connect with a strike, Atilius had managed to back Justina up until she was almost against the wall. She was no longer returning his parries but instead, seemed to struggle just to block his blows.

Her expression had also changed. Confidence and determination had been replaced with a look of concern, almost bordering on despair. Antonia cupped her hands over her mouth as Atilius pushed Justina back even further, pressing his advantage. She was now unable to keep up with his strikes. She missed a block, and Atilius' sword found its mark against her leg. Antonia winced. Justina missed a second block and the wooden gladius slammed against her arm. Had it been a real sword, is would have left a deep gash. When she missed a third time, Atilius swung his sword at her head, smashing it into her helmet. Antonia cringed with the sound. Justina's helmet crashed to the ground.

Atilius smiled. Antonia started to shake. Justina appeared dazed, but she would not back down. She held her sword out with two hands to counter his next attack, but the sword was shaking. Atilius swung his own gladius hard, aiming right for Justina's sword. Her grip failed, and the sword flew across the room. Atilius stepped in closer and pressed the tip of his gladius hard against her neck. Justina was on her toes. Had the sword been metal, it would have pierced her skin. Atilius was only inches from her face.

Antonia dared not look.

"This will be the last time I face you in combat." Atilius spat out his words. "You are not my equal. You are not worthy of my time. You are just a stranger in my house."

Antonia peeked through her fingers.

Tears fell from Justina's eyes, but she dared not move. Atilius stepped back, then, without warning, swung his sword at Justina's head. There was a dull thud. Antonia screamed. Blood began pouring from the wound. Justina stepped back, stunned, then fell to the floor.

Atilius examined the blood on the sword. He slowly looked up at Antonia. "Take my gladius and clean it," he barked. "But first, remove your clothes."

When Antonia refused to move, he raised the sword as if to hit Justina a second time. Antonia leapt in front of Justina and reached for the sword. Atilius pulled it back. "Oh no," he said. "First remove your clothes. You can clean my sword when you are properly naked."

Antonia lowered her head, then pulled the tunic from her shoulders, letting it fall to the ground. Atilius violated her with his eyes. She went to cover her naked breasts, but he swiped her hand away. Then he pushed the sword into her. "Use your tunic to clean it," he commanded.

Antonia took the sword and began to wipe off Justina's blood. She kept her eyes on the sword. She could not bear to see the smile on his face, or the lust in his eyes. Tears were falling, and she was beginning to sob.

She fell to her knees.

"One day slave, you will learn that you leeched onto the wrong member of this household." Antonia shuddered when Atilius' helmet and breastplate dropped to the floor beside her. "It is I you should be visiting late at night," he said and then left the room.

Antonia finished cleaning the sword, still sobbing. Afterward, she pulled her tunic back on. She looked over at Justina who was huddled in the corner of the room, the blood running down the side of her face.

"Your brother has left, Domina," Antonia said, as she picked up Atilius' gear and placed it in the closet.

"You call me, Domina?" Justina asked, looking up.

"I am a slave and always will be. Our fantasies of anything else are simply that," Antonia said and walked to the door. Before she left, she turned and looked back at Justina. "You'd better go see the Medicus and attend to that wound."

CHAPTER 21

"*D*o you have time to discuss our history, almost revealed?"

The Medicus was mixing herbs when Cato appeared in his doorway. "You may enter," he said. "But be mindful of your words. Best use quiet tones."

Cato entered the Medicus' room. It was meager surroundings. Along one entire wall were shelves containing glass bottles, mainly filled with herbs, though some had strange-colored liquids and other things Cato could not, and did not want to identify. A small table contained a collection of pestles and mortars that were used to crush herbs when making medicine. The table also had cups, bowls, and several wooden spoons. The only other furniture in the small room was two cots, one for him and one for the family member being treated. Cato chose the cot set aside for patients and sat down.

He had been in the Medicus' room many times in the past and every time felt he had entered into the world of Pliny the Elder. It was not a place he felt comfortable, but he had seen what the Medicus could do with a handful of herbs and he trusted him.

Between the three boys and Justina, the Medicus' services were well utilized.

"Had you any idea there were others like us still of the living?" Cato asked.

"Many travelled with us," the Medicus said, looking up from his mortar and pestle. "Is it not realistic to think there may be some who yet find themselves within the borders of Rome? Still, I did not expect it to be her."

⚘

*J*ustina made her way toward the Medicus' room, pressing a torn sheet against the wound to stop the bleeding. She had tried to push herself up against the wall but was unable to gain her footing. Her head was throbbing, and her legs were weak. She crawled across the floor after Antonia left. She fell twice before finally pulling herself upright. After she caught her breath, she leaned against the wall until her knees stopped shaking. The wall kept her upright as she made her way down the hallway. Drawing close to the room, she heard voices inside. One was the Medicus and the other was Cato.

"The smart ones kept going and found lands far from Rome's reach," said the Medicus. "I often wonder what would have become of us if we had not journeyed to Rome."

"We have done well for ourselves here in the house Livius," replied Cato. "We are well taken care of, know what is asked of us, and in turn, are not beaten or treated poorly. This is a good family, and we did well in our searching them out so many moons ago."

Justina stopped just outside the room.

"Still," Cato continued, "Our freedom, albeit brief, was wonderful to behold. Fighting alongside such a great warrior was a feeling unlike any other I have ever experienced. Nothing brings my heart warmth more so than knowing one of his last commands came down to the two of us."

"A command we honor to this day," the Medicus added.

Cato had never talked much about his past. Justina had always wondered how it was he came to be in their house. She had heard the rumors of Cato having once been free, but if it was in fact true, why would a man who had gained his freedom, so easily give it away? She knew it was wrong to listen, but curiosity had gotten the better of her and she couldn't stop herself.

"Commanded," Cato repeated with a chuckle. "He granted our freedom and never commanded us do anything but what our free will would allow."

"I was once kept busy tending to thousands of injuries and wounds. Now, but a scrape here or there consumes my days."

Justina was having a hard time concentrating on the words being spoken. As the hallway began to spin, she pressed herself harder against the wall, but it was no use. Once the spinning began, there was no stopping it, and it didn't take long for her world to turn black. When it did, she fell hard to the floor.

❀

*C*ato jumped from the cot at the sound and rushed to the hallway. He found Justina on the floor, the bloody cloth next to her head. Without hesitation, he scooped her up in his arms and brought her to into the room.

"The Gods!" the Medicus exclaimed. "What has happened? Bring her over and let me have a look."

Cato laid Justina on the cot and almost tripped backward trying to move out of the Medicus' way. She had a sharp cut on her head, and it was clear she had lost quite a bit of blood. "Go to the preparation room and get me some oranges and a lime," the Medicus told Cato. He rushed from the room. When he returned, he found the Medicus making a salve from the herbs and oils in his jars.

The Medicus looked up when Cato entered.

"Cut those in half and squeeze the juice into this cup," he said, handing Cato one of the vessels from the table. Cato did as he was told.

Having finished his salve, the Medicus moved over to Justina and began applying it to the wound he had cleaned while Cato was gone. The act brought Justina back to consciousness with a start.

"Ow!" she yelled and tried to sit up.

Cato turned, relieved to hear her voice. The Medicus placed a hand on her shoulder and gently pressed to stop her. "Lay down," he said. "Sitting up is not yet wise."

"It stings," she said.

"It is the mint," the Medicus explained. "Discomfort will soon turn to relief."

Cato stepped over to the cot. "How did this happen?" he asked. "With whom were you sparring?"

"How did you know.." She stopped when she realized she was still wearing her full gear. "I owed my brother a debt, one that was not repaid this day. I overstepped. My thoughts and my skills are not of the same function."

Cato knew the culprit, but he asked anyway. "Atilius, I would imagine?"

Justina nodded.

The Medicus finished applying the salve. "Okay, now let's try to sit you up." Cato took hold of her arm and the Medicus placed his hand on her back. The two men helped her to an upright position.

"How is your head?" the Medicus asked.

"It feels like I was kicked by a Cappadocia Warhorse."

Cato laughed. The Medicus motioned for the cup and Cato handed it to Justina. "Drink this slowly." the Medicus said. "You will begin to feel better shortly. Head wounds always bleed terribly but look far worse than they usually are."

Seeing that Justina would be all right, Cato was able to catch his breath, but it wouldn't last long. *How long had she been outside the room*, he wondered. There was one way to find out. "Justina, ever the warrior," he said. "You take after your father."

"I do?" Justina asked, sitting more erect. "How well did you know my father? I've heard only a few tales of the great Legatus."

Cato and the Medicus exchanged a quick glance.

"Your father was a great soldier and leader," Cato said. "He is the reason I made sure of your safety in getting you to Rome."

Justina's face fell. "Yes, this I know. This I have been told many times. But at what point will I finally hear more about my father and his battles? I am almost eighteen years old. All I am told is how he fought so bravely and was taken by the Slave King Spartacus. The coward Spartacus, like an eel, slithered into my father's base camp and killed him while asleep. Some king he was."

"You will know the truth soon enough," vowed Cato. "The day will come when all will be revealed, but that day is not today.

"Nor is it any day near coming," Justina added, crossing her arms.

"Right now, I would say you need to focus on that head injury," the Medicus said.

"And perhaps a bit more training before you pick a fight with your brother," Cato added.

"Shall we see if you can stand?" the Medicus asked, and flashed Cato a disapproving look.

It may have been salt in the wound, but it was nonetheless true. He helped the Medicus get Justina to her feet, holding onto her arms until she felt stable. "How do you feel?" the Medicus asked. "Any dizziness?"

"No."

"Then finish the drink and go change out of that gear. The weight is not good for you."

Justina downed the concoction in one large gulp, then handed the cup to the Medicus. "You are right, Cato," she said. "More training is what I need. I won't let anyone hurt Antonia. She is too good of a friend to me."

She had said the comment purposely trying to get Cato to bite. He didn't. Though he hated to hear her talk that way, he knew now was not the time to correct.

"Thank you, Medicus," Justina said and walked to the doorway.

Cato walked over to the door. "Do you need help, Domina?" he asked.

"No," she replied. "I'll be fine."

Cato watched as Justina made her way down the hall, when she was out of sight, he turned back to the Medicus.

"Do you think she heard us?"

"Possibly, but with that head wound, she was probably too dazed to comprehend much of anything." The Medicus went back to his table and put down the cup. "Did you see how her face lights up at the mention of her father? How long do you think you can hide the truth from her?"

"For all of our safety, it is best she never knows the truth."

"Wouldn't her father want her to know? Do you not see how Justina views slaves? It reminds me of someone quite well."

"Do you not recall your vow?"

"Of course I do," the Medicus said, annoyed at the accusation.

"Then keep your mouth tight," Cato ordered and left.

CHAPTER 22

$\mathcal{T}$he house was still when Livius walked into their bedchamber. All but Cato had long ago retired. Livius had been gone all day, had missed dinner, without message. Alba rolled over to face him and lit a candle by the bed. "It is late," she said.

Livius had started undressing. "Pardon my noise. I did not intend to wake you."

Alba leaned onto one elbow. "I have not been able to find slumber. How did your meeting go? Will we be the talk of the town?"

Livius did not answer right away. Instead, he placed his tunic and robe over a nearby chair and began dressing in his night-clothes. Alba watched her husband, waiting for his response. He had strong arms, developed through wielding a gladius in his youth and, later in life, a butcher's ax. When Livius grabbed you, there was no getting away. How those arms made her feel safe when they first met. Livius was taking his time answering her. She knew her husband. She knew his silence was not a good sign. Her hopes of status began to fade.

After he dressed, Livius finally spoke. "Caesar has forced an impossible decision, one where no beneficial outcome is perceivable."

"I do not understand," Alba said. "Of what decision do you speak?"

"He asks that I convince Herminius to share information gathered while under employment of Pompey."

Alba sat up in the bed. "Why would he request that? Spying on Pompey? That doesn't make any sense. The Triumvirate is celebrated in Rome. Having two armies come together as one, with the purse of Crassus behind them, has only led to a prosperous Rome."

Livius walked over to his side of the bed and sat down. "Caesar wants only what is best for Caesar. He proved that today and all previous days. He believes his word, his will, is the only one worthy of leading Rome into future glories."

"You fought under Pompey. That played a part in Herminius' employment with him. Now to have him spy on Pompey...that could put this household in danger."

"It is not the worst of it," Livius said. "He also threatens Fabricius' standing if his wishes aren't obeyed."

Alba was shocked. This morning, an invitation from Caesar had brought a sense of hope and possibility. Now, it had resulted in fear and apprehension. With one option, he places Herminius in danger. With the other, he causes irrevocable damage to Fabricius' career. How could this have happened? Alba looked to Livius for answers, but there were none to be found. There, however, something else he wasn't telling her. She could see it in his eyes.

"There is more?" she asked.

"He asks Brutus' mother to have Brutus be the bearer of whatever information Herminius obtains. He uses leverage on Brutus, knowing his disdain for Pompey, the man responsible for killing his father. Poor Brutus will be more than happy with this arrangement."

"Servilia was there?" Alba asked.

"Yes," Livius responded.

"This meeting with Caesar included her?"

"Of course," Livius answered. "Caesar asks both influential parents to make sure their children do what is best for the republic."

Alba got up from the bed. If the first part of the news was not bad enough, now it was clothed in remembrances of past infidelities. Servilia was a name bitter to her tongue. "Did you know she was going to be there?"

"How would I have known she would be present?" Livius asked. "You saw the note from Caesar. There was no mention of Servilia."

"And yet, she was there."

"It would seem Caesar had many surprises in mind when he requested my presence."

"Were you alone?"

"Briefly, then Caesar joined us."

"Of what did you speak?"

"I have already told you what Caesar requested."

"Not Caesar," Alba said. "What did you and Servilia speak of when you were alone?"

"She asked of you and the children," Livius replied dismissively. "I complimented Brutus. That is all."

Alba stared at her husband. The man who this very day met with an ex-lover then arrived home long after the day had concluded. Trust had already been broken once in their relationship. Broken with this very woman.

"Has she aged well?" Alba asked.

"Who?"

"Servilia. How did she look? It has been quite some time since you two laid eyes on one another."

Livius signed, then stood and walked over to Alba. He took her in his arms. "I come to my wife of well over twenty-five years to let her know about the most powerful man in Rome commanding me to do something that will affect my sons, as well as the rest of this family. Something against my own will, asked to betray a man who I called commander in my youth. And you want to know details on the appearance of someone I was involved with decades ago? Is that what is to be taken from this conversation? Petty jealousy?"

Alba pushed Livius away. "It is not petty," she barked. "She once shared your heart, and your bed, at a time when I shared those as well. Your involvement with her was a betrayal, and now, you treat her son as if he was your own."

"I show Brutus respect, nothing more. He has not had someone to call father in over twenty years. Must we bring up things that happened so long in the past? You are my wife and always have been. But now you are being ridiculous. Sleep is calling for me," he said and walked over to his side of the bed.

"And yet, you have not answered the question. You have not said how she looked. Did she remember you?"

"Dim the candle and come to bed."

"I do not feel it wrong to ask."

"Alba, dim the candle!"

Alba extinguished the candle and climbed into the bed next to her husband. He was laying on his side, his back to her. She lay on her back, starring up into the darkness. "It is not wrong to ask," she repeated.

Livius sighed a second time. "She looked amazing," he said. "Doesn't look like she aged a day in the past twenty-five years, and she remembered me clearly and fondly. Now sleep!"

That was the last thing Alba wanted to hear.

CHAPTER 23

*J*ustina had not found sleep. The Medicus' ointment had minimal soothing effects and her head had throbbed for most of the night. She sat up in bed slowly, and it was then that she saw Lucilius standing in her doorway.

"What do you want?" Justina asked, pulling the covers up around her. "You know where Atilius' room is."

"It is not Atilius that I seek," he said. "I come to apologize. May I enter?"

Before Justina could respond, Lucilius stepped into the room but remained near the door. "Apologies for my treatment of your slave friend," he continued, "and for making you go to the square. Your brother, along with too much wine, clouded my thoughts that evening."

"It is not I who need the apology," Justina said frankly. "I am used to Atilius and his antics. I've seen you around this house enough over the years to know you are quite the same in thoughts and actions as he. What happened the other evening, the verbal insults, is nothing new out of his mouth. Coming from your mouth just echoed his feelings. It was the actions, both in my room, and at the square that perplex me."

Lucilius looked down at the floor and rubbed the back of his neck. Justina watched through dubious eyes. This was not the Lucilius she had come to know. Something was up. She decided to press a bit further. "Does your hatred for slaves stem from the killing of your parents," she asked, "or is this something deeper, something longer than just the past week's events?"

Lucilius took another hesitant step into the room. "My parents warned me from a young age about slaves, about their hatred for Romans. Regardless of their treatment, good or otherwise, they want us to the afterlife. Seeing how friendly you were with that slave just added to my anger. But I know now, it is not my place to discipline your slaves. That is Livius and his son's choices."

Justina watched Lucilius closely. Something had happened, but she was not sure what it was. Perhaps Antonia had told Cato and Cato had spoken to father. Perhaps it was the sight of the slave—someone he knew very well—suffering on the cross. Justina was more than a little confused at Lucilius' confession and his apparent change of heart. Still, she did not truly trust him, and her anger had not yet subsided.

"That slave you abused has a name," she said. "Her name is Antonia and she has become as close a friend to me as any Roman. Both you and Atilius try to drive a wedge between that friendship. If you are truly sorry for your actions, you will call her by her name, not slave."

Lucilius paused, looking first at the floor, then back at Justina. "Antonia," he finally said. "It is a name I will not forget."

Hearing Lucilius speaking Antonia's name softened Justina, and she relaxed a bit. Maybe there was a chance she had been wrong about Lucilius. Perhaps he had experienced a profound change.

"I hope you and I can put our past behind us and move forward. I come with a gift to accompany my apology." He held out a piece of parchment. "I have invite to the great gladiator spectacle being held just three days from now in the Roman Arena. It is an amazing sight to behold. I was to attend with my family, but now I invite yours. In fact, I would insist that you bring Antonia along, to show good faith and true apology."

"Gladiators are a little barbaric for my taste," Justina said.

"Is it not you who spends free time with sword in hand?" He touched the side of his head and smiled. "By the looks of your head, it appears a few more lessons may be in order."

Justina grinned.

"You can view great warriors as they compete for the entertainment of Rome," Lucilius continued, "And I really do insist you bring Antonia, and the other slave, forgive me, what is his name? The large one?"

"Cato?"

"Yes, Cato. I have heard Livius call him that. Please invite him as well. My parents secured spectacular viewing seats, not more than two podiums away from the great Caesar himself."

"I will ask my father," Justina said with a smile. "The invitation is well received as are your words. Perhaps your kindness will rub off on Atilius and maybe, if you spend enough time in this house, my empathy for slaves will rub off on you as well."

"One can only hope," Lucilius replied. "Now I must take leave as I am on patrol early tomorrow."

"Wait," Justina said. She got out of bed, walked over to Lucilius, and hugged him. He seemed to hesitate at first, but then he hugged her back.

Lucilius was about to leave but turned. "Next time you spar with your brother," he said, "if you can survive his first onslaught, you can defeat him. He gets winded quickly." Lucilius smiled and left.

Justina's mood was light. The apology had been unexpected, and she couldn't wait to tell Antonia all about it. Her head no longer bothered her.

CHAPTER 24

MARCH 9, 55 BC

"*T*hank you for coming, brother," Brutus said. "Please have a seat."

Herminius sat in the chair offered. He had never been to the house Brutus shared with his mother. It was smaller than he expected.

"May I offer you wine?" Brutus asked.

"A cup of wine this early?" Herminius questioned. "I am not yet a politician. Water would be just fine, gratitude."

At Brutus' request, a slave brought a decanter of water. She poured a glass and placed in front of Herminius. He noticed she did not fill Brutus' glass from the same decanter.

"Something to eat?" Brutus offered.

"You know my mother Alba all too well," Herminius remarked. "She would not see any of her family leave the house without being properly fed."

Brutus laughed, then waved off the slave. Herminius was doing his best to make light of the situation. He knew that Brutus could easily have spoken to him any of the times he had come over to his father's house. Being called here meant Brutus intended to speak to him of something he was not comfortable doing in that environment. There was no telling what that could be, but Herminius had been around politics long enough to know it usually wasn't good.

"I hear congratulations are in order," Brutus said. "You now work for the great Pompey. That is quite the feat for someone of your young age. I have always found you of keen mind but didn't know that others had realized it as well."

It was the jam on the bread. Brutus was offering him the sweet in exchange for something he wanted. In politics, that something is always information. Brutus knew Herminius was working for Pompey, but apparently, how the commission was received remained a mystery. Herminius could see no danger in revealing the source of his new position.

"I would like to say it was my wits that got me this position, but my father aided in the deed. I'm sure it had much to do with his fighting under Pompey in his younger days."

Brutus' eyes widened, and he sat more erect in his chair. "I had not realized your father served under Pompey."

"Yes, he fought for Pompey during his entire military career. Much like Fabricius, he rose to the position of centurion in quite a timely fashion. I have always said that Fabricius gets his battle skills from father and I get my skills as a thinker from my mother."

"From what years did he serve?" Brutus asked. "I was under the impression he was a butcher since youth? Wasn't his father a butcher?"

"Well, he has been a butcher since my birth," Herminius said, a bit surprised the news came as revelation to Brutus. Having spoken to his father on so many occasions, it would seem natural the topic would have come up at some point. "He gave up military after I was born," he continued, "My grandfather too was a butcher and eased my father's way from cutting down our enemies to cutting down horses and pigs."

Herminius meant the comment as a lark, but Brutus did not react. He was suddenly distant; the recent news seemed to occupy his thoughts. "Is all well?" Herminius asked.

Brutus smiled quickly. "Apologies," he said. "My thoughts were elsewhere." He took a drink then continued, "Let us discuss the reason I requested your visit. As you may know, I have sights on the senate myself. My mother's friend Caesar has made it clear that he can make this happen faster than I could on my own. Although he detests the senate, Caesar still understands the need for their existence, for now," he paused. "Down the road, emperor is the only title with which Caesar will be happy."

"My new boss will make sure that never happens."

"That is my impression as well. However, Caesar proposes an exchange of information for political gain."

Herminius was about to take drink when he suddenly stopped. "Caesar wants information," he asked. "On Pompey?"

"He does," Brutus confirmed. "In exchange for political rise, Caesar has asked me to gather information on Pompey." He paused, allowing Herminius to take it all in. After a moment he continued, "The only person I know, and trust, to do so is you."

There it was, the reason he was called here. Herminius' reaction was swift and immediate. He stood, forcing his chair backward. "You want me to provide you with information on Pompey? Forgive me, Brutus, but this meeting is over. I will not spy on my employer. Pompey is as much to fear as Caesar. Betraying him will not assist my career to the senate."

"Please," Brutus said, reaching out to Herminius. "Do not leave. Has your father not told you of his meeting with Caesar the other day?"

Herminius had turned to leave, but Brutus' words stopped him. "What are you talking about? I know father met with Caesar, but he has told me nothing of the meeting."

"Then I apologize for being the bearer of such news," Brutus said. "I just assumed you knew. Please, sit."

Herminius sat back down, more from being stunned by the news that from a desire to stay.

"That was the gist of the meeting," Brutus continued, "My mother informed me of this and in time, your father may approach you as well."

"Caesar asked my father and your mother to use the two of us as pawns for his benefit?"

Brutus leaned in to Herminius and placed his hand on the young man's arm. "Listen to me," he said in softer tones. "Our strength is our wits, neither of us being strong with sword. Here we are, you in your twenties and I just hitting thirty with the ear of the two most powerful men in Rome. I trust you. I trust your family, and I hope you feel the same about me."

As the shock wore off, Herminius realized Brutus had a plan.

Brutus pulled away his hand and continued, "I do not have many friends or associates and I consider you a brother. Caesar only thinks the world capable of betraying others, yet, for two individuals to have access to all of Rome's secrets. Well, this could be very beneficial for both of us."

"I am in no rush to reach my goals, Brutus. I appreciate your trust, but this does not seem the best course of action for a political career."

"Our hand is forced brother. Any senator under forty without wealth to assist his rise has done such deeds. It may be our only course."

Herminius did not like that answer. "There is always another course."

"Then think of your older brother."

"Fabricius?" Herminius asked. "What does he have to do with any of this?"

"He fights under Caesar's command. You choosing to not assist in this deed may lead to your brother finding more, shall we say, difficult and dangerous assignments. Never to rise above his current position."

Herminius hadn't thought of that, and the realization hit hard. "Your boss is a jackal!" he exclaimed. "He has made my choices no longer my own. They are now tied to my entire family's fortune."

"This is the reason we must follow through with our plan," Brutus reassured him. "Pompey will never suspect a thing. He knows I am friendly with your family and he knows your father's loyalty to Rome. Although the great Caesar will think this benefits him and none other, you and I will be the wiser. Our association will lead us to the heights of Rome and to the senate."

Brutus extended his hand across the table and offered it to Herminius. He looked at the offering for quite a while without taking action. "Or to the depths of Hades," he finally said, then shook Brutus' hand. When Brutus was about to pull away, Herminius tightened his grip. "You have Caesar's ear, when knowledge is exchanged, be sure Fabricius shares in the spoils. Understood, *brother*?" he said emphasizing the final word.

Brutus smiled. "Understood."

CHAPTER 25

*L*ivius was reading when Justina found him sitting in the large chair of their main gathering room. She had fond memories of that chair. As a little girl, she would slide in next to her father, her arms filled with a pile of books. The two of them would sit together reading for hours, her father teaching her the words and helping her sound out the letters.

When she saw her father in the chair, she slipped in beside him, though she didn't fit as well as when she was little. Still, her father made room and placed his arm around her.

"How is my daughter?"

Justina rested her head on his shoulder. "I have completed my chores for the day."

Livius smiled. "That is not what I asked."

"I am well," Justina said. She loved her father, loved him very much. Though he was not her biological parent, she had never seen him as anything but her father. For his part, he had shown her the same love, always treating her as his natural daughter. Whenever she felt like an outsider in the family, it was her father who made her feel welcome, who brought her back to the fold. He encouraged her to be whatever she wanted to be. When her desire led to learning how to wield a gladius, it was her father who showed her, taking the time to make sure she held it properly, thrust it the way it was supposed to be thrusted, showing her the proper footwork. He even saved up to buy her armor that more suited her build.

"Then why has my daughter been walking around the house the last few days with a large wrap on her head?" he asked. "I assume there is a story to go along with such an injury?"

Justina moved in closer. "Really, I am well. This injury is merely motivation."

"Motivation?" Livius repeated. "How so? Are you looking to become the Medicus? Attempting to learn how to properly attend bandages?"

Livius chuckled at his own wit. Justina smiled.

"I am motivated to get better at my combat skills."

"Is that so? To what end? I cannot have you and your brothers beating each other up. How would that look upon my household? Taking my family to the square only to have wandering eyes question all the injuries that stem from this house. They may suspect me the culprit, and I only beat up dead animals these days."

This time his wit caused Justina to chuckle.

"Do you not want your daughter, your only daughter, to know how to protect herself?"

Livius paused before speaking. "Your mother and I are of few agreements of late. However, we are as one in our hopes for our daughter to find a man worthy of her to wed and make us grandparents someday. We have told you numerous times, women do not need to know battle skills. They need to know how to raise children and be a good partner to their husband. I allow for you to play with swords as a hobby, but anything more than that, Justina, is but a dream."

Justina pulled away slightly and turned to her father. "So my destiny is to be a wife and mother, and run a good household as does my own mother?" she said, a bit louder than she had intended.

"That is the destiny of all fortunate Roman women," Livius replied. "You should consider yourself among them."

This was a conversation Justina had hoped to avoid. While her mother seemed to make it a top priority in all their interactions lately, Justina always hoped her father would feel differently. Why, if this was what he had intended for her all along, had he encouraged her to be anything she wanted in her youth.

Justina stiffened.

"There is no future in fighting, Justina. Not for a woman and, ultimately, not for a man. I would trade all my days of battle for just one more with my family by my side. I want only what is best for you. True happiness is found in a loving family, not on the field of battle."

Her father's words softened Justina, and she once again melted into him. Livius smiled. "Will you be there on my wedding day?"

Livius looked down at her, surprised at the question. "Of course I will."

Justina smiled. "Am I to have slaves in my household?"

"If fortune affords them, and your husband acquires enough status, then yes."

"And if I were to ask for a slave as a wedding gift, would you be gracious in my request?"

"If your husband allowed for it, then yes."

"What if I requested one of the slaves in this house?"

"Speak your mind, Justina," Livius said.

Justina sat up. "I would have Antonia be by my side in my next household. Would you afford me that luxury? As a wedding gift, of course. And with the permission of my loving husband."

Livius smiled in the way only a father could. Justina was laying it on pretty thick and she knew it. She formed the face she used when she wanted something from him, doe-eyed with just the slightest of smiles at the corners of her mouth. He was powerless to resist it.

"You and Antonia have grown up in this household almost as sisters," he finally said. "You seem to forget at times that she is a slave and not an equal. I fear that if she were to accompany you in your next household, your husband may lose out on attentions he deserves."

"She is a good person," Justina said quickly, "and I like being around her."

"And she likes being around you...too much. We each have our place in the world Justina, our own roles to fill. It is the way of things."

"Are slaves not people?" Justina asked. "Dogs to be beaten when they disobey? I have witnessed your treatment of slaves in this very house, father. It has always been merciful."

"A slave is just a status, Justina. Being a slave does not make a person any less human. Still, at times, discipline is needed."

Justina was taken aback. She had never heard such words coming from her father. "Have you...beaten slaves, father?"

Livius took a deep breath. "I have only once had cause to use violence to keep our slaves in line. You were quite young, and I am grateful your eyes did not view it. We are blessed that has not been needed since."

"I am surprised to hear this," Justina admitted. "You are such a gentle man. In fact, it is one of the things I have always admired about you. I like that I am the daughter of someone who does not use violence."

Livius smiled. "You forget I was once in the military, Justina. While I am not an admirer of violence, I am no stranger to it. I find myself fortunate that I was able to serve under Pompey during those times. Although I did not always agree with his commands or tactics, I did as commanded, and it has made me who I am today." He caressed Justina's cheek with the back of his hand. "You can rest assured, the days of violence and Livius are long past."

Justina liked the feel of her father's touch. It was comforting. She melted into his arms. "And am I to do what I'm commanded?"

"To live a happy life, with a family by your side is not a commandment Justina. It is a wish fulfilled."

"A wish for more than just Romans."

"All right, Justina," Livius conceded. "If that is what will make you spend less time with a gladius and more time meeting a possible suitor, then yes, you have my blessing that when you get married, I will gift you Antonia."

Justina's smile took over her face. She threw her arms around her father's neck and hugged him as tight as she could. He kissed her head. "My blessing was answered the day Cato and the Medicus arrived on our doorstep with baby Justina. Your parents tragically killed by the Slave King Spartacus. You will be happy to know that, although I had been retired from military for several years at the time, Pompey came to me for advice and plan to end Spartacus. I was more than happy to oblige."

The news came as a surprise. "I know so little about my parents," Justina said. "In fact, I think I know more about the man who killed them. The gladiator, trained by Rome, who used those skills to kill thousands of Romans."

"It was a tragedy that, luckily, came to an abrupt ending."

Moments such as this, where Justina had her father all to herself, were becoming rare. She felt safe in his arms, happy, and wanted. She was content to simply sit with him and would have been willing to do so for the remainder of the day. As she relaxed, her mind drifted to a future where Antonia would be by her side, as her equal. She was cherishing the moment, when Lucilius' offer popped into her head.

"Lucilius came to me last night with a peace offering," she said.

"Has there been tension between the two of you?"

"A little, but nothing that need cause worry."

"So tell me of this offer."

"Lucilius has invited all of us to the arena to watch the fights. At first, I said no, but I think it would be a fun experience for the family."

"Fun?" her father questioned. "Are you certain? Blood is freely spilled in the arena and that blood is often accompanied by death."

"I've witnessed enough blood, mostly my own, to last me for a while. However, I would like to attend. Lucilius said he has admissions for all of us, including Cato and Antonia."

She allowed her father to ponder the proposition.

"If it is truly what you desire," he said, "then make arrangements with your brothers. I will see if your mother wishes to join as well. Keep in mind, Cato and Antonia will be standing behind us the entire viewing."

Justina virtually leapt from the chair. "Gratitude father," she said with a grand smile.

"I am still surprised this offer came from Lucilius."

"Perhaps being in this household for a few days has made him realize he needs to choose a different path in life. I may have misjudged him. Maybe he is a good man."

"Maybe," Livius said.

CHAPTER 26

MARCH 11, 55 BC

Servilia removed the sheets, revealing her naked self. "Oh, great one, come back to bed and let us continue what we started last night."

Caesar stood by his desk, reviewing parchment. He had pulled on a tunic when he rose and, rather than making her leave, he decided to let Servilia sleep. He looked over at his naked concubine. She was a sight to behold and lying there, with that look, proved more than minor temptation. "If life were only that easy," he said.

It would have been easy to give in to carnal desires. However, if he wanted to stay ahead of the senate, he needed to keep his wits about him. Just as in battle, plans needed to be examined from every possible angle to ensure their soundness. Caesar never let anything take him by surprise on the battlefield, and he had no intention of allowing the senate, or the Triumvirate, to break that streak.

"Oh, poor Caesar, he has not five minutes for pleasure,"

Servilia said in her best seductive voice. She moved her hand slowly up her thigh as she spoke.

The move had the desired physical effect on Caesar, but he didn't give in. "I will enjoy myself when the senate is no more and I am the emperor of Rome. Then, I will give you five minutes for morning fun. Until then, our arrangements need stay in place."

"You are such a bore sometimes," Servilia said, covering herself. "Will we at least be spending the morning together? You do need to eat."

"I have already had fruit. I need you to find your clothing and make your exit. My wife comes in today from her villa just outside of town. We are to attend the fights at the Arena in a few hours."

Servilia pulled the sheets around her and stood to dress. He had struck a nerve. Servilia only covered herself when he had angered her. It was probably the mention of his wife. If that made her mad, Caesar was pretty sure his next revelation would put her over the edge.

"I have invited your ex to the games," he informed. "I sent one of my soldiers to make sure the invite was well-received. I look forward to seeing him again and meeting his sons."

Servilia stopped dressing. "You invite Livius to join in your box?"

"Don't be ridiculous," Caesar replied. "I would not be seen with a butcher in my box. His seats are close enough, however, for us to run into one another."

"How convenient," Servilia said as she tightened the band around her silk robe.

"I look forward to meeting his wife as well. She will see what a true Roman is like."

"If she is happy for the past twenty-plus years with a butcher, she may faint at the sight of you."

Caesar smiled. "Hurry, I need to finish up here and then meet Crassus before the fights."

Servilia was about to comment when a knock came on the door. Caesar answered the door and was told by a slave that Crassus had arrived.

"I must leave and attend to Crassus," Caesar said to Servilia. "I'm sure you can show yourself out."

"Are you embarrassed of me?" Servilia asked as she hooked jewels into her ears.

"Crassus does not approve of our relationship."

"The rich and powerful Crassus has an opinion of Caesar's whore? Since when do you worry about the thoughts or judgments of others?"

"I am not concerned with his judgment. I simply do not want to listen to his condemnation or his counsel on the matter."

"I will not be dismissed like a common whore," Servilia said. "If you do not accompany me to the front door, I shall not enter that door again."

Caesar walked over to Servilia. He lifted his hand to the back of her neck and pulled her close, kissing her full on the lips. Just when she was about to pull away, he tightened his grip and took hold of her hair, pulling her head slightly downward. She almost lost her balance. He looked straight at her, his eyes cold.

"Do not forget who it is you are speaking to. If you do not desire to find yourself replaced." He let go of her hair and walked toward the door. "You may accompany me, but keep your conversation to a minimum."

❦

"Fine morning to you," Crassus said as Caesar entered the room. He was pleased Caesar hadn't made him wait long. That pleasure vanished when he realized the woman by Caesar's side was not his wife. "To you both," he added, doing little to hide his distain. He turned his attention to Caesar. "I thought to find your wife by your side. Are we taking mistresses to the event

RYAN LEW

today? I was not informed of this new way of gaining Rome's trust."

"Hold your reprobation, Crassus. Servilia was just leaving. My wife is to arrive in the next hour or so."

"Good to see you too, Crassus," Servilia said. She turned to Caesar, bowed, and then gave him a pronounced, purposeful kiss. Then she wiped her color off his lips. "Have fun at your little games."

Crassus watched her leave. When she was gone he turned to Caesar. "You know my thoughts on this. Rome has tolerance to a point, but if this relationship was discovered."

"What would happen?" Caesar asked, interrupting. "Nothing would change. The senate would continue to gossip like always. I would have an unhappy wife, but I wouldn't have to invite her to make appearances with me anymore."

"Tell me you aren't developing feelings for this concubine of yours."

Caesar walked over to the table and took a seat. He motioned for Crassus to follow, then called for a slave to bring them wine. "There are several things that make me happy," he said as the slave poured. "Servilia just happens to be towards the top of that list."

"Traveling down that trail is dangerous."

Caesar ignored the comment. "One of Pompey's old soldiers will be in attendance at today's games. I would like for you to meet him. I have a surprise waiting for him at the fights."

Crassus took a drink from the cup filled before him. Caesar and surprises were not a good mix.

CHAPTER 27

*T*he first match had been grueling to watch and the second was proving its equal. Two men had entered the arena. One was clothed in leather pants, boots, and a battered helmet, his scarred chest and arms left exposed. He held a large net in one hand and a strange weapon in the other. Justina's father had called it a trident. His opponent wore a full set of Roman armor, old Roman armor, but armor nonetheless. His weapon of choice, a gladius.

When the two gladiators entered the ring, the crowd erupted in alternating cheers and hisses, supporting their favorite and booing the other. Justina was in a private box with her family, her father on one side and her brother Herminius, on the other. Atilius sat to the right of Livius. Cato stood behind them, with Antonia, who held a jug of wine.

When Lucilius first invited her to the gladiator games, Justina had been hesitant. Watching two men try to kill each other was not what she considered entertainment. Yet, here at the area, hearing the cheers of the crowd, she had to admit, there was a certain excitement. Two men entered. Only one was intended to leave. Fighting for a cause was noble. Fighting for one's life was something entirely different. It brought something out in a man—something unexpected. Despite her initial apprehension, Justina found herself caught up in the struggle.

The combatants circled, testing their opponent with weak thrusts and parries. The length of the bare-chested gladiator's trident helped him keep the other out of range. But Justina noticed his weakness right away: he had but one move, a thrust.

The armored gladiator waited for the right moment. He blocked with his gladius when the thrust came, then spun to position closer to his opponent. The move forced the bare-chested gladiator off balance. It was a fine move, but Justina noticed it placed him on his opponent's net, certainly not sturdy ground.

The armored gladiator swung his sword with all his might. The bare-chested gladiator leapt backward, but it was not fast enough. The sharp metal tip caught his chest, cutting a downward slash. Blood spattered, and the crowd erupted in cheers. Justina gasped and took hold of her father's arm.

Blood flowed from the gash, but the gladiator seemed unaffected. His attention remained squarely on his opponent. He dropped the net to the ground, stepped on it, and then began quickly spinning his trident in a wide circle. The move was unexpected by both his opponent and Justina. The armored gladiator reared back, then took a swipe at the trident. He missed, but instead of thrusting, the bare-chested gladiator scooped the net with the tip of his trident and pulled it with all his might. The legs of the armored gladiator came out from under him and he fell hard to the ground, landing flat on his back. The crowd erupted yet again, and Justina found herself moving to the edge of her seat. She was digging her nails into her father's arm.

The bare-chested gladiator twirled the net high above his head, spinning it until it flattened out. In full swing, he launched the net at his opponent. The armored gladiator tried to stand, but it was too late. The net fell atop him, covering him completely. His opponent wasted no time. As the crowd cheered, he ran forward, planted his trident in the ground, and used it to pole-vault on top of the armored gladiator. He stepped on the man's outstretched arm—the one holding the sword—and positioned his trident inches from the armored gladiator's neck.

The crowd erupted in cheers. Justina tightened her grip. Livius winched.

The bare-chested gladiator remained in position; blood had covered his chest. He waited for the sign of mercy, or the pronouncement of death. The armored gladiator lay there for a moment, then slowly lifted two fingers. The crowd cheered, then began to chant, "Mercy, mercy, mercy."

Livius pulled his daughter's hand from his forearm. "The crowd is feeling generous today."

Justina turned to her father and only then realized she had been digging her nails into his skin. She pulled her hand away. "Apologies, father."

Livius laughed. "Your mother did worse the first time I brought her here."

"Why did mother not attend today?" Herminius asked.

"I invited her to join us, but she was not feeling well and preferred to rest at home," Livius explained.

The two Gladiators left the arena and preparations were made for the next conflict.

"How does Lucilius afford such amazing viewing seats?" Livius questioned aloud.

"He said his parents had these seats waiting for them."

"I never knew his parents to attend the games."

"Well, then he probably spent a month's wages just to show gratitude for your hospitality," Justina said. "It is the least he should do."

"Mind your words, girl," Atilius barked, leaning to look over at Justina. "He owes us nothing. We offer shelter and council because it is the right thing to do."

Livius placed a hand on his son's arm.

157

Atilius leaned back in his seat. "He did not pay for these seats," he said. "They were given to him by his commander, Braccius."

"That is Fabricius' commander as well. Is it not?" Livius asked.

"It is a shame that Fabricius was summoned into patrol today. He may have enjoyed these fights," Herminius said.

"How is it that a commander would come by such seats, and why would he then surrender those seats to an underling?" Livius wondered aloud.

Herminius leaned back in his seat so he could see Cato. "Have you ever witnessed gladiators, Cato?"

Justina turned in her seat as well, eager to hear his response.

Cato didn't blink. "I have seen gladiators," he answered, then directed his comments to Livius. "Gratitude for the offer extended to myself and Antonia," he said and bowed his head. "It has been many years since my eyes witnessed these competitions."

"We are happy to have you," Livius replied.

Justina turned to Antonia and whispered, "Are you well?"

"Gratitude, I am well," Antonia answered. She was standing just as Cato, keeping her eyes forward while holding the wine. Justina had not yet had a chance to give her the good news, but she knew, when she did, she would have her friend back.

When Justina did not look away, Antonia turned her head and asked, "Do you require anything, Domina?"

"I am fine for now," Justina said and flashed a smile. It was not returned. Justina would have liked to say more, but before she could, Antonia returned her gaze forward.

"I will take drink," Atilius said. Antonia moved to Atilius and poured the wine. Justina leaned forward in her seat. Atilius was staring at Antonia, trying to make his glare as obvious as possible. Though Antonia kept her gaze on Atilius' glass, her hands began to shake. Cato reached out to touch her back. The move worked, and her hands stopped shaking. After she had filled the glass without incident, she returned to her position, smiling gratitude as she passed Cato.

Three more gladiators entered the arena to the cheers and jeers of the crowd.

"These gladiators, are they better suited for combat than the regular Roman Army?" Justina asked her father.

"They spend day and night, honing their skills until their very bodies are weapons," Livius replied.

Justina was confused. "It is amazing to me that Rome was able to defeat Spartacus if his army was formed of such men."

"Rome was fortunate indeed," Livius said. "The majority of Spartacus' followers were simple house slaves with no combat experience. And although he was a respected gladiator, Spartacus' army held few in their ranks. If his numbers had been seventy thousand true gladiators, the outcome may have been vastly different. We may all have been slaves to the man."

The crowd jeered as an unpopular gladiator gained an upper hand. Then cheered as their favorite regained his footing. The battle played out until the favorite was the only man left standing. Glorious cheers engulfed the arena as yet two more gladiators were allowed to limp off with their lives and, for the most part, their bodies intact.

"The main event is next," said Livius. "There will be an intermission before it begins."

Just then, Caesar and two body slaves entered their box.

❀

"How find you today, good Livius?" Caesar asked.

Livius stood awkwardly. "Caesar," he said. "What brings you to our box?"

"Truth be told, I am the reason for your appearance here today. I gave my Legatus these seats for you and your family to enjoy."

There it was. The missing piece in the puzzle. "Gratitude for your hospitality," Livius said.

While Livius' attention was on Caesar, Crassus entered. Livius turned, and the two men locked eyes for the briefest of moments.

"Think nothing of it," Caesar said. "Though I have to admit, good Crassus here owns all of the boxes in this area of the arena. He was kind enough to provide me with these seats."

Livius extended his hand to Crassus. "Then gratitude to you as well."

Crassus stepped forward and took hold of Livius' hand. He squeezed it once, then shook. "It is the least I could do." Livius nodded in appreciation. Caesar's eye's narrowed.

Livius noticed Crassus' eyes move behind him. *Who was he looking at?* Livius wondered. Only Antonia and Cato were behind him. His children stood next to him. Crassus moved his head to the side, looking for a better view. Livius wanted to turn and look as well, but with Caesar present, he thought it better of it.

"Tell me, Livius, have you had chance to think on my proposition?" Caesar asked.

Crassus turned suddenly to Caesar.

Before Livius could answer, his son spoke up. "I am Herminius, Caesar. Yes, father has spoken to me and I am in agreement. Anything for the betterment of Rome."

Livius tried to hide the shock that was, most assuredly, showing on his face. He had yet to speak to his son about the proposition and certainly did not expect Herminius to answer for him.

Caesar smiled and turned to Herminius. "All that we do is for the betterment of Rome," he said, extending his hand. "I look forward to hearing more of your reports in the weeks to follow."

While his son shook Caesar's hand, Livius was once again caught by Crassus's gaze. As before, he was trying his best to look behind Livius. This time, Crassus stepped to the side. Livius kept a wary eye on him but made sure to keep his attention on Caesar and his son.

"I was hoping to hear this good news and, in anticipation of it,

I have given your son a great honor," Caesar said to Livius. "The reason he was summoned for patrol today. Keep eyes on the middle of the arena and see appreciation paid. Now, I must take leave." He turned to go then stopped. "Was your wife not invited?" he asked, turning back to Livius.

"She took ill and needed much rest," Livius said.

"I hope she feels better soon. Maybe one day, I shall meet her. Until then," Caesar said, and turned to leave. Crassus took another step toward Livius, trying to get one last look at whoever was behind him.

"Are you coming, Crassus?" Caesar asked.

Crassus turned first to Caesar, then back to Livius. Confusion painted his face.

"Crassus," Caesar repeated.

Crassus followed Caesar out of the box, walking as if lost. Livius had seen that look before. It came when a man was trying to reach into the recesses of his mind and coax a memory back to life. Livius turned to Cato. He was standing, arms folded, looking forward.

"Jupiter shines on our family brightly!" Atilius said with a broad smile. As his youngest son basked in the family's fortune, Livius glanced quietly at Herminius, his eyes searching for explanation.

"Brutus had already been aware of requests," Herminius said. "He filled me in, and I am in agreement with the arrangement."

Livius wasn't sure what to say. He had intended to speak to his son and explain the situation—the benefits, and the drawbacks. At the least, he had wanted to take part in the decision. He did not appreciate being left out and was about to express his displeasure when the horns blasted announcing the main event. Livius turned to find the crowd cheering, looking at Caesar, who was now standing in his own box.

"*R*omans!" Caesar said. "Gratitude for coming to see the mighty gladiators pay homage to Rome." The crowd cheered loudly. Caesar raised his hands to calm them. "But the great Caesar has another offering for you. Just recently, several slaves have felt the need to betray their masters." At that moment, five chained slaves—three men and two women—were dragged into the middle of the arena and forced to kneel.

"They tried to flee Rome," Caesar said. "We give these ingrates the opportunity to serve us and this is how we are repaid?" The crowd erupted in jeers and boos. "Not while Caesar has something to say about this." His words brought the crowd to their feet. He waited, allowing their cheers to fill the arena, before continuing, "Witness Roman justice by three of my respected legionnaires."

Three men walked into the arena to the delight of the crowd. They made their way to the center and stood behind the slaves. The first of the three removed his helmet. It was Lucilius. Justina gasped loudly. Livius turned to his daughter and found the same stunned look he likely had himself. The second soldier removed his helmet as well to reveal Braccius, the Legatus. He held his gladius up high as the crowd cheered.

The third legionnaire did not remove his helmet. Livius thought he might know why.

"You may begin the justice!" Caesar called out.

Braccius didn't hesitate. He shoved his gladius into the back of one of the male slaves, the pointed end piercing his chest. Blood pooled at the slave's mouth. Braccius placed his boot against the slave's back and pulled out his sword. He held it up to show the roaring crowd. The slave coughed, spit out blood, and then fell forward, dead. Braccius moved quickly to the second man. Coming up behind him, he slid his gladius across the slave's throat, severing his jugular. Blood poured from the slave's neck. The crowd rose to their feet in loud appreciation.

Atilius clapped and cheered, standing all the while. Lucilius followed his commander's lead and shoved his sword into the back of the remaining male slave. The crowd cheered, and Lucilius laughed as the man fell dead. Like his commander, Lucilius held up his sword to show off the blood. He then walked to the front of the slaves and stopped before one of the females. He looked down into her face, then turned and pointed his gladius. He was pointing it at Justina. Livius looked over at his daughter and saw the horror in her face. Herminius stood, mouth agape. Atilius was jumping up and down. Antonia went to cover her eyes but was stopped by Cato. He placed his hand on her arm and shook his head.

Lucilius turned back to the slave and shoved his gladius directly into her chest. She screamed out, coughed blood, and then collapsed. The crowd's cheers were deafening. Lucilius held his sword high and walked around the arena drinking in the crowd. The third legionnaire simply stood there. The final slave was sobbing visibly. Braccius turned to the man. The Legatus motioned with his sword and said something, but the crowd was far too loud for Livius to hear his words.

The legionnaire drew his gladius slowly and walked over to the woman. He looked up at the crowd, and for a moment, Livius could have sworn he was looking directly at his daughter. The legionnaire hesitated, then shoved his sword into the female slave's back, killing her instantly. The crowd roared, then began chanting Caesar's name.

"Caesar, Caesar, Caesar..."

Everyone stood. Everyone except Justina and her father. Livius noticed and quickly stood. He took hold of his daughter's arm. "Stand," he said. Justina looked up at her father. She resisted at first but stood when he pulled her up.

Braccius and Lucilius held their gladius' high for the crowd. The third legionnaire did not follow suit. When Lucilius saw that the soldier was not joining in the revelry, he ran behind him,

163

pulled off the man's helmet, and tossed it aside. Livius was not surprised to see his oldest son revealed.

"No!" Justina cried out. She fell limp.

Cato moved to catch her.

Antonia dropped the jug of wine. It shattered in a shower of liquid.

Livius turned sharply to Caesar. When their eyes met, Caesar smiled.

CHAPTER 28

*S*ervilia was sitting on her couch enjoying a foot massage when another slave entered the room and announced she had a visitor. "Show her in," Servilia said, more than a little annoyed she had to cut the massage short. She dismissed the female slave at her feet, slipped her sandals back on, and sat more upright in the chair.

The slave came back in the room, followed by a woman dressed in flowing robes, nice robes, ones that showed she had an amount of wealth, but not too much. She was a striking woman, with dark hair and piercing eyes. She moved with an air of confidence. Servilia recognized her right away.

"Hello, Alba," she said, without standing. "Welcome to my home."

Alba's face betrayed her surprise. "Apologies for coming unannounced."

Servilia always enjoyed having the upper hand—something she learned from Caesar. She relished it now, watching Alba try not to be caught off guard by her instant recognition.

"You have a lovely little place here," Alba said. "Seems cozy for both you and your son."

"Please, have a seat," Servilia motioned toward the chair next to her. "May I offer you drink?"

"Gratitude."

Servilia motioned for a slave to bring wine. As Alba's glass was filled, Servilia examined the woman who had stolen Livius' heart so long ago. She was attractive. More so than Servilia had expected. Servilia hadn't actually recognized her—having never seen her before—but she had the distinct look of a woman protecting her territory.

Alba took a sip of the wine she had been poured. "This is quite nice. You have good taste."

Servilia smiled. "My good taste is not limited to wine only."

"That seems to be true." Alba said, without hesitation. "At one point, my husband was to your taste."

"Ah yes, the one that got away," Servilia said, pausing a moment as if to reflect. "We were but kids when we found admiration for one another." Her mind quickly went to the last meeting between her and Livius, as if it had just occurred. He was so handsome in his youth. Strong and virile. The attraction had been both mutual and immediate. Their affair was one not soon forgotten. But that was not what she was recalling just now. That was not the case with their last meeting, the one where he told her Alba was with child. The one where he told her he could no longer see her. The one scorched into her memory. She let him go that day without one last kiss.

"Too many moons have passed since those feelings," Servilia said and took a slow drink before continuing. "I would assume your presence is due to our meeting the other day? I assure you, I had nothing to do with it and was as surprised as Livius appeared to be."

It was Alba's turn to take a slow drink.

"Were you not bound for the arena today?" Servilia asked, deliberately breaking Alba's pause.

Alba sat back in the chair and crossed her legs. "I did not

suspect you would call for such a meeting. Livius should have earned Caesar's respect over the years. He is a good man, a good father, a good provider, a good Roman."

"The arena?" Servilia said, ignoring Alba's comment.

"It was mentioned to me, but fights of that nature bore me. I thought it time you and I meet. Your son is a frequent guest in my house, and I am reminded of your previous admiration for what is now mine."

Servilia smiled. "You know I am spoken for these days."

"I know what I hear from several Roman mouths," Alba countered. "Your boyfriend is quite married. That cannot be easy for you."

"His marriage is for show," Servilia said easily. "His feelings are mine to command. He is a very powerful boyfriend."

"One who looks to make an enemy of Pompey. Does that seem wise?" Alba asked as she took another drink. "If I recall correctly, you were once married to someone who sided against Pompey. That didn't turn out well. It would be a shame for you to side against Pompey a second time and see worse come your way."

Servilia's eyes narrowed. She considered standing, taking Alba by the hair and slamming her glass into her face but resisted. She had played these games before and was much better at them than this would-be pretender. "Are you here to issue empty threats and drink my wine? Or did you come to get a glimpse at the woman who first had Livius' heart? Truth be told, if I had not been blessed with seed of Brutus' father, I may have ended up with Livius myself."

"You actually believe that?" Alba asked.

"I do," Servilia said. "If you had not become pregnant with Livius' second child, it is almost certain this would have become our paths. The Gods blessed you during those times, not me."

"They not only blessed me back then, but for many years to come."

Servilia kept her gaze.

"Gratitude for your wine," Alba said, uncrossing her legs. "Now that I see you first hand, I should have believed my husband when he assured me I had nothing to worry about."

Alba stood and placed the glass on the small table next to the chair.

"I know your life has not been easy," Alba continued, "If your husband had not been for the afterlife, you may have seen your family celebrated over all these years. Possibly more than two slaves at your side and only one child."

"I often wondered what type of woman stole Livius' heart," Servilia said quickly. "Now that I have met you, I can only imagine how quick you were to spread legs and get seed to trap such a great man. He may be in his forties, but he has many great years ahead. Be sure to keep leash tight." She took another drink.

Alba glared at Servilia, but Servilia did not return her look.

"Know this," Alba said. "I was privy to information that affected your life. I am sworn to secrecy, of course. That is, unless I am forced to spread lips, much like I spread legs so many years ago. I pray that I never have reason to share such information."

Servilia looked up from her glass. Alba caught her gaze, forming a slight smile. The two women remained locked in a glare, then Alba turned and left.

Servilia remained seated, staring forward. She took another drink.

CHAPTER 29

*J*ustina could hear them in the next room, laughing. She imagined Lucilius recreating the day's events, shoving his sword into the male slave over and over again. Describing to Atilius just how glorious it felt to kill innocent slaves, defenseless human beings. It sickened her, just as it had sickened her to watch the spectacle earlier.

She remembered little about the walk home. Most of it in silence, except for Atilius, who could not stop talking about how the slaves got "what was their due." That is, until their father admonished him. After that, no one spoke.

Justina was sitting on the floor against her bed when her door opened slowly. Antonia was on the other side, and Justina could see she had been crying.

"Why?" Antonia said, almost in a whisper. "Why would you invite me to such an event?"

Justina motioned for Antonia to enter, then patted the floor next to her. Antonia entered and sat down.

"It was offered as a gracious gesture," Justina said. "One well received at the time. If I had known intent, I would not have made offer, nor would I have accepted for myself."

"I have lived in this household my entire life and, until recently, never feared harsh treatment. But now, this house seems filled with people to fear."

Justina turned and took Antonia's hands. "Your concerns should be with Atilius and Lucilius and no one else."

"How can you say that? I hear, and now witness, Fabricius' killing of slaves. Once admired, I now fear that he has grown to enjoy his position and the benefits that come with it."

"Fabricius was only doing as commanded," Justina assured her. "Caesar made request, thinking it a favor to my father."

Antonia's eyes widened. "Is it such a great honor to your people to watch slaves killed because we pursue freedom from chains, beatings, and death?" Her tears were welling.

Justina moved her hands to Antonia's arms. "Do not be upset. Lucilius will not be in this house for long. Atilius joins the Roman Army in a week and his time here will be shortened."

Antonia began to sob. Justina pulled her close and wrapped her arms around her. "This all will pass," she said, but it did little to calm her friend. "Is it Fabricius that caused you concern?"

Antonia nodded.

"Fabricius would never harm a slave unless commanded to do so. You saw how he hesitated in the arena and would not remove his helmet."

"He chose to not remove his helmet to hide his true intentions. His true feelings."

"You are wrong," Justina said quickly. "I know my brother. He does as commanded. As a good Roman soldier should. You saw how the Legatus and Lucilius celebrated the killings. Fabricius killed only one, and he did so because he was commanded. You need not fear him." Justina said the words, but she was not sure she believed them herself.

Antonia's cries deepened. "Are my days numbered?" she asked through sobs. "Am I for the afterlife to join my parents in the months, weeks, or days to come?"

Tears rolled down Justina's cheeks. It was hard to see her friend in such pain. "I am here for you. I will never let anyone hurt you."

Antonia cut her off. "You cannot protect me, Justina." She pulled away and was suddenly calm. "Atilius and Lucilius dominate you physically in this house. They also stifle your voice. Your mother closes ears to your desires as well."

Justina squeezed Antonia's hands and smiled. "I have news that will wipe your tears away for good. My father is the only voice that matters in this house and he and I have brokered a deal."

"A deal? What type of deal?"

"When I marry, you are to be gifted to me and waiting husband."

Antonia's face lit up.

"I will make sure future husband knows we are as one," Justina continued.

"And if he refuses?" Antonia asked.

"Then he will have cold nights in his bedchamber."

The two shared a laugh.

"Is this true?" Antonia asked.

"Yes. You and I will be together. You will be treated as sister in my new household."

Antonia hugged Justina.

"You need not worry about your future," Justina said. "I will ensure it is a pleasant one."

The mood in Justina's room lightened briefly, then Antonia pulled back. "Marriage? How are you talking marriage? You have yet to date, let alone show any affection for any male. Do I have time for you to discover what a woman should desire? This sounds like a great dream, but a dream none the less."

"I will make changes. I know I do not present myself well, but that will change. My mother and father want to see me find love, and I shall begin that search. It is important to me to rid myself of living under a roof where slave killings are celebrated. I do not like the abuse of slaves. I know it is celebrated in our culture, and I should share same mind and feeling, but I do not. I would imagine my real father, the Legatus, would be disappointed in me."

"Well, I am grateful for you and your true heart. I hope the day arises soon where someone of your mind comes into your life and the two of you find love."

Antonia and Justina hugged once more. Just then, a knock came on the door. Fabricius stuck his head inside. "Apologies for the late appearance," he said. "I have just now arrived from my day's duties."

Antonia moved closer to Justina and took hold of her hand.

"Is there something you need at this late hour, brother?"

"I need to share a word with you before I find slumber," he said and half-stepped into the room. "Antonia, would you please excuse us."

Justina squeezed Antonia's hand and nodded her approval. Antonia stood and walked toward the door, her head lowered. Fabricius stepped aside. His attention was on Justina. Once Antonia left, he entered the room, closing the door behind him.

Justina got up from the floor and sat down on the bed, arms folded.

"You need to know I was not made aware of my assigned duties for the day 'til just moments before." He sat down next to Justina. "When Braccius told me I had been selected, I asked if the assignment could be given to another. He told me Caesar himself had made request and that it would be unwise for me, or my family, to deny such a request. I had hoped to keep my helmet firmly on so none of you would see who delivered the last blow on the slave."

Justina was flooded with emotions she did not expect. She wanted to hug her brother and comfort him, but at the same time, she was doing all she could not to slap him hard in the face. She

understood he had been put in a situation with no possible beneficial outcome. Still, he had killed a defenseless human being.

"Had you been told their crime?" Justina asked. "Their
real crime?"

Fabricius stiffened. "We have laws in this land, Justina. Laws
that hold for Romans as well as slaves. Breaking those laws brings
punishment. I do as commanded, not as choosing."

Justina was quiet. Fabricius moved closer. "I need you to know
that isn't who I am. It is your opinion and none other that vexes
me at night."

Justina looked up at her brother. "Why is that?"

"I love all in this house. Most of all, I love you and your way
with Antonia. I respect our slaves, but that is a relationship that
would be forbidden outside these walls. Slaves and Romans are
not to become best friends, yet you do not care. She has become
sister to you, and I admire that." He paused and took hold of Justina's hand. "I admire a great deal about you."

Justina smiled shyly. She loved her brother. He was an accomplished soldier, yet there was gentleness about him—much like
their father. She squeezed his hand. It was hard for her to stay
mad at him for any amount of time.

"You are a good man, brother. Your heart is kind. The woman
who steals that heart will be very lucky indeed."

Fabricius smiled shyly.

"You are into your twenties now," Justina continued, "with a
highly-respected position in the Roman Army. You constantly
bother me about finding a man, yet, I have not seen you with, nor
mention affections toward any females. Why is that?"

Fabricius took a deep breath. He was unable to look his sister
in the eye. "Honestly," he began, "I have met a few and had chance
to entertain the opposite sex." He paused.

"What is it?" Justina asked.

"I compare them to you," he finally said and looked up at

Justina. "Your beauty, your intelligence at such a young age. Your unchained attitude."

Justina laughed, and Fabricius joined her.

"I am flattered, dear brother, to hear these words from your mouth. Your love for me has always been strong and appreciated."

Fabricius smiled. "It is stronger than you know." He leaned in. Justina leaned in as well, expecting a hug. What she got was a kiss —on the lips. She pulled back, her eyes wide.

Fabricius pulled back as well. "Apologies."

Justina was suddenly filled with an unexpected wave of emotions. Fabricius had overstepped his boundaries. He was her brother. Yet, the feeling of his lips was not unpleasant, and she had to admit, what she felt for him had always been different from what she felt for their father, or even Herminius. She was always happy in his presence, always safe.

But he was her brother.

The confusion must have shown on her face. Fabricius was standing, looking both embarrassed and distraught. As he moved toward the door, Justina spoke, softly at first, "Is this not forbidden?" she asked. "Could brother and sister find a different kind of love?"

Fabricius sat back down. "There are many things in this world we must adhere to. None of those matter in the case of the heart." His eyes dropped to her lips. He leaned in, took her in his arms, and kissed her. This time, Justina kissed him back. His lips were firm but soft. It was her first real, passionate kiss and it felt amazing! Time vanished and all she could feel was Fabricius' strength and passion. She allowed him to engulf her.

When it was over, she let the feeling linger, then she slapped Fabricius on the chest. "You should apologize!" she barked. "You take actions without even asking me on proper date."

The comment brought them to laughter.

"Well," Fabricius said with a smile, "we will have to rectify that. I have an offer that may satisfy your request. Atilius celebrates his eighteenth the day after tomorrow. I am sure anything but being present with him and his friends would be ideal. What if I tell father I am going to take you to the market and for a horseback ride so you do not have to attend the festivities?"

"This is quite the romantic offer," Justina said. She was smiling brighter than ever before. "Getting me away and using your youngest brother as the excuse. You are so clever."

"It is a date then?"

"Yes, I would love to go on a date with my brother," she said and laughed. Fabricius joined her.

"Maybe we should lose the brother and sister and use our names," he suggested.

"Oh yes, mighty Fabricius. I would be honored to go on a date with you." This time, it was Justina who initiated the kiss, cupping Fabricius' face. When they were done, Fabricius ran his hand through her hair, softly brushing her cheek. Justina closed her eyes and smiled.

Fabricius stood, smiled, and left the room, closing the door behind him.

Justina let herself fall onto the bed. Maybe marriage wasn't going to be such a bad option after all.

CHAPTER 30

MARCH 12, 55 BC

*C*aesar hated being here. He hated the building, the Senate
Building, and he hated the people who occupied it. These
pompous, overstuffed, cretins, all vying for position. Rome's elite,
the senators. Nothing more than an assembly of old men, gathering in an old building. It was all he could do to sit there among
them with a face not twisted from distaste.

The building itself was fairly small, built by a dictator who
died more than a quarter century ago. It was so small that half the
senators were forced to stand. Had more been in attendance,
which was typically not the case, they would have met in the
nearby temple. The senate was loud. The white marble building
echoed with the voices of its occupants. Everyone was talking—
most of them at the same time—and if that wasn't bad enough, the
doors to the outside were open, allowing all of Rome to enter if
they so chose, as was tradition. He made a mental note to replace
this building one day.

On this occasion, all the seats on the benches were taken

except the two next to him. One of those was meant for the blowhard Pompey, but he was already sitting among the senators on the other side, in full view of Caesar. He did that mostly to spite Caesar, but also, Caesar guessed, to hedge his bets, just in case.

Crassus made his way into the room, catching the attention of almost every head. He walked purposely over to Caesar and sat next to him. As the voices quieted, Caesar stood.

"Thank you all for being here today," he began. "I hope you enjoyed the fights at the Arena yesterday. It was quite a celebration for Rome. Gratitude to Crassus for making yesterday happen and all of your attendance possible."

Many of the senate clapped. Pompey did not. Caesar took note.

"I hope you were all satisfied with your seats," Caesar paused, waiting for the applause to subside. "That is all the business I have to share today. I open the floor to any other senators."

Caesar sat down as another senator stood and began speaking.

Crassus leaned into Caesar. "Gratitude for recognizing me in front of such esteemed men."

Caesar smiled. "Your purse continues to make me look good. Why would I not return the favor?"

Crassus and Caesar listened to a senator go on about some worthless item of business meant to eventually line his own pockets. Caesar was bored. Unlike Crassus, he did not have the patience to sit for hours listening to men who mostly said nothing, waiting for just the right moment to hear just the right thing, to gather just the right information. He was a military man, and as such, craved action above all else. There was little action in the senate.

When it appeared as if Caesar was about to stand, Crassus again leaned into him. "The family you introduced me to yesterday, who were they? And why would a butcher's family be of interest to you?"

"Interesting," Caesar said. "I do not recall introducing him as a butcher."

Crassus smiled coyly. "You do not think I have people with information as well? You may have access to my purse, but I do spend my own money when it suits me."

Caesar returned a knowing grin. Crassus had made an unintentional slip, but he let it pass. Instead, he logged it in his memory along with the interesting handshake Crassus exchanged with Livius the day prior. "Let us just say the man is a friend of a friend, and his son is now working for Pompey."

Crassus looked across the room to the third member of the Triumvirate. "So, you offer favor to his family for much needed information?" He turned to Caesar. "Must I remind you that you and Pompey are on the same side?"

"Are you aware how many men detest the way you made it to the senate?" Caesar asked. "Do you know how many men in this room feel you purchased your seat? Only a few of us know better. I know of your battle with the Slave King Spartacus. I know you drew sword and spent many months away from comfort of home. And yet, who is celebrated for such victory? The man you say is on our side." Caesar looked across the room at Pompey. "He is a snake and will strike the moment it suits him. I prefer to be informed before his attack."

Crassus turned away. After a few moments, he spoke, "You play dangerous games, Caesar. All of Rome is at your feet, but betrayal of Pompey may change those feelings." He paused a moment, then continued, "I would also hope you come to senses in terms of your mistress. Women like her tend to have loose lips."

Caesar smiled and let out a small laugh. "I play my game and everyone else is simply a pawn. Present company excluded. And as far as my mistress and her loose lips, I prefer lips like that. Makes for better sex." Crassus was not amused. "You needn't worry," Caesar continued, "I tend to her every financial need and she will never give that up. Now, must we stay longer? I grow weary of politicians."

"Humor me. Stay the whole meeting for once. Maybe you will hear something of interest. And if not, maybe you won't anger the entire group of men before you."

CHAPTER 31

*L*ivius was sitting in one of his favorite spots in the house, finally finding solitude in his chair. Too much had happened in the last few days. A web had been spun, and webs tended to be sticky things. This particular web had put his son and his house in danger, and that did not sit well with Livius.

He was so lost in thought, he barely noticed Cato's approach. The other slaves had been dismissed and Livius guessed it was Cato's doing. That was not good news. Cato usually did this when he had something important to discuss. It was not what Livius needed right now.

"Dominus," Cato said. "Might I have a word?"

"Pour yourself a cup of wine Cato and join me."

Cato did not move.

"Is there a problem?" Livius asked.

"Apologies," Cato said. "It is just that in all the time I have known you, you have never offered wine."

Livius thought for a moment. "Then it is I who owe you an apology. Please, join me."

Cato brought the wine to Livius and topped off his glass.

Livius motioned for him to fill his own. He did so, then took a seat.

"Gratitude for the wine," Cato said and took a sip. "I have not had wine in quite some time."

"I hope the taste brings back pleasant memories."

The two men sat for a while, enjoying their drinks before either of them spoke.

Livius was the first. "How long have you been under my roof?"

"Since Justina and Atilius were but babies."

"And how do you find my accommodations?"

"Your household has been fair," Cato said without hesitation. "We all appreciate that you choose not to stand by the whip."

Livius smiled. "When I was younger, violence often proved the best deterrent. Now, as I get on in years, simple words find same results."

"I am glad that is your way, Dominus. However, I fear your loins may have found original path."

Livius knew exactly of what Cato spoke, though he was a bit surprised at the comment. Surely he understood that Fabricius did as commanded, that the slaughtering of slaves was not in his nature. "What you saw in the arena was a command from a very powerful man in Rome."

"I know of Caesar and his reputation from many years ago. However, this is not the first slave killed at the hands of your son in the recent past. I am worried this is becoming a thirst."

"Nonsense," Livius said sternly. Though he treated Cato as a confidant, he was more than a little annoyed at his boldness. "I know my son. You know my son. He is of good heart. But he is a soldier, and a soldier does as commanded, whether or not that command is welcome. Soon enough, he will be a leader and you will not see same choices made."

Cato took another sip of wine. After a few moments, he spoke again, "And what of your youngest son? I do not mean to speak out of turn, but he longs for the Roman Army and the ability to kill. He took much pleasure in seeing the killing of those slaves yesterday."

Cato was right, more than Livius wanted to admit. "Living under this roof, under my rules cannot be easy. He is ready for the next stage in his life. He has yet to find a girlfriend, which would ease built up tension."

The two men shared a knowing laugh.

"He worships his brother and looks up to Lucilius," Livius continued, "He is more bark than bite."

"It is his bite that has caused injury to both Antonia and Justina in recent days."

The news was not completely unexpected. Justina had been bandaged after all. She and Atilius had been at each other's throats the last few weeks, and those feuds often ended in the sparring room. It wasn't entirely her fault. In fact, Livius himself had routinely pointed the boys to the same spot in their youth. It was a good place for energetic boys to settle feuds. Not so much for girls. But he had not heard of harm coming to Antonia, though it did explain Justina's recent plea.

"Apologies for any harm that has occurred to Antonia. I was unaware. She is quiet and respectful. A good addition to our home. I fear that her association with my daughter may have invited confrontation. If further harm comes to her, or any slaves at Atilius', or his friend's hand, please inform me. We do not harm slaves unwarranted in this household."

"Gratitude," Cato said. He was about to take another sip of wine when Alba entered the room.

"Is this what you choose to do now after simple argument between us?" Alba demanded.

Cato jumped up so fast, he almost spilled his drink. "Apologies Domina," he said and bowed his head. He turned to Livius. "Thank you for your counsel, Dominus."

Livius raised his glass and nodded.

Alba watched Cato leave the room, then returned her attention, arms folded, to Livius. "My husband sits in general conversation with a slave? Drinking wine as if a senator was occupying the next seat?"

"You act surprised by my actions."

"Surprised? If the outside world were to learn that you choose to share wine with slave and not wife, it would ruin us."

"Cato is a better confidant than most Romans. He has been loyal friend to me and to this house for many years."

Alba remained standing. "Your wife is the only confidant you need. You should remember this. One argument and you choose to avoid me, our bed."

It was true, Livius had been avoiding the bedroom since the other night. It was easier to slip in once Alba was asleep and leave long before she rose. It was partially due to the fight and partially due to seeing Servilia again. The meeting had stirred memories he thought long ago buried, and he was looking at his marriage through a different lens.

"We have had several years of coexistence," he said without looking at his wife. "To say our total years peaceful together would be a ruse. You are the mother of my children, and thus, I do everything to make sure we remain as one. If avoiding our bed for a few nights helps in that cause, then let it be."

Alba unfolded her arms and slid into the seat next to her husband. "Our complex past is filled with many secrets," she said softly. "We harm one another if secrets were to be revealed to wrongful people."

Her words caught Livius' attention. "It is you who speak of jealousy for Servilia. A relationship born over twenty-five years ago, and dead almost as long."

Alba sat up straight. "You speak of jealousy as if it were confined to my side of the bed. Was it not you who found two slaves in our bedchamber with me as the third willing participant? You neglected my needs so that even I stooped to such a low level for satisfaction."

It was not a memory Livius wanted to re-live. Walking in on his wife engaged in intercourse with two slaves was bad enough. Having one of those slaves be male, did more than hurt him, it wounded his pride. It cut him deeper than she could ever know. Anger sparked in his eyes. "To find one's wife in that position was not one of jealousy, but anger. Have you not been full of jealousy since the first day I took Justina into this household? You no longer being the only female of my attention."

"You and I have not seen eye to eye on numerous things," she swiped back. "We do for our children as we must. I long for the day that your favorite child leaves, the one not born of this house or from either of our loins."

Livius let Alba simmer. He took a slow drink before continuing. "I have recently had words with her about this. She is set to purpose."

The news clearly took Alba by surprise.

"You have been a good wife and mother to all of our children," he paused, "all four of them. I would not want otherwise. In fact, tomorrow as we celebrate Atilius' eighteenth, I have preparations to make it even better. Fabricius told me not thirty minutes ago that he intends to take Justina to the square and for horseback ride. I know that Atilius will be happy to have her absent."

"Well, that is good news," Alba replied. "Fabricius always the peacemaker. Maybe you are right. Maybe I overreacted to news of you and Servilia meeting up. It was not of your doing, nor hers. She beds a very powerful man. And why would she ever want to be with the man responsible for killing her husband so many years ago?"

Livius frowned, and his eyes narrowed. "I shared that information with you after too many glasses of wine, to calm your jealousy of my past women. You said you would never mention that again, and yet here we are, and it comes spewing from your lips."

"As I said, Livius. We are a team. But make no mistake, your past is very clouded." She stood. "Facts like these and others would cost you the respect of your family, and love of your daughter. I offer gift tomorrow to Atilius and you will honor said gift with open arms. Any other reaction, and revelations will come forward." She turned to leave, then paused. "Find yourself in guest chambers tonight," she said and left.

Livius took another drink and wondered if any of the choices he had made in life had been correct. Suddenly, his chair did not seem so relaxing.

CHAPTER 32

MARCH 13, 55 BC

*A*fter months of pestering, Livius had surprised him with the horse. Fabricius was but a child of twelve. They had found a good, clean stable to house it, and he had come to see it every day since. It took some time to learn how to ride it properly, but Fabricius had put the time in willingly. The stables were his escape. Being atop Arion as he ran was one of the grandest moments he had ever experienced. He didn't know what flying felt like, but he imagined it was something like this and couldn't have been happier had he been on the winged Pegasus itself. Sometimes he'd be lost for hours, rushing home to face the consternation of his parents.

He had hoped to join the Equites unit but couldn't bear to see his Parthian Stallion in battle. So he told no one of its existence. Only his mother and father knew of the horse. "Let's keep this as our little secret," his father had told him.

He snuck away often in his youth to ride, groom, or just be alone with his Arion. His favorite meal was barley, and Livius kept him well stocked. That is, until Fabricius took over the financial responsibility himself. Lately, Fabricius would visit Arion before his patrol, but often afterward as well, before he went home. The animal helped him relax.

"Keep them closed," Fabricius said. He was holding his hands over Justina's eyes. She had a hold on his arms, trying with all her might to pull his hands away. She was having little luck.

"Where are you taking me?" she asked.

"It's a surprise."

"I already know we are around horses," Justina said. "Their odor betrays them. Besides, you invited me on a horseback ride, did you not?"

"That I did, but I did not tell you on what horse," Fabricius said and pulled his hands away. In front of Justina was a beautiful, strong chestnut horse with a dark, brown mane, standing nearly eighteen hands high. His black tail almost wagging.

"He's beautiful!"

"He's mine," Fabricius answered. The horse's ear twitched, when he spoke.

Justina turned to Fabricius. "What do you mean he's yours?"

"He's mine. Father bought him for me when I was a mere youth."

"And you have never shared him?"

"I was not allowed to tell anyone of his existence."

"Anyone?" Justina questioned.

Fabricius smiled. "Only mother and father know."

The horse walked over to Fabricius and nibbled his ear. Justina laughed. "He is certainly fond of you."

Fabricius stroked Arion's face. "He well should be. I see him every day and ride him most days."

"Can I touch him?"

"Of course, he loves to be petted."

Justina laid her hand on Arion's muzzle. It was soft and warm. She pet him several times. Fabricius smiled.

"What is his name?"

"Arion," he said.

"The horse in the *Illiad*?"

"The very one." Fabricius was pleased Justina knew the origin of the name.

"He is just lovely."

"I am glad you like him. Are you ready for a ride?"

Justina nodded. Fabricius moved to check Arion's saddle.

"What have you planned for me?" she asked. "Honestly, take me to the sewers and I will be grateful. Anything but being with Atilius and his jackal friends."

Fabricius stopped his preparations and turned to Justina. "I over-reached in planning then. A simple sewer tour and you would have been happy? I shall remember that for our second date."

"So this is a date," Justina said and smiled. "I wonder how father would feel. Should I go let him in on that fact? And what of mother? Always trying to get me out of the house and meeting a man. Would she be pleased to know I have met a man, that is of her blood?"

"If you are going to tease me the entire day, then we should make this brief. Atilius would be glad to have you alongside him for the day."

Justina smiled coyly. "Truth be told, I tease you to calm my nerves. If I were to date anyone, why not someone I already know and love?"

Fabricius took Justina in him arms. "I have a nice day scheduled for us. Hopefully it will last long enough for you to miss the birthday festivities." Before she could answer, Fabricius lifted Justina up onto the horse, positioning her just behind the saddle. He placed his foot in the stirrup and, in one single move, was in the saddle in front of her.

She placed her arms around his middle and kissed him on the back of the neck. Her kiss was warm and unexpected.

"Today is going to be a day we will not soon forget," said Justina. "I am already blessed by the Gods in Atilius' absence this morning. Though I at least wanted to wish him a happy birthday."

"He was too excited to wait for breakfast. Lucilius took him down to registration so he can officially start his training this upcoming week."

Fabricius pulled the reins and led Arion out of the stable. When they had reached the open field, he stopped the horse. "Hold on," he said. Justina tightened her grip and leaned into him. He gave Arion the command and the horse bolted forward, so fast that Justina almost lost her grip.

"Your horse is well-named."

Fabricius led Arion around the field, over hills, and through streams. Arion did not miss a beat. He followed Fabricius' commands just as they occurred, either from rein or heel. It was as if the two were of one mind, one purpose. Time flew as quickly as did Arion, and before they knew it, they had reached the market.

Fabricius dismounted first, then helped Justina slide off the horse's side. She walked over and cupped Arion's face, then kissed him on the muzzle. Fabricius led the horse as the two walked slowly around the colorful booths, eyeing the wares.

"I love the market," Justina said.

"Do you?"

"I do. I have ever since Cato took me here as a young girl. The sounds of vendors barking, the smell of herbs and oils. It is the only place you can catch a glimpse of the world outside Rome."

It is a world, Fabricius imagined, Justina longed to see. She was walking down an aisle when she paused before a table of jewelry.

"Has something caught your eye?" Fabricius asked.

"No," Justina said quickly.

Fabricius laughed. "Do not lie to me. We have passed dozens of tables and yet this one gives you pause."

"I have no desire for materialistic things. I wear father's gifts over the years with pride."

Fabricius picked up the necklace that seemed to have caught her eye. "Maybe it is time for you to receive gifts from someone not your father." As he placed the piece around her neck, Justina lifted her hair. The necklace looked beautiful on her.

"Do you like it?" Fabricius asked.

Justina did not speak. She was smiling brightly.

"Of course she likes it," the vendor said. "Can you not see it in her eyes?"

"He's right," Fabricius said. "You do love it."

"No," Justina said. "I mean yes, I like it, but no, it is far too much for you to spend. I do not need it."

"We do not buy because we need," the vendor chirped in. "We buy because we desire."

"You deserve it, and I want you to be happy," said Fabricius. "Your brother will be receiving many gifts today. I would not have you feel left out."

Fabricius turned and haggled with the vendor, before Justina could object further. Maybe it was his size, or perhaps the horse standing stalwartly behind him, but the vendor gave Fabricius what seemed more than a fair price.

"It is yours. Justina pulled him into her and kissed him. They kissed so long that Arion even seemed to blush.

As they continued down the aisle, Fabricius led them to a vendor selling food. He bought enough for two, plus wine and an apple for Arion.

"What have you planned?" Justina asked coyly.

"Come," he said, and led Justina and Arion away from the market.

"Where are you taking me?"

"Someplace quieter so we may be ourselves."

When they reached an open spot, Fabricius lifted Justina back on Arion and then jumped into the saddle in front of her. He led

Arion out of the city into the countryside, back toward the stables, then took a turn up into the hills surrounding Rome.

When they stopped, he slid off Arion and helped Justina down as well. As Justina was taking in the views, Fabricius removed Arion's saddle and blanket, opening it up on the grass. He placed the food and wine on the blanket, then went over and handed Arion the apple. As Justina turned around, she saw Fabricius whispering something into Arion's ear.

"Do you and Arion share secrets?"

"Yes," he said without hesitation. "And we always have."

Justina laughed as Arion walked across the field, eating the sweet grass.

"Aren't you worried he'll run off?"

Fabricius had already taken a seat on the blanket. He looked over at Arion. "Who him? No, Arion would never leave my side."

"So you've done this before."

"Not this month."

Justina feigned insult.

"Come, sit," Fabricius said.

Justina sat down as Fabricius readied the meal.

Justina's mood suddenly turned solemn. "Can we actually do this? I know we are not of blood, but we are recognized as siblings."

Fabricius smiled and placed a hand on Justina's cheek. She held his hand leaning into it.

"I have always looked out for you, cared about your well-being. When we were children, I looked upon you as something that needed taken care of."

"So I'm a pet?"

Fabricius ignored the comment. "As I grew older and went out into the world, I saw what Rome had to offer. But I could never get you out of my mind. And everyone I met could not compare. My brotherly love went away many years ago, replaced by one that held no boundaries." Justina kept his gaze. "Still, I assumed I could never act upon it, so I kept it to myself. Then you approached your eighteenth year with not yet a suitor and I realized I could wait no longer. I could not take the chance that you would be taken from me. I do not care if our relationship is frowned upon. If the Roman Army won't have me, then I will take up butchering at father's side. I would do whatever is needed for you, Justina. That is the depth of my love."

Tears began rolling down Justina's cheeks.

Fabricius wiped them away with his hand. "Why do you cry?"

"I cry because I am happy. I cry because I am loved. But it is father who I am concerned about, not the army you fight for. Most of those men are barbarians who would jest and laugh at the thought. Father and mother may not allow such a relationship. Then what?"

"Father loves us both very much. He may be disappointed, but I cannot see him abandoning his children. However, it is best we keep our feelings and desires in the shadows for now. I have saved my coin. In short time, I can afford my own place and you can come live with me."

"You would have me as a guest?"

"I would have you as a wife."

The two leaned into each other and embraced. It was an embrace that quickly turned into a kiss, and then, as Fabricius leaned backward and Justina forward, a passionate kiss. He kissed Justina with abandon, wanting nothing more than to feel her lips against his, his arms around her body. They had been kissing for quite some time when Fabricius stopped. "I think it best we get back," he said. "This is our first date. I would not have us venture further."

"If I had known my body's reaction to such desires, I would not have waited so long," Justina said and smiled. She moved in and took one last kiss.

Fabricius cupped her cheek and gazed into her eyes. He

smiled. "If we leave now, we will be home before the party is over and we can give birthday wishes."

Justina frowned. "Through all this, I had forgotten about Atilius. For several hours, you have made me quite happy. I already long for more like this."

⚘

*A*s Fabricius saddled the horse, Justina allowed the emotions of the day to once again fill her senses. She had fought against the thought of marriage for so long, of belonging to a man. Now, she suddenly saw the entire world in a new light. If she had to belong to a man, she could choose none better than Fabricius. Antonia was not the only one with a bright future.

CHAPTER 33

They had been going for the better part of the day, swordplay, rough housing, gossiping about women, all the things young men do when together. Alba had a feast in the ready, laid out on tables in the dining room. The centerpiece was a tower of the finest meats—boar, veal, goat, and hare, along with peacock and pheasant. Mussels and clams filled bowls on either side of the meats, along with bowls of liquamen for dipping. In smaller wooden bowls were almonds, figs, walnuts, grapes, and olives, as well as parsnips, pumpkin, and turnips.

Readied were canters of mulsum, a wine mixed with honey, and of course, regular wine, though Alba had it watered down. The last thing she wanted was a bunch of drunken eighteen-year-olds in her home. Standing behind the tables, ready to serve, were the house slaves. Except for Cato. Livius demanded he be allowed to stand off to the side to remind the boys to keep their festivities under control. As the sun set, Alba called the revelers inside, telling them it was time to feast.

Atilius carried a grin sufficient to the day he was having. He had enrolled in the Roman Army with Lucilius and would soon be on patrol. He had all his closest friends at his house to celebrate his long-awaited day of manhood, and his parents had prepared a feast worthy of a senator, a feast his father would be spending the next several weeks paying back. And the best part was that Justina was nowhere to be found. This was truly a special day.

As Atilius walked into the room, Lucilius came up behind him and placed an arm around his back. "You have skills with the sword, my brother. You will make a good recruit, and I shall request you by my side once you are ready for patrol."

Atilius couldn't help but smile even broader. "I shall welcome that. My father has kept me two extra years from battle, and while I have much catching up to do, I do not fight as a naive sixteen-year-old as most recruits. I shall be the toast of this group of new soldiers and my stock in much demand."

The two walked over to the large table already filled with Atilius' friends. Slaves brought cups of wine, and as Atilius reached the table, the group cheered and raised their cups to toast. Alba motioned for Livius to make a speech.

Livius stood, cup in hand, a broad smile on his face. The group quieted almost immediately. "My son. You became a man in Roman eyes two years past. And while you were eager to take your place alongside your brother, you obeyed my wishes and waited until I thought it best. That time has come." The group cheered as Livius continued, "My youngest son is ready to part the heavens and take Jupiter's spot." The group cheered louder. "I am proud of you to follow in my footsteps. For the glory of Rome!" Livius raised his cup at his son. The entire table stood and cheered, yelling "Atilius! Atilius! Atilius!"

Livius took a drink and sat back down. Alba smiled her approval. As the rest of the table sat, she motioned for the slaves to begin service.

"Where are your brother and sister?" Lucilius asked. "Do they not wish to celebrate their brother's big day?"

"I await their arrival. I am sure their trip into the market is to find the perfect gift." Atilius stood and walked to the end of the table where Herminius was sitting. "However, my other brother sits quietly. Does he have my gift?"

"Gift?" Herminius asked. "Was I required to bring a gift? I was not informed that gifts were a necessity."

Atilius punched his brother in the arm, a little harder than he intended. Herminius winced, causing the group to laugh. Though embarrassed, he stood, pulled a dagger from his cloak, and handed it to his younger brother. "Of course I have gift for you," he said. "A dagger, once held by the great General Lucius Macedonicus."

The gift caught the attention of the crowd and left Atilius speechless. He held the dagger as if it were a gift from the gods themselves. His smile replaced with a gaping mouth. He looked from the dagger to his brother. "Lucius, the man responsible for enslaving 150,000 people? You honor me, brother." Atilius grabbed his brother's hand and then pulled him in for a hug. The group cheered yet again. Atilius held the dagger high. "I have opened all the gifts from my friends. I now await gift from my other brother and my parents."

As the meal began to wind down, the group took cups of wine and headed to the gathering area. "Where is Fabricius?" Alba asked Livius. "Taking Justina away for a while is acceptable, missing the entire event is not."

"I'm sure they are near." No sooner had Livius said the words when Justina walked into the room, followed closely by Fabricius. "There, you see?" Livius said. "All is well."

⚉

*J*ustina was hoping the party would be long concluded by the time they arrived home. She was less than pleased to see it still underway. Seeing all of Atilius' friends, especially Lucilius, brought a sour note to her joyous mood. *What a terrible way to end a most pleasant day,* she thought to

196

herself. Fabricius had sent her on ahead, saying he needed to get something from his room. Atilius' present no doubt. She had drug her feet so much that Fabricius had caught up to her.

"Well, our timing was not perfect, but the party seems to be coming to a conclusion," she whispered.

"Quiet your lips and give this to your brother," he said and handed Justina a large shield. "Brother," he said loudly, walking over to Atilius. "A toast to your future on your special day and a gift from your sister and me. We hope you use it well in the days and weeks to come."

Justina handed the shield to Atilius. "Happy birthday," she said with pasted smile. Atilius snatched the gift from Justina and turned to Fabricius.

"Wow!" he exclaimed. "First a dagger and now this. My brothers know me too well. Gratitude, centurion," he said taking Fabricius' arm.

"Gratitude to your sister as well," Fabricius said patting him on the shoulder. "It was of her choosing."

Justina knew the last thing Atilius wanted to do was thank his sister or even speak to her on his day, but there were too many eyes watching and he was forced. "Gratitude to you as well, my sister."

Justina caught the jab and was about to return it when Fabricius' look of warning halted her. She bit her tongue and instead simply nodded as the group headed over to Atilius to congratulate him and admire the shield. She gladly stepped out of the way.

While the group centered around Atilius, Justina searched for Antonia. She was standing in line with the other slaves at the back of the room. Justina tried to get her attention, but Antonia was set to duty and did not look up or around. No doubt following Alba's instructions. Cato, as usual, stood in the corner of the room, far enough in for his presence to be noted, but not so far as to make it obvious.

Herminius had walked over to the group and was standing by

Fabricius. The brothers took forearms, then Fabricius patted him heartily on the back. Alba and her father were sitting off to the side of the group and seemed to be engaged in conversation. It was not a conversation that seemed to be going well. Her father had a worried look that quickly turned to anger. Justina tried to get close enough to hear what they were saying but was hesitant to get so close as to be noticed. Just then, her mother stood.

"May I have your attention?" Alba said as she walked over to the slaves.

Justina moved next to her father. "What is mother up to?" she asked. Livius did not answer, but kept his focus on his wife.

"My son," Alba continued, "You have shown great patience over the past two years. While all of your friends go into the army, you were stuck here. Your father keeping you as a boy instead of the man that you are. We both feel great regret, and because of that and due to your maturity, we have decided to give you the best gift we can. I present you your own slave." Alba grabbed Antonia's arm and pulled her from the line. Antonia almost tripped and fell in the process. Alba yanked her over to Atilius and pushed her toward her son.

Cato's eyes widened.

Justina was about to yell out, when her father placed his hand on her shoulder. She had to cup her mouth to stop from screaming.

"Is this not our feelings my husband?" Alba asked, looking over to Livius. The crowd turned as well. Atilius especially awaiting a response.

Justina looked to her father for answers. "Apologies, my daughter," he whispered. "I have no choice." He turned to Atilius. "You are a Roman, my son. You deserve your own slave to command. Enjoy!" he said and raised his glass. The group cheered.

Justina's confusion turned to tears. She looked to Antonia and saw nothing but fear, devastation, and betrayal on her face.

Livius flashed a glare at Alba. She returned a smile.

"I may be the last of our group to join the Army," Atilius said, "but I am the first with my own body slave. I will make sure she protects me, especially in the late evenings."

The group laughed.

Justina ran from the room.

CHAPTER 34

APRIL 4, 55 BC

*E*verything changed after Atilius' party. Everything. Betrayed by her father, Justina had nowhere to turn. So she stayed in her room, not even venturing out for meals. In fact, it had been several weeks since Livius could recall seeing his only daughter. But then again, he hadn't been spending much time at home either. Cato had been sneaking her food—despite the wishes and directions of Alba. "If she wants to eat, she can come to the dining like a proper person," she had told Cato. Livius made sure Cato did not follow those orders.

Now with Alba out of the house at market with Cato, Atilius at training camp, Herminius working with Pompey, and both Lucilius and Fabricius on patrol, Livius decided he needed to speak with Justina. Her door, as it had been so often lately, was closed. Livius knocked. No response. When he knocked a second time and got the same, he opened the door. Inside Justina was lying face down on her bed, uneaten food scattered about the room.

Livius knocked once again on the inside of the door. "May I enter?"

Hearing her father's voice, Justina turned. "It is your house," she said. "You may do anything you choose."

Livius stepped further inside the room. He had little idea what to say, but knew something needed to be said. He attempted humor. "You have been living only in your room of late, are you not satisfied with the size of this house? Shall we look for a larger one?"

Justina did not appreciate his attempt. Instead she asked, "Why did you adopt me?"

Livius stepped around plates of food, making his way over to Justina's bed. She pulled up her legs, and he sat down. "From my youth, I dreamed of having a daughter. With each pregnancy I prayed, but every time the gods saw fit to gift us with a boy. I love my boys, but I began to believe my desires to never have a chance of fulfillment. Then opportunity presented itself, and I did not hesitate."

"Did mother approve of this decision?"

Livius looked down for a moment, then back up at his daughter. "She was not of shared excitement," he admitted.

"Is this the information you fear coming to light?"

"It is not."

"Then what? What could possibly force you to allow her to break my heart in handling of Antonia?"

Livius let out a deep sigh. No father wants to look weak in front of his children, and no parent wants to admit faults—especially grievous ones. But he had allowed himself to be placed in a position where he had little choice. His daughter needed an answer, and he needed his daughter's pain to be soothed. He needed that look in her eyes, that longing, to go away, to be replaced by the sparkle he loved.

After a few minutes, he finally spoke, "I made poor decisions in my past, Justina. Some were commanded and some were of my own doing." He paused. Justina kept her gaze on him, her eyes longing, begging for answers. "The way you always look at me. It is what every father wants from a daughter. It is, well, heartwarming. I never wanted to do anything that would remove that look. I never wanted it to go away. Your mother forces my hand in several areas now, and I will see her choices balanced once again. She is a good woman but needs to be reminded of her place in this house."

Justina's face showed hope. "So you will reverse her gift and have Antonia answer only to you?"

Livius lowered his head. "I cannot at this time. The damage would be too great to your brother."

"And what of the damage to me?"

Livius reached over and took his daughter's hands, happy that she let him. "I come here to offer gift. A gesture I hope you will find of equal balance."

"What could you possibly have to offer that would be of value equal to Antonia's life?" Tears were welling in her eyes.

"Your oldest brother, Fabricius."

Justina suddenly looked up, the surprise on her face obvious.

Livius continued softly, "I know of his intentions. This house is big, but not so big that I do not see what is going on between the two of you. How you two try not to look at each other. I am not so old as to have lost my ability to recognize young love."

Justina looked back down. "I do not know what you mean."

"The relationship your brother would like to have with you is frowned upon, but not forbidden. If you both shared same blood, I would not consider this. However, you are adopted, and you do both seem quite happy together."

Justina looked up at him. The pain in her eyes was gone.

"Do not flaunt it around your mother or brothers. This secret must remain between the three of us. If you both find truth in your hearts and decide to be as one, then I will soften awkward blow within family."

Justina hugged her father. He wrapped a strong arm around her.

"Gratitude, father," Justina said. "I do find deep feelings for Fabricius. He is a great man, and his affections for me seem real. But this does not change the position Antonia finds herself in."

"I have told you, there is little I can do about that. If you find your brother treating her poorly, let me know, and I will try and counsel him. We do not treat slaves harshly in this house. No matter who owns them."

He looked down at this daughter and she up at him. They smiled.

"I must get to work," Livius said. "Remain here for a moment. I have a surprise for you." He kissed Justina on the forehead, stood, and headed to the door. On the other side, Antonia was waiting. He smiled and motioned for her to enter.

❀

*J*ustina never took her eyes off the door. Her heart leapt when Antonia stepped into the doorway. She wanted to run and hug her friend, but something about Antonia's demeanor stopped her.

"Please come in," Justina said.

Antonia walked slowly into the room. Her gait was not light, not as it had been on the many occasions she entered the room in the past. Now she was walking wearily, as if preparing defense for some as yet unseen strike. The comfort she had always had in Justina's presence was long gone, replaced with apprehension.

"How are you?" Justina asked.

Antonia stood stiffly, holding her arms close to her body, rubbing one hand up and down the other arm. She did not look at Justina when she spoke. "Little has changed since my ownership went from beloved father to hated son. He is busy with his training and is either gone or too tired to command. I still remain living amongst the slaves and do house chores as commanded by your mother. But his training ends in two days, and he will then be spending more time here again."

"I have spoken to my father and he..."

Antonia suddenly turned to face Justina, anger replacing apprehension. "Your father," she said cutting Justina off, "Your father who promised me to you if you were to marry? Is that the father you speak of?"

"He has told me that if improper treatment comes to you that he should be notified. He will respect Atilius' choices; however, he will do what he can to ensure they are better ones. I also have Fabricius' ear. Atilius looks up to Fabricius. I can have him talk to Atilius as well."

Antonia forced a smile, but her stiff body betrayed her. "Gratitude for what you are trying to do. I hope that someday the two of us can look upon these trying days and remove them from memory."

Justina slid closer to where Antonia stood. She wanted nothing more than to hug her. "You are my sister. I will not let anyone hurt you."

"I am the sister of the sister of my master. Yet, he has never considered you a sister. Therefore, I am just property. Cato tried to warn me, but I refused to listen. He was right." She looked directly at Justina. "Your promises to protect me have proven ineffective. Your mother and brother remind me daily of my true status. Now, please excuse me, I must attend to my daily chores."

Justina's eyes pleaded for her to stay, pleaded to hug her. Antonia turned and walked away but stopped at the doorway. "Gratitude for the years of being my sister in spirit," she said without looking back. "It made me forget for awhile that I am truly a slave."

"Do not give up on us, sister," Justina said through tears. "I will see that we are together as it should be."

Antonia did not turn. She left the room and did not look back. Justina collapsed on the bed.

CHAPTER 35

"Why don't the two of you make yourself at home?"
Caesar said as he entered his dining room.
Seated at the table were Servilia and her son Brutus. They had
been in a joyous mood, eating, drinking, laughing, and joking.
When Caesar entered, the mood changed.

"Oh we have," Servilia replied with a smirk. Her son was
visibly tense in Caesar's presence. Servilia was not.

"I am glad I can be so hospitable to the two of you," Caesar
noted. He looked specifically at Brutus and said, "I know what
your mother does to stay in good favor, but I have yet to see
benefit to your attendance."

Brutus stiffened and spoke quickly. "I have word that Pompey
sends invites to several senators for private gathering."

Cesar smiled. "And this gathering? Would it be in two days?"

Brutus' eyes widened. He looked over at Servilia. She
shrugged. He looked back at Caesar. "How did you know?"

Caesar laughed again, only this time, his laugh seemed more
menacing. He walked behind Brutus, gripped the back of his neck,
and squeezed. Brutus tightened his neck muscles, but Servilia had felt

Caesar's grip; it was like iron. Brutus winced. Servilia sat straight up, her jovial mood gone. She wanted to rush to her son's side to protect him but knew better. As Brutus' face tightened, Caesar suddenly released his grip. Then he slapped Brutus hard to the back of his head. "What did you do that for?" she barked. "He is doing as commanded."

Caesar turned his attention to Servilia. "Your son gives me information that is already known. You think I would let my future ride in this idiot's hands? He is but one of dozens who keep me informed." Caesar spoke directly to Brutus. "And if you are going to give me yesterday's news, you are worthless to me."

He walked behind Brutus a second time. Servilia willed her son not to flinch. "Maybe your inside connection is not as good as you claim," he said to the back of Brutus' head. "You asked me, no, begged me for more responsibilities to speed your road to the senate. And this is all I get?"

"It is all I have been given by Herminius," Brutus answered.

Caesar turned to Servilia once again. "I show generosity to your friend the butcher. I allow his son to be a part of the executions at the games. I even give his family great seats at the arena. If this is how I am to be repaid for everything I have done for his family, as well as yours, then maybe it all should come to a swift end." He turned back to Brutus. "Either bring me information that will be useful or find yourself no longer in my presence," he said forcefully. "Now get out."

Brutus almost leapt from his seat in his haste to leave. It was times like these, times when Caesar demeaned her only son, that Servilia wondered why she stayed, why she allowed this to happen. But she had to admit, there was part of her that was disappointed in her son's inability to stand up to Caesar. Brutus did not understand, but Servilia did. When standing in the face of power, weakness is abhorred. Servilia got up slowly and took her time preparing to leave.

Caesar took a seat across the table from her. "You may stay, Servilia. You serve a different need."

Servilia waited until Brutus left the room. She placed her hands on the table and leaned in to Caesar. "I will not have my son talked to and treated this way. I know you to be under a great deal of pressure, so I will allow this one act to go without notice, but I do not expect it to happen again." She stood, straightened her clothes, and turned to leave.

Caesar let her get halfway across the room, then spoke, "I suggest you meet with the butcher again and emphasize the importance of this assignment. Do not return until you know exactly what I want and need from you and your son."

Servilia paused. She looked at Caesar intently, then turned and left.

CHAPTER 36

APRIL 6, 55 BC

*I*t had been a while since she sat at the dinner table, but the conversation with her father had given Justina hope. If there was a way she and Fabricius could be together, then perhaps there was a way she could break Antonia of this bondage to Atilius. It required only thought and careful planning. There was a way, Justina only needed to find it.

It was the first family dinner in quite some time where everyone was in attendance. Livius sat in his usual spot at the head of the table, Alba was to his right. Atilius sat next to his mother, with Lucilius on his other side. Justina took her seat between her older brothers.

As the house slaves placed plates of meat and fish on the table, Fabricius leaned in and whispered, "My heart swells seeing you back to normal. I see that you finally saw fit to bathe as well," he said with a smile.

Justina returned the smile. "I have great news from father that

I will share with you later this evening. I hope your patrol today didn't leave you wanting an early slumber."

Their mother flashed them a disapproving look. "What are these whispers?" she asked. "Do we all now keep secrets in this house?"

"Apologies, mother," said Fabricius. "I was just telling Justina how nice it is to see her dining with us."

Justina was about to respond, when she caught her father's cautionary look. At the same time, Fabricius gave her leg a quick squeeze.

Antonia entered the room with a jug of wine. She walked slowly but deliberately to the table. Her shoulders were sunk, and she had the look of one resigned to her future. Justina tried to make eye contact, but Antonia's gaze was fixed on the ground.

"Slave, bring me wine," Atilius ordered. Antonia moved to Atilius and filled his cup, her hands shaking as she poured. "Leave the jug for another slave," he said when Antonia had finished pouring. "Go to my room and wait there 'til commanded."

Lucilius chuckled. Both Antonia and Justina looked to her father, but he remained expressionless.

"Did you not hear your new master?" Alba chimed in. "He commands you to go and wait his arrival in his room. Do not look elsewhere for guidance."

"Wait at the foot of my bed on your knees," Atilius added. "This will be your new resting place."

"We have suitable quarters for all of the slaves in this house down the hall, Atilius," Livius offered.

Alba jumped at her husband's comment. "Are you now telling our son how to use and enjoy his gift? Did your father do that to you?"

The attention of the entire table was now focused on Livius. Justina waited with eager anticipation to see if her father would do as promised. Cato raised an eyebrow. Livius' eyes narrowed, and he exchanged a look with Alba that seemed to last an eternity.

Two forces clashing for control of the household. The mood of the house was changing.

Justina felt a change happening in the household, one that began when Lucilius darkened their door. His ideas on the treatment of slaves was having a strong impact on Atilius. He was becoming power hungry. He was beginning to see them as something other than human. And worse yet, their mother seemed to be taking his side in the matter. The even-handed treatment their slaves had come to know and expect with Livius was quickly disintegrating and everyone—slave and master—could sense it.

Livius waited an unusually long time before he answered. "Do as commanded, Antonia," he finally said.

Justina's heart fell. Alba smiled. Fabricius was about to speak when Livius flashed him a stern look.

"This slave and all should be sleeping at our feet, like the dogs they are," Lucilius said, suddenly embolden. "We were blessed to be able to execute them just weeks ago in front of so many Romans."

Livius sent Lucilius a stern look, but with Atilius and now Alba on his side, the look had little impact.

"I never got to thank you for the seats at the arena," Justina said suddenly. Fabricius again squeezed her leg.

"You are quite welcome, Justina," Lucilius replied. "I hope they were to your satisfaction."

"Very much so. They enabled me to see what a donkey's ass you truly are."

"Justina!" Alba yelled out.

Lucilius only laughed.

"May I be excused?" Atilius said to his mother. "I have many things that need doing and with only one slave, she will be quite busy for the next several hours."

"You may be excused. You as well, Lucilius. In fact, I shall take leave. I grow tired of eating next to my disobedient daughter."

Justina was smug. She waited until all had left, then addressed her father directly. "Father! What has happened that power shifts to that side of the table? You are the Dominus in this household. I sit next to a great mind in Herminius and a great warrior in Fabricius. Across the table are just two foot soldiers and an angry old woman."

"Do not speak of your mother like that!" Livius barked.

Justina was undaunted. "She treats you like her slave and yet you defend her? What makes you cower like a beaten dog?"

Livius put his head down. Fabricius squeezed Antonia's leg even harder. It had no effect.

"Answer me, father!" she demanded.

"Justina!" Fabricius yelled.

"Justina," Herminius added. "Father has his reasons. Though they may not be evident to us, they…"

Justina addressed Herminius, "They may be his reasons, but they are having an impact upon the entire house. You, me, and everyone else are suffering the effect of those decisions." She turned to her father. "What secret does she hold, father? What does mother know that forces an honorable man to cower and dishonor his promises?"

"Justina!" Fabricius yelled a second time. "You push too far! Father…"

"Stop!" Livius yelled. The entire table went quiet. Livius took a deep breath, then spoke, "I am the reason Antonia is without parents."

The revelation came unexpected.

"What is your meaning?" Justina asked. "How could you be responsible for that?"

"I'm confused, father," said Herminius. "Did you fail to provide adequate care in their illness?"

Livius took a very deep breath. "We used the excuse of illness for cover," he said looking first to Herminius, then to Justina. "Your mother and I were having…problems. You were just a baby, maybe two years of age. Alba and I were no longer sharing bed.

One night, she decided to bring both of Antonia's parents into her bedchambers. I heard noise coming from that room, so I entered, finding all three naked and in hot desires." He paused, taking a drink of wine. The table was silent.

"I was infuriated. I wasn't thinking. I grabbed Alba and threw her from the bed. Antonia's mother jumped and ran to the corner of the room. I was left with Antonia's father, on the bed before me. My bed. The bed I shared with my wife." Justina cupped her mouth. Fabricius sat still. Herminius' eyed widened in anticipation.

Livius paused. It was clear the tragic events were playing back in his mind. "He tried to explain the situation, but I wasn't listening. All I saw was a man in bed with my wife. I hated him more than I had ever hated another human being," he said and bowed his head before continuing. "I suppose the soldier in me took over. I retrieved a dagger I kept hidden in the room and..." He paused, then looked directly at Justina. "I killed him."

Fabricius reached over and placed a hand on his father's arm. Justina started crying. He took his other arm and placed it around his sister. Livius continued, "The next morning, I sold Antonia's mother to a slave trader so she would be taken far away. I made Alba promise to not ever share this information. All of you were young and did not witness, so hiding excuse was easy. I never realized it was your mother who commanded Antonia's parents to join her in the bedroom. In my rage, I had forgotten that slaves do not act on their own, but only as forced. They did not deserve the end they met." He looked down. "I will always regret my decisions leading up to that day and my actions that night. I live with the burden of what it is like to truly kill an innocent man and to condemn another to her death," he said looking specifically at Fabricius.

Justina suddenly jumped up and ran to her father, throwing her arms around his neck.

"You need to know that after that night, I swore I would never

213

harm another person again, and I have not." There were tears in his eyes. Justina hugged her father even harder. She couldn't imagine what it must have felt like to carry such a burden. She had always known him to be kind and gentle. To kill an innocent person, even in the heat of passion, the weight of guilt must have been unbearable.

"Now, she knows your feelings for Antonia and tries to hurt you," he continued, "She also tries to put wedge between you and me."

"We all make choices throughout our lives father, hoping they are all for the better. This one act, although awful, has made you a great father and a wonderful owner to our slaves," Herminius said. He stood and shook his father's hand. Livius smiled appreciatively at his son.

"You are a great man and a great father," Fabricius added. "That will never change." Livius nodded his appreciation.

❦

With the secret out, Livius' burden had been relieved. The fact that his sons had not viewed him in less light meant more to him than they would ever know—that is, until they had sons of their own. But it was Justina's hug that had given him the most comfort. It was her disapproval that he feared most, so it was her forgiveness that he cherished.

"I knew it was in this family's best interests to keep Atilius from the Roman Army for an extra two years. He has shown his immaturity and lack of ability to own a slave. I must rectify that situation. Go now," he said to his children. "I have much to ponder and a bit of a mess to straighten out."

After they all left the room, Livius looked over at Cato. "Please, come sit," he said.

Cato walked over from the corner of the room where he had been standing and took the seat adjacent to Livius. They shared a knowing look, then Livius poured him a cup of wine. "Am I a monster?" he asked as he poured.

"That is not for me to decide," Cato told him. "I have always been aware of the actions from that night. Although I have never shared details with anyone, I let any slave who enters this house know that their master is still a Roman."

Livius nodded. Cato's caution to the slaves was not unexpected. Still, it stung. Livius looked at his head slave. He couldn't help but wonder what a man like Cato could have accomplished if his birth hadn't limited him so. He stood and held his cup in toast. Then turned to walk away.

"I am grateful for the past dozen plus years that you have not had reason for such punishment to any others," Cato said.

Livius turned and placed his hand on Cato's shoulder. "You are a good friend."

CHAPTER 37

abricius followed Justina to her room, eager to learn what she and father had discussed. She rushed inside, while Fabricius closed the door. When he turned, Justina was sitting on her bed. "Will you not join me over here, mighty Fabricius?" she said and patted the space next to her.

Fabricius smiled, then sat on the bed. "I am eager to hear what news you have," he said. "But with Atilius and Lucilius in the next room, we best keep our voices to a whisper."

hey took their time getting to their room. It was Lucilius' idea. He wanted to make Antonia spend an especially long time on her knees. When they opened the door, they found Antonia sitting on Atilius' bed.

"It appears your slave does not know how to listen to orders given," Lucilius said.

Atilius moved past Lucilius, grabbed Antonia and pushed her to the ground. "I told you to be on your knees at the end of my bed," he barked. Antonia quickly moved to that position.

Lucilius sat on his own bed. "Your father, although respected, has gone soft on these slaves for far too long."

"You are not wrong, brother," Atilius replied. He ordered Antonia to remove his shoes. She pulled the shoes of his feet and placed them by the side of the bed. When she turned back, Atilius rubbed his feet in her face. "This is where you will be for the remainder of your worthless life slave. You will be at my feet to do as I command."

Lucilius laughed.

❀

*J*ustina tried not to pay attention to the laughter coming from her brother's room. Fabricius heard it as well and tried to distract Justina by offering her a foot massage. He removed her shoes and began to gently rub her foot. His touch was soft but firm, just as his lips had been. She closed her eyes. "This is where you belong," she said, "at my feet. You can be my personal slave."

"Oh, I see," Fabricius said. "Now you want a slave as your own? And just how would you command me?"

"You are off to a good start. But you have on far too much clothing for my liking."

Fabricius was a little taken aback; still he was happy to do as commanded. He let go of her foot and started removing his robe.

"Oh, don't stop," Justina said. "Can't you do both?"

Fabricius smiled and picked up Justina's foot, massaging it with one hand and removing his robe with the other. Justina watched, a great grin on her face. Fabricius had a soldier's body; a well-trained soldier's body. His chest was tight and his stomach showed every muscle, as did his powerful arms. Fabricius caught Justina looking and smiled. "Is this what Domina wants?"

"It's a start."

217

"While I do as commanded, why don't you share with me what father said?"

Justina smiled. "He knows about you and me. He is not happy with arrangement, but he will not interfere if we believe our love is true. He will also keep secret from mother and loving brothers."

Fabricius returned her smile.

❀

"We have a new toy," Atilius said. "I have been so busy training, I have not had chance to play with it yet. What games shall we partake with new toy?"

Antonia looked down, slumped shoulders, knowing all her fears were about to be realized.

"We have this dog in front of us, yet, she is fully clothed. Is this how you plan to allow your slave to be seen?"

"My brother, you are correct. You assist me in the error of my ways," Atilius said, then to Antonia, "When you are in my room, you are to be fully naked. Now, remove your clothing."

Antonia did not move. Her body began to shake.

"Your slave does not seem to understand who is in charge. Maybe a firm reminder will help."

Atilius stood, and Antonia quickly removed her clothes. He grabbed her arm and pulled her to her feet. When she tried to cover her private area, he slapped her hand away. He eyed her up and down, then nodded his approval. Afterward, he made her turn so Lucilius could also get a good look. When she turned back to face Atilius, he suddenly slapped her hard across the butt. The sound echoed in the small room.

"When you are commanded to do something, you will not hesitate. Do you understand?"

Antonia nodded yes, tears streaming down her cheeks.

❀

"*N*ow slave, remove my top," Justina said. "It has been a long day, and I need to be free of this clothing." Fabricius put down Justina's foot and moved closer to her. She raised her arms as he lifted off her top. She lowered her arms and covered her bare breasts as Fabricius tossed the top to the side of the bed. Her bravado had wavered a bit when the top started coming off, and she found herself slightly embarrassed.

Fabricius took hold of her wrist and gently lowered her hand, revealing her full breasts. He smiled, then lifted his gaze to her eyes. "What is my next command, Domina?"

"Lay on your back and shut your eyes."

Fabricius did as commanded, lying on Justina's bed with his hands behind his head, a huge smile on his face.

"Wipe that smile from your face, slave," Justina said, then swung her legs up onto the bed. Fabricius stopped smiling. Justina slowly made her way on top of Fabricius, sliding her hands up his body as she moved. Touching, feeling every muscle. She stopped when she had made it halfway, straddling his pelvis. She then bent down and began to kiss Fabricius on the stomach, moving up to his chest, and then his neck. He turned his head to give her access, and she eventually made her way to his lips. Kissing him slowly at first, then passionately, as Fabricius took hold of the back of her head and pressed her into him. She was lying flat on top of him now and could feel him grow.

As the two kissed, Fabricius moved from her mouth to her ear and whispered, "We must remain as quiet as possible. Are you sure nobody will come through your doors?"

"The doors are sealed as are my lips. For now."

❦

*H*aving a girl take her clothes off was much easier than knowing what to do once those clothes were off.

Atilius and Lucilius were both sitting on their beds. Antonia was back kneeling on the floor, her head bowed.

"You know," Lucilius finally said. "For many Romans, a slave is their first encounter."

"What do you mean?"

"It is better to train and learn how to be a great lover on a slave. A slave will not gossip. A slave will not complain if you do not satisfy. Some of these Roman women will make a mockery of your efforts if not done properly."

"I have already been with many women."

"You have not been with any," Lucilius answered quickly. "Do not worry. It is not a problem. You have not had opportunity. Until now," he said motioning toward Antonia. "You have a desirable woman, naked in front of you. I shall stand watch outside of doors." Lucilius stood and walked over to the door. When he reached it, he stopped and looked back at Atilius. "Remember, she is yours to do as you please. You do not ask. You take. You are a Roman," he said and closed the door behind him.

Atilius stood. "Go to my bed," he told Antonia. She stood, not wanting to incur Atilius' wrath and moved over to the bed. As she climbed on top, she began sobbing.

"Lay on your stomach, but keep head up and eyes open," Atilius said as he disrobed, then climbed onto her.

❦

*T*heir bodies moved as one, like a wave rolling along the ocean. He was on top of her now. Moving in and out, pushing harder and harder with each thrust. Justina was doing her best to control herself, biting down hard on her lip to stop from moaning, but even that wasn't working. When the wave finally crashed upon the shore, their bodies succumbed to the energy of the climax. Fabricius collapsed on top of her, sweating and breathing hard.

"Apologies for performance," he said through measured pants, "but I have yet to be with any woman."

Justina chuckled, trying her best to catch her own breath. "I have nothing of which to compare your performance."

"I am your first?"

"You are," she confirmed. "But I would not have had it be anyone else, my centurion."

✸

"*Y*ou do not have to do this just because your friend says you do," Antonia said.

"You need to keep mouth shut," Atilius answered. While he had heard much about bedding a woman, he had never actually done it, or seen it done, and he was not sure what to do first.

"Please," Antonia begged him. "We have known each other from childhood."

"And that is when desires started. Now, my mother makes dreams come true." Atilius placed his hand on Antonia's bottom, and she immediately started to cry. "Keep your voice down. I do not want discovery."

He was on top of her now, sliding himself between the cheeks of her buttocks. He had little idea where to put himself and even less idea how to get it there. But it felt good where he was, so he continued to thrust. Antonia cried out, so he placed his hand over her mouth to silence her. On one of his pushes, he felt himself enter something tight and continued to thrust. Antonia cried out through his hand. It was hard to enter, but he pushed and pushed, thrusting seemingly deeper and deeper. After a few seconds, he climaxed, spilling himself all over her behind.

Antonia was crying uncontrollably. Atilius climbed off her and let her cry as he dressed. When she finally stopped sobbing, he commanded her to dress herself. She stood and pulled on her tunic; her tears were no longer falling.

"You performed adequately," he said. He was embarrassed, but tried to act smug.

Antonia turned to him, her face as red as a ripe apple. "There is no wonder this family has always looked upon you as the slow one," she said. "You are too stupid to even know where to put your tiny little cock."

Antonia's words and the force with which she spoke them shocked Atilius.

"I do not have anyone to gossip to," she continued, "but I can tell other family members of what you just did and how pathetic you were."

"You will not speak a word of this to anyone," he commanded. He tried to sound firm but was beginning to panic.

"The only way someone like you gets a woman is if he owns her."

Atilius moved suddenly to Antonia and punched her in the stomach. She doubled over and fell to her knees, trying desperately to catch her breath. Hearing the sound, Lucilius opened the door to find Atilius grabbing Antonia by the hair and pulling her head back sharply. He clapped.

"This will be one of your duties 'til I marry," Atilius said, inches from her face. "I will be inside you, no matter where I choose to stick my cock. This is your life from now 'til the day you die." He pushed her head away. "You were fortunate to receive my seed." He looked up at Lucilius who was laughing.

"Bravo, brother." he said.

"In fact," Atilius continued, "tomorrow, as a gesture to my best friend, he will also be inside you and free to use you as he pleases."

*T*hey were laying next to each other now, hands clasped. Justina was on her side, outlining Fabricius' muscles with her finger. "It is getting late. I should take leave," he said. "But know we have many more days like this ahead of us." He leaned over and kissed Justina, then stood. She watched him as he dressed. When he was finished, he walked back over to the bed and kissed her on the forehead. "Until then," he said and left her room.

"*N*ow take leave," Atilius said to Antonia. "I do not wish to lay eyes upon you until tomorrow."

Antonia hurried to the door, happy to be free from Atilius if only for a moment. As she opened the door and stepped out into the hallway, she saw Fabricius leaving Justina's room. He looked at her for a moment, then moved past her on his way down the hall. Antonia watched him walk away. She wanted to tell him what had happened. She imagined him entering Atilius' room and beating him until he was unconscious. Telling him that he didn't deserve a woman as fine as she. Telling him that she belonged to him now, then taking her to his room. She imagined all that, but knew none of it would ever happen.

She moved over to Justina's door and softly leaned her head against it, not wanting to make a sound. If only she had listened to Cato. She placed her hand on the door, then kissed it. She stayed there for only moment, then let her hand fall and walked away.

*A*PRIL 7, 55 BC

CHAPTER 38

APRIL 7, 55 BC

When Justina entered the dining area, Livius and Alba were already seated. Justina was in a light-hearted mood. The best she had been in weeks and it showed. Livius was happy to see his daughter smile again. He was also happy to be free of the burden the secret had placed on him all these years. She passed Cato with a smile and headed to her father. She kissed him on the cheek.

"Good morning, father. Mother."

"Good morning, daughter," Livius said. "How did you sleep?"

"Magically. Best sleep I've had in weeks," she answered, taking a seat at the table. "And how did father sleep?"

"I found that once a huge weight was lifted from my chest that breathing came easier. I too slept quite well."

Justina and her father shared a smile, as a house slave brought her food.

Alba was visibly annoyed at the exchange. She glared first at

Livius, then at Justina. "What brings you two such happiness? Your outburst yesterday will not go unpunished, Justina."

Justina took a piece of food, then looked up at her mother. "Father told me he will not tolerate Atilius' treatment of Antonia under his roof. If this does not change, he will lose her as his slave."

Alba was surprised at the revelation. "Is that so, Livius?"

"It is," he confirmed. It felt good to once again have the upper hand. "We shall find something else for our son to treasure. So far, he is not showing us that he is mature enough to have his own slave."

"Are you sure you want to go against my wishes?"

"I do. Antonia was not a gift from the two of us."

Alba's face turned red. "Has the slave not endured enough in her young life? Now you want revelations to come forward, thus ruining hers and your relationship with our daughter."

"My decision has been made," Livius said and took another bite of food. "I will let Atilius know of my intent when he arrives home tonight. He either treats her as I treat the rest of our slaves, or she becomes Justina's gift."

"Then you force my hand. I feel it time your daughter learns about the actions of her father."

Livius did his best to look worried. Justina stopped smiling.

Alba turned her attention to Justina and spoke bitterly. "I know you worship your father, think he a caring man. Has he ever shared with you the fate of Antonia's parents?"

"Why yes, mother, he has."

Alba's mouth dropped. She had clearly not expected this answer and was at a loss for words. She looked at Livius. He smiled. She looked back at Justina. "He murdered Antonia's father."

"I am quite aware," Justina said interrupting her. "He also told me of your whoring days with slaves."

RYAN LEW

"Justina," Livius cautioned his daughter, but he was smiling the entire time.

Alba just looked at Justina. "A secret holds no power when it is no longer a secret," Justina said to her mother and laughed. "May I be excused?" she asked Livius. "I am too excited not to share news with Antonia."

"You may go find her and let her know."

Justina almost leapt from her chair.

Livius turned to Alba. "You will learn your place in this household or find yourself present here no more. Justina knows all my secrets and still accepts me as her father. You, on the other hand, act anything but a caring mother." Livius returned to his breakfast.

Cato allowed himself a smile.

Alba sat there, her face blank.

CHAPTER 39

Justina looked everywhere, but she couldn't find Antonia. She looked in the preparation area; she was not there. She looked in the slave's quarters, she was not there. She even looked outside the house, but Antonia was nowhere to be found. Then it hit her, Antonia was probably in Atilius' room, doing chores he had no doubt left for her. When she arrived at the room, the door was closed. She knocked, but got no answer, so she opened the door. What she saw made her scream.

Antonia was lying on Atilius' bed in a pool of her own blood. The dagger he had received as a birthday present was embedded in her chest. She ran over to Antonia. Her eyes were open, and she was still breathing.

"Who did this to you?" Justina asked.

Antonia turned to face Justina. "You could not free me, so I freed myself," she said. "I heard conversation at table only moments ago. You knew your father killed mine and yet you laugh at given information?"

Justina took Antonia's hand and squeezed it hard. "I was informed only last evening. I was bringing news of you being returned to father and free from Atilius. The laugh, a slight at my mother."

Antonia tried to take a deep breath but only coughed blood. "You take me from one monster and hand me over to the man who killed my parents," Antonia managed to say. "I do not know which one is worse." She was having a hard time getting enough air to speak. Justina moved in closer. "This house is full of lies. You need to open your eyes, Justina. Follow your heart. You do not act as Romans do. Romans are evil; you are not evil. I shall await you in the afterlife."

"No! Hold on! I will get help," Justina said, then yelled for help as loud as she could.

Antonia smiled. She tried to touch Justina's face but could no longer control her arm. Justina screamed for help. She cradled Antonia's face in her hands. Antonia managed one deep breath, then let out her last.

"No!" Justina yelled and called out over and over again until her yells turned to sobs.

❀

*L*ivius ran down the hall as fast as his legs would carry him. When he arrived at the room he found his daughter hunched over the body of Antonia, the dagger still visible. "Cato, find the Medicus," he yelled. Alba arrived shortly after. She looked in the room and laughed.

Livius glared at her. "Are you satisfied?" he asked. "You have crushed your daughter."

"I did not put dagger in heart," she replied. "And you can refer to Justina as your daughter, not mine."

Livius placed his hands on Justina's shoulders. She looked up at him. Tears were streaming down her face. He was about to kneel next to her when Alba spoke again. "The slave takes the easy way out."

Livius turned sharply and moved purposefully to Alba. He did not stop until he was inches from her face. "You think this funny?" Alba did not answer. She was trying to keep a stone face, but Livius was beginning to breathe heavily. The veins in his neck were bulging and he had that look, the same one she saw the night of the slave's demise. Livius raised a clenched fist. Despite herself, Alba leaned back slightly. "Now it is my turn to show you the results of your actions," he said, and with that, he walked out of the room, so forcefully that had Alba not moved out of his way, he would have knocked her over.

Alba took a deep breath, then, composing herself, looked back at Justina. She was covered in blood. "She is gone, Justina," Alba said. "See yourself cleaned and then to your chores."

CHAPTER 40

*H*e was not sure what he had meant when he threatened Alba, but he knew he had to leave the house right then. What had his wife turned into? Where was that woman he had once found himself attracted to so many years ago? Sure, the years hadn't all been great, but they hadn't all been that bad either. As Livius walked the streets of Rome, he thought back to that day when he had decided to tell her that it was over. That he was in love with Servilia and wanted to be with her.

"I have something to tell you," he said to her, unable to look her directly in the eye.

"And I you," she said. He had not expected that. Nor had he expected what she told him next. His heart leapt when he heard he was to be a father again, leapt at the possibility of a daughter, then fell when he realized what exactly that meant. His conversation with Servilia went about as well. But he had learned to love Alba over the years. At least, he thought he had. If that were true, then why was he standing in front of Servilia's house about to knock on the door.

*S*ervilia was more than a little surprised when the slave announced Livius at her door. A little surprised and, truth be told, a bit leery. Had she not just been ordered by Caesar to speak with Livius about his son's lack of useful information, she would have been more inclined to believe it a coincidence.

"Livius, what a pleasant surprise," Servilia said as her old love entered the room. "Would you care for a drink?" She was lying on the couch in a house robe, sandals off. Her legs bare to the upper thigh. She did not stand.

"I may need the entire jug," Livius said, "but a cup would be a nice starter."

Livius hardly noticed her. He was a man preoccupied. Lost in thought. It was all over his face. She had seen it more often than she cared to remember. Powerful men facing life or death decisions. Average men facing life-altering consequences. The look was the same.

A slave brought in two cups and filled them with wine. Servilia motioned for the slave to place the decanter on the table and leave the room.

"To what do I owe this surprise appearance?"

Livius drank the entire cup of wine before speaking. Whatever was weighing his mind had nothing to do with Caesar. No, this was a personal issue.

"My wife has taken me to the brink of hostility," he said with heavy breath. "I have not been this mad since my military days. She thinks she now runs my household."

"And why would she think such a thing?"

Livius filled his cup a second time, then took a seat in the chair next to the couch. "My daughter held one of our slaves in great esteem. The two girls grew up together, almost as sisters. Against my wishes, Alba gave this slave to my youngest son as gift for his amusement and just now she takes her own life."

"This is what has you so flustered?" Servilia said lightly. "A

231

slave killing herself? Slaves are but property to do as we command. If your slave has killed herself, go to the square and buy another. You certainly are of means to do so."

"It is not the death of the slave that weighs on me. It is the heartbreak my young daughter must now feel. It is the fact that none of this was necessary, that the only reason the incident even occurred was due to Alba's jealousy."

"I'm confused," Servilia said. "Your wife was jealous of a slave?"

"My wife is jealous of my daughter."

Servilia laughed in spite of herself. "Oh good, Livius, your wife is jealous, but it is not of your daughter. The day you attended the arena, she made excuse of illness to make a surprise visit to my house. Much like you do today."

"She came to see you?"

The surprise on Livius' face was genuine. "She has not told you," Servilia said with a smile. She wondered, was it the tigress protecting her territory, or the cat making a desperate attempt to appear brave?

"She has not," Livius admitted.

"She wanted to be sure I was not to put my claws back into you."

Servilia gave Livius time for the revelation to sink in, and as he contemplated his situation, she filled his glass. He drank it mindlessly. She sat back down on the couch and pulled her robe back to expose her legs.

After several soulful minutes he spoke, "Sometimes, I feel jealousy for your position in life. No responsibility to a significant other. You come and go as you please. You are free like the wind."

"Ironic how the people we hold dearest do us both harm in recent times."

"What do you mean?"

"Caesar is not happy with information being supplied from your son to mine. He threatened to sever our deal and make life difficult for both families. My arrangement in jeopardy." She took a slow drink. "Would life not have been easier if I had become pregnant by you instead of Alba holding second child?"

Livius chuckled. "I do not know if I could have kept up with you and your ambitions back then. I do not think I can keep up with them now."

This time it was Servilia who chuckled. "I cannot be paraded in public. I share bed and time behind closed doors. There is not much to keep up with." She took another drink and continued, "I long to be seen in public as more than a whore to the great Caesar."

"We all do what we must in this world. Although some of your choices may not be ideal, you are a wonderful woman and mother." For the first time since he entered the room, Livius really looked at Servilia. She watched as his eyes moved up her legs to her soft, full breasts. When their eyes met, she smiled. Livius blushed.

"Brutus loves you and you are still as sexy and desirable as the day I met you," he said.

Servilia moved her leg to reveal even more skin. "Has good Livius had too much to drink already?"

Livius left his chair in favor of the couch. Servilia sat upright. "We cannot turn back the years, nor would I want to. But we are here now. In this moment, free to do as we choose."

Livius put his cup down and slid even closer. He took her cup and placed it on the table as well. He kissed her. Timidly at first, then forcefully. She kissed him back. His lips were just as she remembered, soft, yet firm. Livius had always kissed her as a man freed from decades in the desert and she a flagon of cool, fresh water. With each kiss the years slipped away, until Livius was once again a soldier and she a maiden. Then, just as he had done so many years before, he made love to her.

When they finished, he lay holding her on the couch. She folded into him, allowing his strength to engulf her. She was comforted in a way she had not known for many years. Not since the last time she had been in his arms. The day he told her he was staying with Alba, she knew she would never feel it again. She spoke to push the memory away.

"I do not recall you of such skills in the bedroom," she said. "Had I known."

They both laughed.

"A lot has changed over the years," Livius said. "But your own skills in that area, I have never forgotten."

They laid there for the longest time. Livius running his hand along Servilia's body, caressing her back, her bottom, and her thighs, every so often kissing her shoulders and neck. This is how her life should have been. Here with this man, in his arms. This is how she should have felt, but it wasn't. Livius wasn't her man, and this wasn't her life.

Servilia became suddenly solemn. She sat up and pulled over her robe. "So what is next for our saga?" she asked. "Was this a one-time deal to get back at our partners?"

"I am done with Alba," Livius said. "She goes too far, and I must move on. All of my children are old enough to accept the consequences of her actions."

Servilia stood. She walked to the table and took a drink from her cup. "You never said what she had over you to cause such injury."

Livius sat up and pulled his clothes to him. "What do you mean?"

"I would assume she knew something about you that caused you to allow the gifting of the slave."

Livius stood and dressed. "She knows a secret or two. None of worth anymore. She has no more power in house Livius."

Servilia smiled. There was more to it than what Livius was willing to reveal. "Does that mean you are free for a proper Roman woman to court? Even one of questionable past?"

Livius took Servilia in his arms. "I would not have it any other way," he said and kissed her fully. "Let us have a few days to clear head. Then we shall approach subject again."

He gave Servilia another kiss, then left.

As he walked out of the room, Servilia recalled the conversation they had oh so many years ago. She wondered if this time, she'd finally get the man she once loved.

CHAPTER 41

The cot used by the Medicus for the sick now held Antonia's motionless body. Why hadn't she listened to Cato? Why hadn't she taken his advice? Had she listened, all of this could have been avoided. Drawing attention to one's self was a dangerous move as a slave. It was better to blend in, to go unnoticed, to almost seem invisible. It is never good to stand out, to invite contention. Maybe it was his fault. After all, he was the head slave. If anything happened in the house, it was ultimately his responsibility. He had let this girl down.

And now she lay there before him. Her trip to the afterlife secured. The Medicus had removed the dagger, cleaned the blood, and even placed an ointment on the wound to hide it as best he could. Now preparations were needed to dispose of the body.

"What will happen to her?" Cato asked. He sat on the cot next to Antonia, unable to take his eyes off her. The instrument of death at her side.

"I'm afraid she is destined for potter's field," the Medicus said from behind his table. "Unless Livius will pay for her cremation."

It was the fate that awaited all slaves. Still, the thought of Antonia's body being dumped into an open pit turned his stomach. It was not deserved. But Livius was not a man who would pay for the burial of a slave, especially one who took her own life.

"It is unlikely," he said.

Cato was so intent on Antonia that he didn't even see Justina enter the room until she was already kneeling by Antonia's side, her cheeks painted with tears. Cato placed a hand on her shoulder.

"Why would she do this?" Justina asked. "It was supposed to be us together under my roof in our future. My brother has not the brains of a sleeping two-year-old. He is certainly not worthy of taking one's own life."

So much had changed in this house lately. While there had always been a bit of contention, it remained between family members and only once migrated to the slaves. But that was not the case anymore. A cancer was infecting house Livius. What started in Cato as a concern was quickly turning into a fear.

"Your brother follows the example of his father," Cato said. "The Medicus and I thought we brought you to a good family so many years ago. For the most part, we were correct. But there is more to this family than we have known. Your father confesses of the killing of slaves. Your oldest brother does it for sport in the arena. And now the youngest forces hand of Antonia."

Justina turned to face Cato. "What do you mean?"

"Caution Cato," the Medicus said.

Cato did not heed the caution. "When Antonia returned to our quarters last evening, she had been crying," he continued, "After some prodding, she confessed your brother had raped her at the convincing of Lucilius."

"My brother is not capable of such a thing," she said.

"The Medicus has verified the wound," Cato explained.

Justina looked at him, mouth agape. "Last night?" she asked. "Why would she not tell me?"

Cato cut her off. "She did stop at your room, Domina but did not confide."

"I don't know what to make of this," Justina said, her gaze fixed on nothing. "I don't understand."

"All in your family, from your parents to your brothers, are capable and willing to kill slaves. They are Roman, make no mistake of it."

Justina focused on Cato. "I am not capable of harming a slave. It is not in my heart. I do not care that my natural parents were Roman."

The Medicus spoke up. "You have noble blood running through you, Justina. You are of good heart and mind. Much like your natural parents."

No, Cato thought to himself. *Now is not the time.* He sent the Medicus a disapproving glare and shook his head. The Medicus remained quiet. Justina seemed lost in thought, and Cato was happy to let the situation slowly pass. Then, out of nowhere, Justina asked, "Who was I named after?"

Cato almost laughed. "Your birth parents named you," he said. "They were expecting a boy, and when cock didn't appear, they made change to awaiting name."

"What was I to have been named?"

"Your father wanted to name you Justus," the Medicus said.

"That is a strange name."

"He believed the world was not right and that his son would make sure things were just in his life," the Medicus continued, "He felt the name would be a constant reminder."

"What Roman does not feel the world just?" Justina asked.

The Medicus had said too much. While the time might eventually come when the truth could be revealed, doing so now, with atmosphere as it was in house Livius, was reckless. No good could come of it. He was about to change the subject when the Medicus began coughing violently. So much so that he had to take hold of his table to prevent collapsing. Justina stood. Cato rushed to him and poured a cup of water.

"Is all well?" Justina asked.

The Medicus took a drink from the cup. "I have been under the weather of late," he said. "It is something that will pass in a few moons." After several minutes, he regained his composure. Cato patted his old friend on the back. He didn't like the sound of that cough and liked the Medicus' dismissal of it even less.

Justina turned to Antonia and kissed her on the forehead. She would be cold by now, her skin having lost its soft shine. "Apologies," she whispered. She stood and turned to Cato and the Medicus. "Gratitude for all that you have done for me over the years. You two have been angels in my life, helping guide and watch over me. I know I can confide in either of you with my true feelings and I will get honest response. Father is a good man, please try and remember that. So are Fabricius and Herminius. We shall get through this tragedy together."

Cato walked over to Justina and placed a hand on her arm. "I will never place my trust in a Roman. It lies with you and what you do," he said.

Justina looked at Cato strangely, then turned to the Medicus. Their eyes met briefly before he looked away.

After Justina left the room, Cato turned once again to Antonia. How sad it was when a life is taken from this world. Sadder still when the life taken is but a child. He bent down and, just as Justina did, he kissed Antonia on the forehead. It was at that moment he noticed the dagger was missing.

CHAPTER 42

"Greetings Alba," Livius said as he walked into the bedroom. She was lying on the bed in her bedclothes reading.

Alba looked up. "No honey or wife as greeting?"

"No, I think the best greeting for us now is by first name," he said as he started to undress. "Not to worry, it will not be for long."

"What do you speak about? Are you ill?"

"Never better. In fact, Servilia thinks the same."

Livius waited until she was struck by the realization of what he had done.

"So now the great butcher of Rome takes side whore like Caesar?" she said placing the book down. "I do not think so. I will allow for one last visit between the two of you. That visit will consist of you telling her you will never see her again, in this life or the next."

Livius enjoyed Alba's anger. "You hold nothing over me now. Justina knows everything. You cannot damage that relationship as you have tried. In fact, we will be stronger for it. You and she will never be close."

Alba stood and walked over to Livius. She stood right in front of him, face to face, just as he had done to her earlier. "I do not care for other people's children, only my own. Justina is one step above slave in my eyes. She was your gift to yourself having nothing to do with my feelings or me. I showed no reservations because she came with a slave and the Medicus as package.

"You have selective memory," Alba continued, "but are blessed that your wife remembers all she is told. If you choose to see Servilia again for other than reason I just permitted, I will be forced to sit down with her and beloved son and let them know of your actions so many years ago. Senators and politicians like taking credit for a great many things. Some of those things they had nothing to do with.

"Pompey takes credit for death of Brutus The Elder back some twenty plus years ago. A death that still haunts poor Brutus, his son. A death that changed Servilia from the talk of the town, to the whore in the streets. What might they think if they knew the truth? That you were solely responsible for that death. You alone planned it so that you and she could be as one. Only to find that I was pregnant with our second child. Your best laid plans gone sour. You were lucky that Pompey was willing to take credit for your actions back then."

Livius' heart fell. In one moment, just as before, his future had been snatched from his grasp. He had forgotten the confession he made one drunken night. The realization hit him hard.

"I await your return to our bed," Alba said and slid under the sheets.

Livius removed his clothing and climbed into the bed next to her. She moved over and placed her head on his chest. "You may dream of Servilia in your next life, but in this one, it is you and me." Livius placed his hand on his wife's side and stared straight ahead. The balance of power had shifted once again.

CHAPTER 43

*J*ustina was sitting on her bed, holding the dagger, the events of the past several weeks running through her mind. The guilt she felt was stifling. The pain, almost unbearable. So much had happened lately; she did not know where she stood. She had always felt safe here, but after today, after seeing her best friend lying lifeless on the cot, there was no place she felt safe. She also didn't know who to trust any longer. It seemed that just as she placed her confidence in one person, it was betrayed.

Even Cato was holding secrets from her. The incident on the cross was never sufficiently explained. Then there was today. What did he mean when he said his trust lied in her and what she did? What secrets did he know? House Livius had become a house of secrets and of death. Justina was so lost in thought, she didn't hear the light tap on the door.

When he didn't get an answer, Fabricius stuck his head in the room. "Greetings," he said. "Apologies for the late hours, but my patrol went long."

Justina quickly slid the dagger under her pillow as Fabricius slipped into the room, closing the door behind him. "Is something wrong?" he asked.

"Antonia is dead."

Fabricius sat on the bed next to her. "I am sorry to hear such news." He tried to take her in his arms, to comfort her, but she pushed him away.

"Are you, brother? She is just a slave and you are Roman. Should it matter?"

"Of course it matters. She was part of this household. You grew up together. How did such a thing happen?"

"She took her own life. A wise decision versus the choices she had."

"I am confused. I know Atilius is a foolish boy, but father was to take her back."

Justina looked at Fabricius with hard eyes. "Your brother is a monster," she said forcefully. "His actions caused her death. And she was not aware of father's intentions. It was too late when I found her." She didn't mean to yell at Fabricius, but she was angry, and she needed to take it out on someone, anyone.

"This is terrible news," Fabricius said. "I shall go talk to Atilius."

"Do not waste your breath. What good will it do? He will not care. Antonia was property to him. Less value than a dog itself. He raped her, Fabricius. He raped her, and she killed herself because of it. His only loss is now he will have to do his own chores."

Her brother was at a loss for words.

"Please leave my room," Justina said and turned away from him. "I need to be by myself."

Fabricius stood and slowly walked to the door. He took hold of the handle and paused. "And what of us?"

"I may have gone too far in being with you last night. Had I been there for her, she might still be alive."

Fabricius said nothing. He left the room, closing the door behind him.

Antonia had depended on her, and she had promised her protection. But she hadn't delivered on that promise. Lucilius beat her and all she could do was stand there and watch it. She had promised Antonia a bright future only to have it snatched away by her mother. She had allowed herself a moment of pleasure and it had ended in tragedy. All she could think of was what horrors Antonia must have been made to endure at Atilius' hand. She should have protected her friend, her sister. The dagger should be in Atilius' chest. Justina jumped from her bed, pulled Atilius' dagger from under her pillow, and rushed out of the room.

❀

"Hello, Justina. It is nice of you to join us," Atilius said as she stormed into his room. He was sitting in a chair next to Lucilius who was lying in his bed. "Did mother tell you the good news? I am to get a new bed in a day or two. This one has been stained."

Justina ignored their laughter. It was nothing more than the cackling of imbeciles. She stood there in front of Atilius, letting the anger rise, holding the dagger behind her.

"It is a shame the last gift expired so soon," Lucilius added with a smug smile. "We had great plans for it." The two exchanged another great laugh.

"I think I may have found another gift of yours," Justina said and lunged toward Atilius. Her swiftness caught him off guard, and before he knew it, she had the dagger pointed directly at his throat. Fear painted his face.

As Atilius sat frozen, Lucilius laughed even harder. "I had wondered where that went," he said. "Thought it was lost in your slave. Gratitude, Justina, for finding it and returning it."

She ignored Lucilius, focusing all her attention on her brother. She fixed her eyes on his, but it was to her detriment, for Lucilius had rolled off the bed and taken hold of his gladius. He now held it against Justina's temple. "Hand over the dagger to proper owner or face dire consequences."

Justina did not move, nor did she take her eyes off Atilius. They were focused, with sole intent. Her weight was against Atilius' neck and the edge of the dagger was just short of breaking skin. How easy it would be to push it into his throat, to cut the jugular, and then join Antonia in the afterlife. Lucilius pushed the point of the blade into her temple, not enough to pierce the skin, but enough to remind her it was there. She lowered the dagger and handed it to Atilius. Lucilius lowered his sword.

Justina turned and headed for the door. Emboldened, Atilius leapt from the chair and grabbed her arm, spinning her around. "The next time you point sharp instrument at me, you best use it because I will be pointing one at you with deadly intent."

Justina yanked her arm from Atilius with such force that he was unable to hold his grip. She stepped into him, face-to-face. "I know what you did last night. Actions have consequences, even for Romans." Atilius' bravado disappeared, replaced by concern. "The next time you lay your hand on me will be the last," she said, then turned and walked out the door.

CHAPTER 44

$\mathcal{T}$he market was abuzz with people buying, bartering, and generally looking at the wares offered. A little girl stole a piece of fruit, causing a huge commotion as the vendor chased her through the crowd. Justina heard a familiar laugh coming from behind a vendor's table. It was Antonia. She rushed to the table. Its wares were spread out before her, daggers, knives, and swords. They were all very fancy, most of a make Justina had never before seen.

"Hello, Justina," Antonia said casually. "Would you like to buy a knife or perhaps a sword?"

"What are you doing here, Antonia?"

"I am selling my wares. Here is a nice sword for you," she held up a wooden practice sword. "Best not use a real one. You might get hurt."

Justina did not understand. Why was Antonia behind the table? "You better get home Antonia before you find yourself in trouble."

"I have no home," she said. "No home, no parents, no friends."

"You have me."

"Perhaps a nice dagger," Antonia said. She presented Justina with the very dagger she used to take her life. "Perhaps you can use it to stab someone in the back."

"No Antonia, it was not my fault."

Cato suddenly appeared behind her. "Come," he said to Justina. "This is not why we came."

Cato led her to a clearing just past the market. A slave was hanging from the cross. Atilius and Lucilius were standing at the foot of the cross looking up at the slave. She could see them laughing and pointing. She looked up at the slave; it was a girl, a young girl with long brown hair. She stepped closer to get a better view of the slave's face. She knew that girl. She was that girl.

❦

*I*t was unbearable. There was simply no way to relieve it. No position that didn't cause gut-wrenching pain. She looked over and saw the nail that had been driven into her hand. She could not move her fingers. She turned to the other hand. It too had been nailed in place. There was laughter coming from below. She could hear it; even from up here, their voices were clear.

"This is what we do to slaves that do not listen," Atilius said.

"But is she not your sister?" Lucilius asked. The question brought a hardy laugh.

"As far as I know, she is not even Roman."

Justina closed her eyes, but the tears wouldn't come. When she opened them again, Atilius and Lucilius were gone. Alba and her father now stood in their place.

"You did all you can for this slave," Alba said.

"I am fortunate I did not have to kill her like the others," Livius replied. "To think of all the time and money we spent on this one. It would have been easier to just buy her instead of pretending she was our daughter."

Alba and Livius shared a laugh, and then walked away.

247

"No!" Justina called out. "I am not a slave!" She started to cry, but her eyes were too dry to form tears. She sobbed heavily, the pain racking her body with each heave.

Herminius and Fabricius approached the cross.

"I heard you bedded this one," Herminius said.

"I did," Fabricius confirmed. "I spoke of love and only being with her."

The two brothers laughed.

"Add her to the long list of slaves you have had your way with. This one took longer than most."

"She did not know she was a slave. She thought herself Roman."

Her brothers laughed again and walked away.

Cato stood alone in front of her. "This is what all of our sacrifices bear?" he asked her. "I could have been free from this place many moons ago if this was to be your fate."

Cato was mad at her, but she did not understand why. "I thought I was Roman. How did I become a slave?"

"You were never Roman," Cato said. In the distance, Livius could be heard calling for him. Cato turned and looked, then returned his attention to Justina. "I have said too much and now must go answer my master's call." He turned and stormed off.

She was alone now. Alone in the blazing heat. Along in her suffering.

After a few minutes, a man walked up to the cross. He stopped and looked up at her. His eyes were fierce, but kind, his skin darkened from years in the sun. He had on leather pants, much like the kind Cato wore and his chest was bare. Various scars adorned his arms and shoulders. She had never seen him before.

He smiled at her. "I have not seen you in many years," he said.

"Do I know you? Are you friends of my family?"

"I am no friend to Romans."

"Then how do you know me? I am Roman."

"Are you?"

"All of my family came to see me but called me a slave."

"Then you are a slave."

Justina shook her head. "But all these years, I have been raised Roman."

"You have been raised," the man said. "But if you do not adhere to their laws and ways, then how are you Roman? Just eating their food and living in their city does not make you Roman. Slaves do the same."

Justina considered his words. "I do not understand how I ended up here."

"You chose your situation. We all do. At least free men and women do."

"Was I betrayed?"

"The only betrayal here is to yourself. You betray your true self, so you deserve what has become of you."

"I don't understand," she said and shifted her weight to relieve her arms. "How would I have fared differently?"

The stranger stepped closer to Justina. He was now face to face with her. "You allow yourself to be weak. You allow others to dictate your life and your choices. What does that make you?"

"A slave," she said, bowing her head.

The man smiled again. He lifted her chin with his hand. "Do you want better?" he asked. "Do you want to be neither slave, nor Roman?"

Justina began to cry. This time the tears flowed.

"You need to look deep," the man continued, "You question your thoughts because of what you can see. Why do you question your heart? It has no eyes. It knows only your truth."

"How did I become a slave?"

"You must change your choices, your decisions." He touched her arm. His hand was warm, familiar, somehow comforting. "I only wanted your safety. If I had known your fate, I would not have let you go."

"Let me go? How did you let me go?"

The man did not answer her. He just smiled. In a moment, he was down at her feet again, looking up at her. "The next time someone offers you freedom, you must take it."

"Will there be a next time?"

The stranger laughed. "I come to visit my daughter for the first time and she wants to know everything."

"Daughter?" Justina said. "Why does a Legatus speak ill of Rome?"

"Do I look like a Legatus?" he asked, and as she looked down at him, he started to vanish.

"No!" she yelled out. "Don't go! I need to know who my father is!"

*J*ustina sat up suddenly, soaked in sweat, breathing heavy. She was in her own room, in her own bed. She patted the covers, still unsure of their existence. They were real. The bed was real. She looked at each hand. The nails were gone, and there were no holes. She took a deep breath, allowing herself to relax. It was now early morning.

"The next time someone offers me freedom," she said aloud, "I must take it. I will not be a slave any longer."

CHAPTER 45

APRIL 8, 55 BC

"Have you come to fight me?" Fabricius asked. Justina was standing in his doorway, having just flung open the door. She was dressed in full combat gear, minus her helmet.

"Good morning, Fabricius. How did you sleep?"

"I did not sleep well." He had tossed and turned most of the night, trying to come up with something that would save their budding romance. He was mostly unsuccessful. Women, in general, were hard enough to understand; this one was worse.

Justina closed the door. She turned and gave Fabricius a coy smile, then ran over to his bed, jumped on top of him, and gave him a deep kiss.

It all took Fabricius by surprise.

"I hope I was not reason for lack of slumber. Apologies if I was. I was not myself," she said and kissed him again.

"If this is how I am to wake from rough night of sleep, then I accept new fate." Justina placed her hands on his bare chest and smiled down at him. "You are in a good mood," he said, "your friend not dead more than twenty-four hours."

"I will mourn Antonia in my own way," she said and jumped off him. "I had a vision last night and need help from loving brother."

"A vision?" Fabricius repeated. "Were your eyes closed and your head on the pillow when this 'vision' occurred?" He leaned on one elbow.

"Of course," Justina said.

"That is called a dream."

"Call it what you want," she said and walked over to the door. "Just get dressed in your fighting gear and meet me in the training room." Justina flashed a smile and left.

Fabricius stood, rubbing the sleep from his eyes. He wondered what Justina was up to, but based on the way she was dressed, knew it couldn't be good. She would want revenge on Atilius and, worse yet, she would want him to help her get it. This was the only possible explanation for her elevated mood. He began to dress, all the while formulating a plan to dissuade her from her course.

When he got to the room, Justina was ready, gladius in hand. He took a deep breath. "Have we not already gone over this, Justina? I thought you were to stop this nonsense and find loving husband. I know of one who is interested in that position."

"I ask one favor of you, Fabricius. And in turn, I shall be loving girlfriend and confidant."

"And what is this favor you ask?" he said, stepping further into the room.

"I need you to give me my freedom."

Fabricius was puzzled. "I do not understand meaning. You ask for freedom and you will be loving and supportive girlfriend? Are they not contradictory?"

Justina laughed. "Far too long I have been trapped in this house. I do as commanded, like a good Roman girl should. I even allow my brother to bully me. I shall have my freedom in this life and no longer be commanded by those who I do not respect."

"Freedom will come, Justina, when we move to our own place, funds for which I do not yet have."

"That is not freedom," Justina said. "Freedom is a mindset. If you empower me with battle skills, I will no longer feel as slave under these walls."

"And what is your intention?" he asked. "What do you plan on doing with these new-found skills? Am I to train you so you can exact revenge on your brother?"

"You are to train me so I do not have to."

Fabricius smiled. He understood the confidence that came with the ability to defend oneself. He knew it in his own life, and he had seen it with the recruits he helped train. Justina didn't want to feel the victim, and the only way to do that was to know you could defend yourself if the need arose. "If this new confidence, apologies, freedom is what you seek, then I will grant it. However, if little girl shall appear and realize vision was but a dream, my favor will be ended, but your portion of the deal will remain. Do we have an accord?"

"We do," Justina said eagerly.

"Know that I will not show leniency with you just because you are a girl. If you want to learn these skills, it will require you to be hurt physically and mentally. I will push you to limits you will not like. But, if you stay true to your purpose, your skills will rival those of your brother and Lucilius. It will take time and dedication. Are you willing?"

"Willing and waiting," Justina said, sliding on her helmet.

Fabricius walked over to the practice swords and removed one from the holding rack. He placed his helmet on his head. "Then let us begin," he said and thrusted his sword forward with all his might.

CHAPTER 46

*B*rutus was slumped in a chair when Caesar walked into the dining area of Servilia's home unannounced. The slave had tried to make him wait, but Caesar was not a man who waited for permission to do anything. When Brutus saw him, he sat up straight as a column.

"Caesar," Brutus said, the surprise evident in his voice.

"Good evening, Brutus. Why does late evening find you away from slumber?"

"I am just now getting home. I know how much you desire information, but I was to you tomorrow with news."

Caesar was intrigued, eager to see if his not-so-veiled threat had born fruit. He took a seat at the table. "What news have you for me?"

"Your partner in the Triumvirate, Crassus, has desires to command army again."

Caesar was impressed. Though the information was not news to him, it had only been spoken between he, Pompey, and Crassus.

The fact that Brutus was able to discover it was a good sign. "Continue," he said.

"Pompey is planning to call for a vote in seven days' time to block such desire. He is concerned for Crassus' health if he were to find battlefield."

"Pompey and myself are of like mind in this." That was all Brutus needed to know. The news, however, did not please him. Blocking such a deal could potentially cut off purse strings for both armies. The move made him wonder as to Pompey's purpose.

"Pompey is recruiting support in the senate now," Brutus added.

Though he heard Brutus, Caesar was still contemplating his options. A warrior's mind preparing for battle. It was that mind that began to think aloud. "Crassus is relying on Pompey and I to make this happen for him," he said. "He once defeated the slave king Spartacus in battle, yet Pompey quickly grabbed credit for history to hear. Crassus desires to be known in the annals for more than just his wealth." He looked directly at Brutus. "I see conversation just a few short weeks ago finally bears fruit. Message must have been received by butcher's son as well."

"We are here to better the glory of Rome."

Caesar cut him off. "Gratitude for information. Now, find me names of each senator that Pompey sways. I will have my time with them as well." He stood. "Is your mother home?"

"She is in her bedroom, asleep for hours according to slaves."

"I shall see if I can awaken her with good news of her son's actions."

Brutus bowed his head.

Caesar made his way across the peristyle to Servilia's bedroom. He tapped lightly on her door. When he got no response, he knocked harder.

"Enter," Servilia said. He had awoken her, and she was still groggy from slumber. When she saw him enter the room, she sat straight up, raised her knees to her chest, and pulled the covers up around her. Caesar entered the room and closed the door behind him.

"This is your bedroom?" Caesar said looking around. "I have never been invited." The room was smaller than he expected, being barely large enough to fit the bed. One small window was located on the west side. The shutters had been closed to block the light. Servilia's bed was draped in sheer silk with patterns of flowers. A vase and several grooming items rested on a small table to the right. "I thought it would be larger."

"It is more than enough for one woman to sleep. Were there someone to join her, then yes, a larger room would be ideal."

Caesar smiled. He wondered briefly what it would be like to live here, but quickly pushed the thought from his mind.

"What brings Caesar to my humble home at this late hour?" Servilia asked.

He stepped closer to the bed. "For each of the last few nights, I had intended to summon you to my quarters."

"And yet, you did not."

"No," he said. "Because you are not someone to be summoned. You are someone to be invited with waited response."

Servilia lowered her knees and allowed the covers to flow downward. "Is the great Caesar becoming soft in his old age?"

Caesar sat on the bed next to her. "I do miss your affections," he said and placed his hand on her leg. "But I also miss your counsel. You are wiser than most men I call advisor."

Servilia smiled broadly. "Gratitude, I have always hoped to be of more use to you than that of concubine." She leaned over and kissed Caesar softly on the cheek.

"Would it be too much to ask for my guards and I to accompany you to my home this evening?"

"I think I can be persuaded. Let me gather some clothing and we can leave." She arose and headed over to a small wardrobe against the wall. She opened the door and began to pull out clothing.

"Besides," Caesar said. "I do not believe your son would care to hear our climaxes."

Servilia laughed. "So, great Caesar wants more than just my counsel this evening?"

Caesar smiled. "I will accept what you wish to give this evening. And," he added, "I hope to make this more of a permanent situation."

Servilia turned suddenly, still holding the robe she had removed from the wardrobe. "What is meaning of statement?"

Caesar stepped closer to Servilia. He placed his hands on her arms. "I am aware I am not the only surprise visitor you had in this house recently."

Servilia's face showed the shock she felt. Before she could answer, Caesar continued, "I know that Livius made an appearance here not too many days past. Based on your son's information today, I would assume your meeting with him was to exchange ideas," he paused, "and nothing else."

Servilia's body stiffened. Caesar noted her stress, but instead of relishing in it, as was his nature, he relieved her of it. "I do not wish to know if anything more happened between the two of you," he said, with more kindness than even he expected. The thought of losing her had been more uncomfortable than he anticipated. His first instinct had been to send Livius to the afterlife, and he nearly made the decision to do so, but thought better of it. Losing the butcher would mean losing his son and that would not be a wise move. Pride could not be placed before power. Caesar knew his history; men who did that had a tendency to fall hard.

"I just need to know that it is over and that you and I will be for each other," he said.

Servilia dropped her robe and threw her arms around him.

"I have told my wife that she may remain in the villa outside of the city. She will no longer make appearance with me or for me. My heart lies elsewhere."

"My ears have been waiting many years to hear such words come from your mouth," Servilia said and kissed him full on the lips. He slipped his arms around her and kissed her back.

Caesar pulled back. The softness had fallen from his eyes. "I do not consider butcher a friend, but he is no enemy, as yet. As long as his son performs as promised, his family will prosper."

"My concern is no longer for the butcher," Servilia said. "I have the greatest man in Rome."

Caesar kissed her again. "Bring clothes for several days. I would have you at my side and residence for more than the evening." He let Servilia return to her packing. "I will wait for you outside. Let your son know of your whereabouts."

🐚

*C*aesar walked out of the room, but left the door open. Servilia returned to her preparations. She had waited for this day for so long, and it had finally arrived. She sped up her efforts, singing as she prepared.

"May I come in?" Brutus asked.

"Yes, of course," she replied, still packing. Brutus entered and walked near the bed. "You must continue to keep Caesar happy," she said, as she folded her robes. "I will do my part on my end." She stopped and looked up at her son. "As I am sure you heard conversation through thin walls." Brutus' cheeks reddened. Servilia continued to pack as she spoke. "If you truly want revenge on the man who took your father from us, then you must uphold your end and provide information."

"I will do what I can, mother," Brutus said. He was lingering in the room.

"Is there something else?"

Brutus looked down. She waited for him to find the right words. "I was not aware Livius had made appearance here."

Servilia stopped. "He came. It was a couple weeks ago."

"Why did you not tell me?"

Servilia returned to packing, a little more quickly than before. "There was nothing to tell. He came over, we talked, and he left."

"That is all?"

"Did you want more?"

"Caesar seemed to think there was more."

Servilia walked over to her son. "Whether or not there was something more no longer matters. Recent revelations from Caesar have secured our future." She kissed her son on the cheek, picked up her clothing, and walked out of the room. "Do not wait up."

CHAPTER 47

APRIL 28, 55 BC

*T*hree weeks had passed since his confrontation with Alba and little had changed. Tension still filled the house, and the relationship between them was strained, at best. Livius had not been able to bring himself to talk to Servilia, and that seemed to have worked out best, as Brutus had explained Caesar and Servilia's current relationship. He may have acted in haste with Servilia, but that didn't change his feelings toward Alba, who he no longer viewed as a wife or confidant. Their evenings were spent in separate rooms except for dinner and sharing a bed at night. The two of them hardly saw each other.

The house itself had grown quite quiet. When Fabricius wasn't on patrol, his nights were spent with Justina in the sparring room. Livius didn't know why they were training so hard, but he thought it best not to ask. There was a chance it wasn't training at all and, quite frankly, that was something he didn't want to know. Lucilius and Atilius spent most of their time on patrol or with other soldiers, doing things young boys did at their age. Livius didn't want to know about that either. Herminius too was away most of the time. In fact, it had been several days since Livius recalled him even being in the house. So when he walked in while he and Alba were having dinner, Livius was very happy to see him.

"Father, Mother, I have news," Herminius said, a grand smile on his face.

"Come sit by me and share," Alba said.

Herminius walked over to his mother. He kissed her on the cheek and sat down beside her. "Gratitude to both of you for all of the years of support you have given me. I am the man I am today because of caring actions from you both. I am set to move into my own home in a few days."

Livius was happy for his son, not only was he moving up in the world, but it would be good for him to free himself of the tension that so filled the house as of late. "I always thought Fabricius would be first to leave from under our roof," Livius said. "Congratulations, you have bested your brother."

Herminius was very happy with his father's response. Alba was not. She flashed Livius an unpleasant look. He ignored it. She turned to Herminius. "You are just starting your new position. Are you sure it wise to leave so soon?"

Livius stood, walked over to his son, and shook his hand. "If mother would have her way, all four of you would remain under roof till departed from this world." Livius shared a laugh with his son.

Alba was not amused. "I knew the day would come when all my children would take leave. I was hoping it would be after they were long married and with children."

Livius ignored her a second time. "Are you sure you can afford to live on your own?" he asked Herminius. "You can come and go as you please here."

"Gratitude. I recently received much-deserved bonus for the job I am doing and expect more of that in the weeks and years to come. If I find struggle I will return, with permission, to my old room."

Livius returned to his seat at the head of the table. "Bonus?" he questioned. "I have known Pompey many years, but have never known him to give such a treat. Maybe he has changed,"

"The bonus was not from Pompey."

"Then who?" Livius asked, but as soon as he did, he knew the answer.

"I know you served under Pompey father and have much respect for him. I appreciate your words assisting in my position. But the future belongs to Caesar and being in the wrong camp could be costly."

"You must be very careful in the games politicians play," Livius cautioned. "You are young to the ways of these cunning men. Guile is their handiwork."

"I do what is best for myself, best for Rome," he said. "I do not feel my hand forced. This family will rise to prominence whether desired or not."

"Finally someone in this household sees benefits of such actions," Alba chimed in. "I long to be revered in the town square."

"We are not looked down upon," Livius said frankly.

"No, but higher status would be a nice change."

Livius grew grim. "I respect that you make your own decisions," he said to Herminius. "I hope you will learn from Brutus and keep friend near."

"I will, father," Herminius said. "Now I must go prepare." He stood and kissed his mother on the cheek. She forced a smile. He shook his father's hand again. Livius gave him a firm grip and a father's grin. Herminius smiled back and left the room.

Livius turned to Alba. He was disgusted with what he saw. "You long for status? Since when? I married you, not Servilia, because you were not obsessed with such a thing."

"When we were young it did not matter to me. Now, I have children leaving nest. I have longed for respect for several years now, and with Fabricius as a centurion and Herminius assisting Caesar, we may reach my goals."

Livius did not answer.

"Speaking of that other woman, I assume communications have ended?"

"She sent note several moons ago that we should not continue talking," Livius said without looking at Alba. "I respect her wishes. She is now a key aid to Caesar."

"Caesar seeks a whore for direction? I must go tell Herminius that he chooses the wrong side."

Livius stood and was about to leave. He turned to Alba. "She is more intelligent than you give her credit. You have your wish fulfilled. Servilia and I will not happen and I am committed to my loving wife." Alba smiled, but tonight, Livius would not share her bed.

CHAPTER 48

APRIL 29, 55 BC

"*E*ver so anxious you are," Fabricius said.

As usual, Justina was in full battle gear. Ready and waiting for him to arrive at the sparring room. She had made great progress in the last few weeks. More even than most of the recruits he had helped train, so he said. When Justina was in the training room, she was of single purpose. Not only did she endure what Fabricius put her through, she craved it. She practiced on her own, so much so that except for time in this room, the two saw little of each other. In fact, the house didn't see much of Justina at all. Dinners and chores, otherwise her time was spent practicing.

Their mother, for the most part, ignored her. Their father seemed to have decided it was his daughter's way of dealing with Antonia's death and it would subside in time, but it did not appear as if that time was coming in the near future. Justina stayed up late and practiced, got up early in the morning to do her chores, then returned to the sword. While Fabricius was impressed, he was also a little apprehensive.

"Sometimes I wonder whether it is me you are excited to see, or the 'freedom' that you are learning."

Justina smiled, then gave Fabricius a long, passionate kiss. "I do get ever so lonely with my big brother playing army while I just swing sword all alone." She tapped him on the chest, then returned to being all business. "Can we begin?"

Fabricius walked over to the rack of practice swords and drew one from the holder. "You have done great work, Justina. You are driven and your skills have improved dramatically." Justina was pleased with the assessment. "Your desire for this freedom has me curious though. This man who spoke to you, not in dream, but in vision. I wonder, once you have your freedom, will you seek him out?"

Justina laughed. "You needn't worry. He is father's age. I prefer someone of younger years." She winked. "Now tell me of my skills again."

It was Fabricius' turn to laugh. "Your skills are strong. I can see improvement from only a few short weeks ago. I would go as far as to say you could best some lesser recruits."

"I do not wish to best recruits destined to see their fate on the battle field. Only true freedom is what I desire, and that will make me as tough as you, centurion."

Fabricius laughed again. "Do you have any idea how many years it has taken for my skills to develop? It is not a matter of weeks," he said, "but years." Out of nowhere, Fabricius swung his sword at her. The movement caught her off guard, and she was barely able to block the blow. He stepped into her and swung again. This time, she managed a block but did not pay attention to his footwork. He caught her leg, and when she transferred her weight, he easily pulled it out from under her. She fell hard on the floor.

Now she was mad. "Your advantage is your mind and your

desire," Fabricius said. "You are smart and will be able to outwit many opponents." He offered her his hand. She took it and when he pulled her up, she turned and thrust her sword at him. Fabricius easily stepped out of the way and slammed his sword hard into her back as she passed. The blow made her wince in pain.

"But you are still far too aggressive. Once we teach recruits how to be animals, we try to harness that anger and aggression so they may become true warriors." Justina turned to face him. She wasn't about to show the pain he had inflicted. "You need to slow down. Plan your attacks. Read your opponent. It is not always about the gladius." He paused. "You have seen many bruises on your brother. I do not wish those same in your lessons. A few minor scrapes are all I offer."

That set Justina off. All this time, while she thought herself progressing, Fabricius had been holding back. "Then you do me no favor. I make one request of you and you taint it with half effort. I love you regardless of your choices for me. If you love me as well, you will show me what it takes to gain my freedom."

Fabricius locked eyes with Justina. He stood there for quite some time pondering his next move. Then, without warning, he lunged forward, attacking Justina in a barrage of swings. She did her best to block everything she could, but was not skilled enough to step to the side and allow the barrage to pass. It took little time for Fabricius to overpower her. To knock her to the ground.

"Freedom," he said, looking down at her, "is being prepared at every move. The moves that you see and those you do not."

Fabricius extended his hand, but Justina did not take it. Instead, she got up under her own power, scowling at Fabricius but cautious at the same time. She had learned from her previous mistake not to charge in anger. She waited for Fabricius to make the next move. She did not have to wait long. She had barely caught her breath when Fabricius charged her a second time, lowering his shoulder and hitting her squarely in the stomach. She stepped back and doubled over. Then, out of the corner of her eye, she caught the sword coming for her. It hit her hard. The force sent shockwaves through her arm and knocked her sword from her hand. She yelled out in pain.

"Freedom is being able to accept pain and continue the fight," Fabricius said. "If a little tap is going to leave you defenseless, then lessons are meaningless."

Despite the sharp pain in her stomach, Justina stood erect. She walked over and picked her sword from the ground, then lunged quickly at Fabricius. He stepped aside easily and because her body was committed to the lunge, she couldn't stop. The pain of his sword hitting her back rippled throughout her body, sending her hard to her knees.

"Your footwork is terrible and you rush your attack. You commit yourself too soon and announce your intentions with your entire body," Fabricius said standing over her. "Maybe we should do our training in the bedroom. Time spent here is a waste." He winked at Justina.

Justina got to her feet and closed her eyes tightly. When they opened, she was calm, her breathing steady. Fabricius noticed and smiled. Justina lowered her head and charged. Fabricius waited for just the right moment and stepped aside. But this time, Justina had not committed to her charge. Anticipating Fabricius' move, she turned and swung her gladius downward, hitting him squarely on the arm, so hard that he dropped his sword.

He smiled. "You are a quick study. Do you see the benefit of using your intelligence and not your aggression?"

"Yes," Justina said, a smile coming to her face.

"Maybe there is hope for you. Now, let us truly have combat."

The two opponents exchanged blows for the better part of an hour. Justina landed several good shots, but Fabricius maintained the upper hand through most of the engagements. He seemed bent on breaking her spirits, but Justina would have none of it. Every time he knocked her down, she quickly got up and engaged him again. She pushed it well past the point where many recruits would have given up.

On one of her attacks, Fabricius swung his sword in a horizontal slash. Instead of trying to block the sword and have the force unbalance her, she ducked beneath the blow. At the same time, she swung her sword and caught Fabricius right behind the knee. His leg quickly buckled, and he fell down hard on his back. The blow, unexpected, knocked the wind from him.

Justina was very proud of herself until she saw that Fabricius was not rising. She flung off her helmet and ran over to him. "Are you hurt?" she asked. "I take it too far."

The pain was evident on Fabricius' face, but his winces quickly turned to laughter. After a moment, Justina joined him. "I thought this was a simple hobby for you," Fabricius said. "I humor you because I love you and want you to be happy. I do you no service with previous lessons, yet today, they all take hold and you show me something I did not think possible. In true combat, you would not best me. However, you would not die as quickly as before."

"Who said this isn't real combat," Justina said and jumped on top of Fabricius, pointing her gladius at his neck. "Do you concede, centurion?"

Fabricius raised his hands in mock surrender. "I am yours to command."

"Yes, you are," Justina said and was leaning in for a kiss, when the door to the sparing room suddenly swung open.

"Justina!" Alba yelled out. "Get off your brother!"

Fabricius and Justina exchanged a knowing look, like children who had been caught being bad. Justina tried not to laugh as she rose and helped Fabricius up from the floor.

"Is this what you two do in here?" Alba asked.

Justina walked over to her mother and stared her straight in the eyes. "I shall become a centurion one day, Mother, and then you can do chores for me," she said and walked over to the rack of swords.

Alba was not amused. "We have one child leave this house. I am afraid you two are destined to be under this roof forever," she said to both of them, and then turned to her son. "Fabricius it is best for you to spend extra free time with a suitable woman so I may become a grandmother. Your brother Herminius beats you out of this house. Do not let him beat you to that task as well."

Fabricius walked over to the rack and placed his sword in its holder. He exchanged another look with Justina, and then he turned to Alba. "Mother, I am quite happy with my dating prowess. I have found a woman that I am quite fond of, and if things progress, you will not only see me to my own place, but many children for you to brood over."

Fabricius glanced at Justina. She smiled. Alba did not. Justina was becoming more and more impertinent, and Alba did not like it. Though she had regained power over Livius, Justina was proving another story entirely. Antonia's death seemed to have emboldened her. She was spending hours in the sparring room, mostly with Fabricius. Alba longed for the day when she would be rid of the usurper once and for all, and she was ready to do anything necessary to make that happen. "Justina, go see the the Medicus. He has become ill over the past few weeks. I would not see him leave this house due to lack of effort by this family."

"*Yes, mother,*" Justina said, placing an undue emphasis on both words, and left the room.

CHAPTER 49

$\mathcal{T}$he Medicus' room seemed quiet, almost solemn. It was not a comfortable feeling. The Medicus himself was lying on his cot, flat on his back. Most of the color was missing from his face, and he looked very grey. His breathing was shallow and seemed labored. Justina walked over and sat down beside him. "Hello, old friend. How do you feel today?"

The Medicus turned his head. "Justina," he said and tried to smile.

She touched his forehead. It was like putting hand to flame. "You are burning up. What must we do to aid you?"

"Only the gods can aid me at this point, child. I have used all my knowledge to keep me going the past week. I fear I will soon join Antonia in loving embrace."

Justina took a cloth from the Medicus' table and soaked it in the bowl of water by his bed, then draped it across his forehead. "Do not speak like that." She tried to put on a brave face, but there was a strange presence in the room and she felt, just as he did, that he wasn't long for this world. "This house has known your services since I was yet a baby. It was you and Cato who delivered me here upon command of loving father. You must stay until I am ready to leave."

"Yes, your loving father. The great warrior."

"Warrior?" Justina repeated. She had never heard her father referred to as a warrior by either Cato or the Medicus.

"You have never harmed a slave in your life. You question Roman ways even living under Roman roof. We speak of Legatus as your father, your Roman father."

"I had visit from him, in my dreams for the first time," Justina admitted. "He was not dressed like a Roman Legatus, but insisted he was my father."

The Medicus took ahold of Justina's wrist. His touch was cold, almost chilling. "You had vision of your father?"

"Yes."

"Did he speak?" His grip tightened.

Justina looked down at her wrist, then back at the Medicus. His eyes were wide and he was staring intently at her. "You are beginning to scare me. Your fever has you maddening."

The Medicus leaned upward. "Did he break words with you?" he repeated with heavy breath.

"Yes," Justina said. She tried to pull away, but the Medicus' grip was remarkably tight. "He said I was just a slave if I did not speak up for myself and fight for what is right."

"Does that sound like the words spewed from a Roman?"

"No," she admitted. "It does not."

The Medicus smiled. He released his grip and laid back down. "Your real father came to visit you."

"My real father? The Legatus dressed as slave?"

"No," the Medicus said and chuckled weakly. "Slave dressed as slave."

"I don't understand," Justina said. "What is meaning of words?

"You are the daughter..." he said and began coughing. It started small at first, then became more violent. He grabbed the cloth from his head and placed it over his mouth.

Justina was scared. She could see blood on the cloth and didn't know what to do. "Do not die," she said, as if her words would force the sickness from his body.

"King," the Medicus said between coughs. "You are the daughter of a king."

"What do you mean, king?" Justina asked.

After a short while, the Medicus stopped coughing and was able to continue, "You do not think like a Roman. You do not act like a Roman. It is because you do not have the blood of a Roman. We made up lie to ensure safety to baby Justina. A man once granted myself and Cato freedom, and thousands of others as well. Cato and I chose to go back into servitude as respect for all the chains cut by king."

Justina's eyes were wide and her mouth agape. All her life she had been told her father had been killed by the Slave King Spartacus. How she had grown to hate even the very name and now the Medicus seemed to be saying that Spartacus was actually her father. "I...I do not understand," she said.

The Medicus took hold of Justina's arm, his grip this time gentle. He leaned up as best he could. "He had but one daughter. You, Justina. He did not want to see his daughter in chains or dead, so choices were made."

Before he could say any more, the Medicus began coughing anew. He tried holding the cloth to his mouth, but his body began seizing. He dropped the cloth to the floor. Justina took hold of his hand, tears streaming down her face. In only a few moments his body stopped shaking, and his hand fell limp. Justina laid her hand on his chest and began sobbing.

CHAPTER 50

MAY 1, 55 BC

*H*is body was still outside in the peristylium, lying on a pedestal surrounded by roses. This was a peaceful place. Violets, bluebells, periwinkles, jasmine, crocus, geraniums, and cornflowers decorating the open space were all in bloom. It was the perfect place to lay his body, as it was also the place where he and Cato grew herbs—some of which were used for cooking and others for medicinal purposes.

Livius had agreed to pay for cremation services to prevent the Medicus from ending up in potter's field. Just as he had done with Antonia, only he had kept that act from Alba, but not Justina. Cato visited his old friend this day, just has he had done when the Medicus was ill. He was there, kneeling by the Medicus' side, when Justina came upon him.

"He was a gentle soul," Justina said. "Always more consumed with our well-being than his own."

"He did as commanded," Cato said without looking up. "As any true slave would. He was a brother to me." Justina moved closer to

Cato and placed a hand on his shoulder. "We have seen much in our lives."

"Would he have been happier being a free man?" Justina asked.

Cato looked up at Justina. "The choice was not our own."

"My father commanded it?"

Cato did not answer. He just looked away.

Justina was tired of the lies and half-truths. Tired of the stories she was told of her origins. Time she knew who her real father was and why that truth had been hidden from her for so many years.

"Why would a man who granted your freedom ask you to become a slave again?" she asked. "My father, the Roman Legatus, must have had you and the Medicus as his slaves. Yet, I have heard through our walls that you and he were free men, albeit briefly."

Cato stood and faced Justina. "What are you saying?"

"I had a vision not long ago. It was of my father, my real father. He was not Roman. He was a slave."

"Your dreams betray you," Cato said.

Justina stepped closer to Cato; tears were forming in her eyes. "My father was not a Roman, was he?"

"Your father was a great man who sought only justice in this world."

"A man who would not command other men to protect his daughter and force them into slavery, but from his actions, men would volunteer to do such a thing. Men such as you and the Medicus."

A tear fell from Cato's eye. "Your father was a great man," he repeated.

"Then tell me of him, so that I may finally know the truth."

Cato did not respond.

"Please Cato!" she pleaded.

Cato was looking at her intently. He lowered his head, took a deep breath, then looked up, and continued, "Your father freed thousands of slaves and had the mighty Roman Empire shaking," he said, placing his hands on Justina's arms. "He knew you would be put into slavery or killed if your true identity were revealed."

"Then it is true," she said. "I am the daughter of Spartacus?"

"It is true," he confirmed. "For such a man, many of us were willing to give our lives. I have but one goal and that is to see you safely through this life."

Justina was filled with a wave of unexpected emotions. At the same time a burden had been lifted, a weight had taken its place. She grieved at the loss of a father she had never known, a father who was never real. A man, once hated, now stood in his stead, and with it, everything fell into place. Now she finally understood why she felt so strongly for slaves, why she never fit into Roman society, and why a gladius always felt so natural in her hand.

As the puzzle began to reveal itself, Justina recalled the scene just outside the market. "And the woman on the cross?" she asked. "The woman who knew my name?"

Cato's shoulders dropped, and he bowed his head. "She was with us, as was her husband," Cato admitted. "We all made the journey to Rome together but separated before we found a place for you."

Justina wasn't quite sure what to do next, but she wouldn't have time to decide.

The clapping drew their attention immediately. "This is quite the story you and the Medicus have come up with, Cato," Alba said as she entered the peristylium. Alba strolled over to the two and stood between them. "So now the question becomes, is my adopted daughter being deceived, or is she the daughter of the Slave King Spartacus?"

"I speak falsely," Cato said quickly. "Apologies, I was speaking lies. Whatever punishment you seek for me, I will accept."

Alba looked hard at Cato. He bowed his head. "Go into the house and prepare meal for dinner. You are a slave and your words have little meaning to this family. Do not speak of this conversation ever again."

Alba moved closer to Justina. She was smiling broadly. "You and I have never been as mother and daughter should," she said and placed an arm around her daughter. Justina stiffened. "You were not from my loins, but Livius so wanted a daughter, I allowed you into our lives. That was the biggest mistake I have ever made. Now to find out this secret. From who you were spawned. I can no longer blame myself for your actions. You are but the daughter of a slave. And from now till you are no longer under my roof, I will treat you as such."

Justina clenched her fists.

"Unless," Alba positioned herself to face Justina. "You cease this ridiculous relationship with my son and remove yourself from this house as soon as you find a new place to call home. If you do not, I will be forced to tell all in our family of your true nature. I'm sure Atilius would love to hear such news."

Tears fell down Justina's cheeks. Her hands were shaking. Had she a sword right this minute, she would gladly have shoved it directly into Alba's midsection. She had never wanted to end a person's life so badly as she did this imposter of a mother. It was Alba who had given Antonia to Atilius to spite Justina. Alba who was pulling the strings. Alba who should by lying dead.

"I will take your silence as an agreement," Alba said and began to walk away. She took a few steps and stopped. "I will have conversation with Fabricius tomorrow, and if his mood does not reflect ending of sick relationship, he will get information that will change his mood." She didn't look at Justina. "You may remain out here for a bit longer so you can mourn your fellow slave."

All of this training had been for nothing. It had not brought her freedom. With one quick comment, Alba had taken everything from her. She had a choice, stay and become a slave, or strike out on her own. She knew exactly what she must do.

CHAPTER 51

She was truly a slave. She just never realized it. Every time it looked like she had the upper hand, like everything she wanted in life was about to materialize, she was knocked down, broken, put back in chains. Antonia had killed herself, and she couldn't protect her. The Medicus died. Her father, the great Legatus, was a lie. She was the daughter of a man she had been raised to hate. She had finally found love, finally understood what it meant to care more for someone else than her own self, and now that too was taken away. There was nothing left.

A soft knock came on the door. It opened, and Fabricius stuck his head inside. "I never thought this day would end," he said. "Only thoughts of being in your arms aided long hours." He walked over and picked Justina up off the bed. Despite herself, she put her arms around him and they kissed. When he put her down, he began to remove his top.

Justina took hold of his top, pulling it back down. "No," she said. "We must talk." She sat down on the bed.

Fabricius' face grew worried. He pulled his top down and took a seat next to her. He tried to hold her hand, but she pulled away.

"Apologies brother, but we can no longer do this." Justina did not look at him when she spoke. She did not want him to see the tears.

"What is it we cannot do?" Fabricius asked. "And why are you suddenly calling me brother?"

Justina took a deep breath and turned to face Fabricius. Her tears were glistening on her cheeks. Fabricius looked worried. "Something has happened and I must leave this house. Your mother does not want me under this roof, and I must abide by her command."

"Mother does not want you here?" Fabricius asked, raising his voice. "This is as much your house as any of us. I shall speak to father in the morning and get to the bottom of this. You are not going anywhere."

"Do not!" Justina said quickly. "Please do not say a word to father. I am no longer wanted here. I must leave. I will take tomorrow to find proper shelter."

"Then I will leave house as well," Fabricius said. "I will not let mother force wedge between us."

Justina stood. "Our relationship, or whatever this may be called must end. We were both foolish to think otherwise."

"Do you not love me? Did I not live up to my end of bargain? Have I not shown you the freedom you desire?"

Justina took Fabricius' hand and knelt beside him. "You have done all you promised and more." she said gently. "You did not owe me affection and love, and yet I gladly accepted it. But it is best if we simply look upon past with fond memories."

"Do you not love me?" Fabricius asked again. "Tell me you do not. Let me hear you say it, and I will find way to accept your words. But I must hear it from your own lips."

"I do love you. With all my heart."

"Then I cannot accept your decision," Fabricius said.

Justina stood and let go of his hand.

"You are not a slave to do as commanded," Fabricius continued, standing. "You are a Roman. You have voice! You are free!"

"I am not free," Justina said and turned away. "I am a slave."

Fabricius stood. "What are you saying? You are Roman. We all must listen to our parents, even when we don't agree. That doesn't mean we are slaves."

"You don't understand," Justina said softly.

"You are correct," Fabricius barked. "I do not understand! Tell me! Turn and talk to me Justina!"

Justina suddenly turned. "I am the daughter of Spartacus!"

Fabricius stood there, eyes wide, mouth open.

"I am the daughter of a slave," Justina said, tears flowing. "Not Legatus as false lips would spew. My father was Slave King Spartacus. I am a slave."

"That cannot be," Fabricius said. "Who told you of such fable?"

"The Medicus," Justina explained, "On his last breath. Cato confirmed this past afternoon."

Fabricius looked down at the floor for the longest time. Finally, he took a deep breath. "I do not care. I only know the person in front of me, not her blood father. I would still have you even if you found yourself shackled."

Justina's heart was pierced, but her head knew better. "You are a centurion in the Roman Army. You serve under Caesar. We live in the heart of Rome. And yet you do not care if people know you are with the daughter of Spartacus? Do not be foolish. Our love is strong, but reality is stronger."

Fabricius took a step closer. Justina looked at his face, it was pleading with her, wanting her. She couldn't help herself. She walked to him, threw her arms around his neck, and kissed him hard. He slipped his arms around her and drew her into him. He held her tightly. She felt safe in his arms. They kissed again and again. Then she pulled away.

"I will be fine," she said to him. "Maybe some time down the road if our paths cross, we can see what future brings. Tomorrow,

I look for new shelter, and the following morning, I leave these walls forever." She started to remove the necklace from around her neck, where it had been ever since he gave it to her.

"No," he said. "Please keep that. I would have you remember me and what we had. It was gift from loving brother."

Justina smiled. Fabricius turned and walked to the door. He turned and looked at Justina one more time. She smiled at him through teary eyes. He turned and left.

❀

*A*tilius couldn't believe what he had just heard. He and Lucilius had returned from patrol and were headed to their room when they heard voices coming from Justina's room. Her door was ajar. When the revelation came, Lucilius had pushed Atilius into their room and shut the door behind them.

"Do my ears deceive me?" Atilius said. "This cannot be true. My brother beds slave king's daughter."

"Lower voice or risk discovery," Lucilius cautioned. "I knew there was something different about her, as did you. She is nothing but a slave trying to play Roman."

Atilius was still in shock. "My brother and Justina together?" he repeated. "Mother must have discovered this secret, and that is why she removes Justina from house. It is about time family came to senses. I would hope Cato to follow her."

While Atilius was thinking only of his immediate future, Lucilius was much more forward in his thinking. "You know, Atilius," he said. "Now that you are part of the Roman Army, this could be a huge boost to your career. What would the senate think of new recruit who brings in the daughter of the most hated man in Roman history? The city would chant your name. You could even find yourself rise through the ranks faster than your brother."

Lucilius' surprised Atilius. "Turn Justina in to the senate?" He sat down on his new bed. "I like that idea. She has played this family for fools long enough." He looked up at Lucilius. "Would there be any backlash for our family harboring such a fugitive?"

"I do not see how. But let me make inquires tomorrow when on patrol. I will make sure that only rewards come to this family. If not, she leaves anyway and you are rid of unwanted slave. Let us meet tomorrow night to discuss plans."

Lucilius began to ready himself for sleep. Atilius just sat on the bed, his head filled with the awards and accolades he would soon receive.

CHAPTER 52

MAY 2, 55 BC

*P*ompey thought he had the votes. He didn't. And now Crassus was the Governor of Roman Syria. This was bound to change things, bound to affect his relationship with Caesar. It was a gamble he thought he had covered. He wasn't sure what happened. Most of the senate had already left by the time Caesar entered. Pompey remained, sitting in the same seat he had occupied during the disastrous vote. Caesar walked over to Pompey.

"I am not one for company," Pompey said.

"I do not plan on staying long," Caesar said and sat down. "You do not look happy, my friend. Did the vote not turn out as you had wished?"

Pompey ignored Caesar, but it was suddenly clear to him why the vote had passed.

"You must have thought private meetings with certain senators would sway influence your way. I too, took private meetings with votes that could be swayed. I guess I am the better politician. I know I am the better general."

Pompey finally looked at Caesar. "Better general? I think not. We both fought many wars, yet the one that will always stand out on record is my victory over Spartacus. The war Crassus could not squash."

"You mean the war you take credit for. Crassus had done all except put final dagger in slave king's heart. You take false credit to boost your standing. Crassus being the great strategist allowed credit to go to you as he felt you would make better ally at the time." Caesar waited for Pompey to respond. He didn't. "You could not even do the job properly."

Pompey turned and faced Caesar. "To what do you refer?" he asked. "Spartacus is long dead."

"Then why does news hit ears once again of the slave king?"

"I assure you," Pompey said, "That slave is serving in chains in the afterlife."

"It is not the man I speak of, but his offspring who still walks among us. Just this morning, my Legatus was given information about a child that had Spartacus as her father. A child that yet lives."

"This cannot be," Pompey said.

"The child will be presented to the senate tomorrow morning. I would suggest you not be present, as it will certainly reflect poorly on you. You wouldn't want to show the senate how you were unable to finish the job started."

Pompey glared at Caesar.

"My soldier is to collect one thousand denarius as bounty placed almost twenty years ago by Crassus."

"Bounty was placed on head of Spartacus at one hundred thousand denarius," Pompey said.

"Yes and one hundred times less for any offspring. For a soldier, that is a small fortune." Caesar stood. "I welcome her crucifixion in the days to come. One more reminder to the people of Rome of my superiority over you."

"Crassus shows support for both of our camps. Now with him set to leave Rome, those camps will be on short purse strings. I long for the day I can finally show who is the superior general," Pompey said and stood. He positioned himself directly in front of Caesar. "I am no longer in need of Crassus' support, nor do I give mine to him."

He turned to leave. He had made it down a couple of steps when Caesar spoke, "Do you not wonder how I knew which senators to bribe?" Pompey turned. "You have spies," Caesar said. "I have better ones."

Pompey stood for a moment looking at Caesar. He suddenly let out a hardy laugh, then turned and walked away.

CHAPTER 53

*W*hen Atilius and Lucilius entered the dining room, Alba was already at the table. She smiled when she saw them. "Come, sit with me. Have some fruit."

As the two boys sat, Cato brought over cups and drink. Alba waited as he finished filling their cups. Instead of giving Cato his typical glare, Atilius was more intent on watching his mother, as she watched Cato.

"Go and meet Livius at his shop," she told Cato. "He is bringing home extra food and will need additional hands for assistance."

"Domina," Cato said and bowed. He put the decanter on the table, walked into the kitchen, and then exited the house.

"Should I go with him?" Atilius asked.

"Do not be foolish," Alba said. "Have you ever known your father to need help bringing back meats? This is opportunity to have Cato out of house when Justina arrives and, ultimately, leaves for good. I would not have opposition."

Atilius smiled. "So you finally remove fake sister from this house? My prayers answered."

"I cannot believe she had relationship with Fabricius," Lucilius added. "It is good that you remove her for such reason."

"Fabricius was beguiled by the slave whore," Atilius said.

"You were aware of their arrangement?" Alba asked.

"Only discovered yesterday through open door," Atilius said.

Alba looked at the two boys. "Might there be other discoveries made?"

Atilius looked at Lucilius. He nodded his head. "We made discovery of Justina's true past," Atilius said, turning back to his mother. "She is not true Roman."

Alba smiled. "Then the three of us share common interest and goal. She is to leave this house and never return."

"With your permission," Lucilius said, "I will aid in even further deed. Many years ago, the wealthy Crassus put a huge bounty on slave king's head. I have come to learn today, that bounty, although smaller, remains on any heirs."

Alba's interest was piqued. "What do you propose?"

"If we were to bring Justina to the senate, they would pay us one thousand denarii. Of course, our Legatus would take his cut, but the bulk to be shared between your son and I. The accolades to be worth even more. This house celebrated."

Alba liked the sound of that, especially the last part. Herminius was already finding favor with Caesar, Fabricius a centurion, and now Atilius handing over descendant of hated slave. Prospects could not be better. She would not only be respected in the square, she would be acclaimed.

"And what of Justina's fate?" she asked.

"She will be sentenced to the cross and dead within a few days. Rome will rejoice!"

If this was going to happen, it had to be done quickly. Livius would never hear of it, even knowing the truth and Cato, well Cato might just fight to the death to defend the slave daughter. Alba turned to her son. "Your father and Cato will not be home for a couple hours. You must restrain Justina and take her some place away from here until you can deliver her tomorrow morning. Keeping her here will only cause conflict. I will make sure remaining slaves are confined to their quarters."

"Fabricius is on special patrol on the outskirts of Rome," Lucilius said. "I heard Legatus ask for volunteers and Fabricius did so immediately. He won't be back for hours."

"Justina arrives shortly," Alba said. She stood and walked over to Atilius. "Be ready for her and be sure to handle this." She kissed him on the forehead. "I am proud of you. All of my sons bring great pride to this house."

"She will not go easily," Atilius said.

"Offer to assist her in her move," Alba said. "Tell her it will go more smoothly."

"She must be alive," Lucilius cautioned. "We can wound her if necessary, in fact, it may look better for us bringing in a bloodied slave."

"Go," Alba said. "Ready yourselves. I will take care of the house slaves."

CHAPTER 54

The house was quiet. Too quiet. Justina went into the kitchen to find Cato, but he wasn't there. None of the slaves were there. She walked down the hall to the sparring room, intent on taking the sword that had been given to her as a gift. It was there. She picked it up. When it was first given to her by her father, it had been too heavy. "You will grow into it," he assured her. She did. Now the sword felt balanced in her hand, and she could easily wield it. She swiped the air a couple of times and smiled. Then she looked around the room. So much had happened here. Lately, it was where she was supposed to have gained her freedom. That would never happen.

She found a place to live, a place that would take her until she could secure an income. It hadn't been easy, and it was not in a nice part of town. Still, she would be able to disappear there, until she could decide what to do next. She left the sparring room and headed to her parent's bedroom, hoping her father would not be there. She knew she wouldn't be able to explain it to him, and she didn't want to chance that Alba would tell him the truth. Alba would anyway. After she left, Alba would tell everyone the truth. She couldn't bear her father looking at her with different eyes.

When she arrived at the bedroom, she found Alba alone, sitting in the bed. "Gratitude Alba for your hospitality over the years. I have done as you commanded, and I leave at first light."

Alba waved her off. Justina turned to leave. Alba looked up just as she turned back around. "Where is Cato?" Justina asked.

Alba smiled. "I sent him on an errand."

Justina headed to her room and did another check to make sure she had everything. She looked at the bed, recalling all the times she and Antonia had spent hours talking. Talking about their future. Talking about how wonderful their lives would be. She also remembered another night on that bed, a night which would be burned into her memory for all her life. A night of pure bliss. She hurried, placing her sword in the pack, wanting to leave before Fabricius came home.

When she turned, she found Atilius and Lucilius in her doorway. She had hoped to be gone before they came home as well. The last thing she wanted was another confrontation.

"We come to assist you with your things, sister," Atilius said.

"You think me the fool?" Justina said. "Get out of my way so I may leave and never see your foul faces again."

Atilius took a step into the room, blocking the doorway.

"Don't make this difficult," Justina said.

A sound came from the main room.

"Who could that be?" Atilius asked.

"I will go check," Lucilius said. "You help your sister out."

It was clear Atilius wasn't here to help her. If that were the case, there would be no reason for Lucilius to see who had just arrived. Justina lowered her pack, positioning her sword closer to her hand. "Step aside," she said. "I do not have time for games."

"That is not going to happen, slave," Atilius said, pulling out his sword. "We know who you truly are, Justina. And now Lucilius and I are for ransom placed on Spartacus and his seed's head."

Justina smiled, dropped her bag, and pulled out her sword.

❀

*L*ucilius was surprised to see Fabricius in the main area. "You are back early," he said.

"The patrol was called off just as it started," Fabricius said. "I am exhausted. Has Justina left?"

"Brother, she has not," Lucilius said. "Why don't I accompany you to the training room to drop off your gear."

"My gear stays in my room," Fabricius said. He looked around and saw the house was empty. No Cato, no slaves, no mother. In fact, the house was unusually quiet. "Where is Cato?"

"Cato runs an errand, sent by your mother."

Fabricius slid his hand down to the hilt of his gladius. "And the other slaves?"

Lucilius smiled. "Fabricius, we know of your love for Justina. We also know that she is not the daughter of a Legatus. The pain she has caused you will soon be repaid with her life."

"Her life?" Fabricius repeated.

"Bounty is too high to ignore. I am sure your brother will give you a taste to help mend broken heart. We take her tonight and turn her in to the senate tomorrow."

"Is that so?" Fabricius said and drew his sword.

❀

"*I* warned you last time you had sharp object in hand pointed at me that it would be your last," Atilius said. "As much as I want the reward, killing the daughter of Spartacus would be reward enough for me."

Justina made the first move. She rushed toward Atilius, slashing downward from high above her head. Atilius moved into a blocking position and when he did, Justina turned and kicked him behind the knee, knocking him to the ground as her sword collided with his. She jumped over Atilius and headed out of the room. She turned left and ran toward the peristylium. Atilius jumped up quickly and gave pursuit.

He arrived only steps behind her, but that was all she needed. "Get away from close quarters whenever you can," Fabricius had told her. "A one-on-one fight out in the open is always preferred. There is more room to maneuver." She had tricked Atilius once, but she knew she wouldn't be able to get away with it again.

"Your skills have improved, slave," Atilius said as he entered the peristylium. He began walking to his left in a large circle, Justina followed suit. "It would appear you and my brother did more in the sparring room than just climb on top of each other."

Justina didn't answer. She just circled. All of Fabricius' training was playing in her head. "Don't look too long at your opponent's eyes," Fabricius told her. "They can be used to deceive you. Best pay attention to his body. Watch how it moves. A fighter reveals his actions by how he shifts his weight."

Atilius took two more steps to the left, and then slowly shifted his weight to his back leg. When he rushed forward, Justina was ready.

❦

"*I* had hoped it would not come to this," Lucilius said and pulled the gladius from behind his back. You make grave error in your choices lately, brother."

"You are no brother of mine," Fabricius said.

"This is no longer business of yours. It would be better if you just remained here and let me assist Atilius. He can be very rash and a dead Justina is of no use to us. I do not want to harm you, but I will if you choose to interfere." Lucilius pointed his sword at Fabricius.

Fabricius moved closer to Lucilius, the sword still pointing at him. He had seen Lucilius in action, practicing with the other recruits. His skills were formidable, but not as good as he thought

RYAN LEW

them to be. He continued forward until the point of the sword was inches from his chest. Lucilius was standing all wrong. Moving forward, Fabricius had taken him by surprise, and his weight was on his back foot. He would have to transfer that weight to his front to make a proper thrust.

"I will give you one chance to get out of my way," Fabricius said, looking him directly in the eyes. He could see the sweat beginning to form on Lucilius' brow. "If you do not move, I will go through you."

"Then you will have to go through me, brother."

"Gladly!"

Lucilius transferred his weight to his front foot and started a thrust. Fabricius spun to the side, blocking the thrust with his gladius, as his body completed the spin, he balled up his hand and hit Lucilius on the side of the head. The blow sent him flying. He was stunned, but he did not fall. Instead, he made a half-hearted attempt at slashing Fabricius. A move, which Fabricius easily countered.

Fabricius sensed that he had stunned Lucilius, and when the boy rushed at him haphazardly, his senses were confirmed. He blocked the slash and countered with another hit to his back; this time, Lucilius crashed into the dining table and if it hadn't been there, he would have fallen for sure. His path free, Fabricius started toward the hall and Justina's room.

Lucilius picked up a cup from the table and launched it at Fabricius, striking him in the back of the head. It was just enough to slow him down. He turned and ran over to Fabricius and, before the centurion could recover, he slashed Fabricius' arm.

***

Justina easily sidestepped Atilius, hitting him in the back with the hilt of her gladius. He winced in pain. When he caught his footing, he turned on her and

292

rushed a second time, slashing with each step. Justina tried to side step him, but he was too fast, and before she knew it, he was on her slashing, repeated blows, one after another. The barrage of strikes was becoming too much. Atilius was too strong for her. One of the blows connected with her arm, slashing a deep gouge. She cried out in pain. Atilius smiled. "If you would like to die tonight, I will accommodate your wish," he said and began anew.

"Slashing is rhythmic," Fabricius had told her. "You have to spot the rhythm, then wait for the opening." One, two, three, the blows came as Atilius stepped closer. One, two, three, they came and Atilius was on top of her. One, two, three. This time, Justina ducked on the third blow. As Atilius was preparing for another strike, she punched the side of his knee, causing it to buckle. She rushed forward and before Atilius could recover, she had pushed through him.

Fabricius looked down at the cut in his arm. The blood was beginning to flow.

"We are both well versed in Roman fighting, brother. I can continue this as long as you."

"I gave you an opportunity to step aside and you did not take it," Fabricius said. "You are leaving me little choice."

"You are ready to take the life of a Roman over a slave. For what? Love? A centurion can never love a slave!"

Lucilius rushed Fabricius, spinning his gladius as he advanced. It was a foolish maneuver. A true fighter never allowed his sword to be loose in his hand. In battle, it was always best to keep a firm grip, lest your opponent snatch the blade and use it against you. Fabricius waited until Lucilius was right upon him before he moved. Lucilius raised his hand above his head and began a downward strike, but before he could get a good hold on his gladius, Fabricius bent down and slashed his sword across both of Lucilius' shins. The pain, unexpected, caused him to lose the grip on his sword. As his arm came down, Fabricius stood and blocked the attack, knocking the sword from Lucilius' hand.

Lucilius fell hard to the ground.

Fabricius walked over and picked up Lucilius' sword. "Stay down," he told him. Blood was coming from Lucilius' shins. He stumbled as he tried to stand. "Stay down!" Fabricius repeated, more forcefully, but Lucilius didn't listen. Once he had firm footing, he pulled a dagger from the back of his waist belt and rushed Fabricius again. This time, Fabricius did not step aside. As Lucilius came, he dropped both of his swords and grabbed Lucilius' arm, flipping him over with his hip.

"Stay down," he said again. Lucilius stood and Fabricius shook his head. Then he realized what was happening. Lucilius wasn't trying to win. He was only stalling Fabricius. How foolish of him not to recognize that. He was wasting time here. He needed to stop Atilius before he killed Justina, or she killed him. He picked up Lucilius' sword. His eyes narrowed. This time, when Lucilius rushed, Fabricius rushed back, and as Lucilius approached, he ran Lucilius' sword through him. Lucilius looked at Fabricius in shock. He clutched the gladius and fell to his knees.

It was not a deathblow. "It was not my intention to kill you," Fabricius said. "You will yet live."

Lucilius looked up at Fabricius. "I will live!" he shouted. "And I will share with the entire world your love and dedication for a slave girl. I will make you the laughing stock of Rome. You have just killed your entire family for your actions. They will be punished!"

Fabricius picked up his gladius. He looked at the blade for a moment, and then walked over to Lucilius, who was trying to catch his breath. "I never got to repay you for removing my helmet in the arena," he said, then thrust his sword into Lucilius' heart. Blood spewed from Lucilius' mouth and as Fabricius removed the sword, Lucilius fell forward. "Gratitude," Fabricius said and ran to Justina.

***

*A*tilius was breathing heavy. He had put all his energy into the barrage of swings and was struggling. She heard Fabricius' words, "Let your opponent make the mistakes. Use his weaknesses against him." Atilius' main weakness was his anger. She could use that.

"Why can't you finish me, brother? I thought you a hero for the Romans. I am but a slave. Can you not beat a slave?"

Atilius' face hardened. "I will send you to the afterlife!" he yelled and rushed forward.

It was exactly what Justina had hoped he would do. "A rush in anger is easily defeated," Fabricius had told her. As Atilius came forward, he raised his arm, preparing for a full, downward swing. Justina waited for just the right moment, and then stepped aside. She spun around, raising her gladius to the right position, and as Atilius passed, she sliced his throat.

She could not see the look of shock on his face as he fell to the ground. Partially because he was not looking at her, but mostly because she was not looking at him. The spin had placed her back toward him. When she turned, he was already on the ground. She walked over to him and looked down. His body was convulsing as the life drained from him. "It is a slave who just sent you to the afterlife," she said.

"No!" The cry came, startling her, as Fabricius ran past. When he arrived at Atilius, the convulsing had subsided. He turned his brother over and saw the slash in his neck. He looked up at Justina, tears in his eyes.

"What have you done?" Alba yelled out, seeing her youngest son in a pool of blood.

Justina rushed over to Alba, clenching her gladius, still dripping with blood. "This is your doing."

"Justina, no!" Fabricius cried out.

Justina kept going. "You made all this happen," she said to Alba. "And now I will have my justice for what you did to Antonia." She lifted her sword and held it against Alba's throat.

"Justina, stop!" Fabricius yelled again. "If you ever loved me, you will not take my mother from me."

Justina looked at Alba, fear was in her eyes.

"Please," Fabricius said.

She looked into his pleading eyes, then closed her own. Everything had been taken from her, and this was the woman who had done the taking. She deserved to die. But Justina loved Fabricius, how could she do that to him?

She opened her eyes and turned to Alba. "You always wanted me to find a man to love. When I did, you took that from me. One day, you will suffer for your actions." She looked over again at Fabricius, and then slashed Alba on the arm. Alba cried out in pain.

"Tonight, I only give you a reminder of what you have done," Justina said and pushed Alba to the ground. "Every time you see this scar, remember that a slave caused it."

Justina walked toward the front door. Fabricius ran to meet her.

"Where will you go?" he asked her.

"That is no longer of this family's concern," she said, turning to face him. "Our relationship is sealed, my hand forced by the actions of another." She looked into his eyes. There was only pain. "I will always love you, Fabricius," she said and kissed him hard one last time.

"She killed your brother," Alba cried out. "Kill her!"

Justina looked over at Alba, then at Fabricius. "I will take my freedom now."

Fabricius did not try to stop her. "Remember me," he said, and watched her run away.

ABOUT THE AUTHOR

Ryan Lew has been a fan of both historical and science fiction since he first saw Star Wars in his youth. In fact, Star Wars had such an impact upon him that he remains a huge fan of the saga to this very day. While Ryan's influences include both movies and television in these genres, none have had more impact than the Starz original series *Spartacus*. It was that influence that started Ryan's writing career and this, his first book. Although most people are familiar with Spartacus and Caesar, Ryan wondered what would happen if he could link those two historical characters together by a common bond, and Justina, Daughter of Spartacus, was born.

WANT TO JOIN THE REBELS?

If you would like to be included on our email list to receive updates and announcements regarding this series, including release notices for upcoming books, purchase specials, contests, and more, go to:

www.IamJustina.com/join-mailing-list

www.IamJustina.com

or

www.Facebook.com/The-Justina-Saga-509893059388005

Email: Contact@IamJustina.com